# *Flaunt*

## CARMICHAEL FAMILY SERIES

**ADRIANA LOCKE**

UMBRELLA
PUBLISHING INC.

*This book is for my readers.*
*Not a day goes by that I don't thank the stars for each and every one of you.*

Sacrifice | Wherever It Leads | Written in the Scars | Lucky Number Eleven
| Like You Love Me | The Sweet Spot | Nothing But It All | Between Now
and Forever

For a complete reading order and more information, visit
www.adrianalocke.com.

# Cast of Characters

*parents*
**Kixx Carmichael**
**Damaris Carmichael**

*siblings*
**Moss Carmichael** [Flirt]
**Maddox Carmichael** [Fling]
**Jess Carmichael** [Fluke]
**Banks Carmichael** [Flaunt]
**Foxx Carmichael** [Flame]
**Paige Carmichael** [Sweet]

# CHAPTER 1
## *Banks*

<br>

"DO YOU WANT TO HEAR MY IDEA OR NOT?"

Milk drips from the edge of my brother Maddox's spoon, splashing into the bowl of cereal below. "No."

"Oh, come on, Mad. This is a great one."

He scoops a heaping pile of Fruity Pebbles into his mouth, chewing deliberately. The crunches echo around his kitchen like he's trying to make a point. *He makes the point.* But that doesn't mean I have to take it.

"They're plastic spiders. Fifty in a bag. And—"

"Banks, *no.*" The spoon hits the bowl with a *ding.* "I'm married now. I can't risk life and liberty every time you want to fuck with Jess."

A slow smirk slips across my face. Maddox pales.

My shenanigans used to be split evenly between our brothers Jess and Moss. They have never been directed at Foxx. *Well, aside for one or two that didn't end well for me.* I was forced to abandon Moss as a target when Brooke moved in. Jess moved Pippa in, so he's not *as fun* to mess with anymore. That only leaves the last Carmichael standing as a target—Foxx.

"I don't even want to know," he says, holding a hand in front of him.

*Too bad.* "Not Jess." My smirk grows larger. "*Foxx.*"

"*You're out of your fucking mind.*"

"It's time." I move out of the way as Maddox takes his bowl to the sink like a good little husband. "We've never done anything to Foxx."

"Because we don't want to eat through a straw."

"Whatever. He probably feels left out."

Maddox lifts a brow. "Really, Banks?"

"I know *I* feel left out now that you and Moss and even Jess have all decided we don't need to be the fearless foursome anymore."

"We were never the fearless foursome." He shakes his head. "What's wrong with you?"

"I'm bored," I say, opening his refrigerator and taking out his last can of Dr Pepper. "And lonely. And I have a lot of time on my hands these days."

"Well, I don't. I have a real estate office to run and a wife to enjoy."

I crack open the drink and stare at my brother. "Ashley ruined my life."

"No, she didn't." He laughs.

"Yeah. *She did.*"

Maddox looks at his phone and motions for me to wait.

I take a sip of my soda and gaze around Maddox's kitchen. We had a lot of good times here. Late-night pizzas, football parties, and one wrestling match that almost ended in a trip to the emergency room. *Thank God for Jess's skills with permanent glue and silver tape.*

But that's all changed now. Everything is changing. No one wants to have fun anymore.

Everyone grew up.

*Fools.*

"Sorry about that," Maddox says, slipping his phone into his pocket. "My appointment got moved up thirty minutes. Love when that happens."

"Is the problem that it's spiders?"

He laughs. "No, Banks. It's not that it's spiders. *It's not even that it's Foxx.* It's that I don't have the energy for the drama right now. The last night you got one of these big ideas, we wound up in jail."

"But not because of the stickers."

"The point is the same, Banks. I'm over all of that now. I'm a newlywed, for fuck's sake. I want to spend time *with my wife*." He grins. "Have you seen her? She's hot."

"Yeah, I've seen her." I roll my eyes. "But she's going to cost you me, you know. I'm going to replace you as my best friend, and I'm not sure you're ready for that."

"Go for it."

Go for it? *Go for it*? "What do you mean *go for it*? Aren't you jealous?"

He shakes his head.

"Not even a little bit?"

"No, Banksy, I'm not. This is good for you, buddy. You can spread your wings and fly."

I glare at him. "I'll fly right through your window and take back my spot on your couch."

"Just don't drop any glitter on the way in."

"Fucker."

Maddox chuckles, way more entertained with himself than I am. "How was work? Did you find anyone to rebuild that carburetor you told me about?"

"Yeah. I got a name of a guy from someone at the marina. No one works on those things anymore. Such a headache."

He grins.

"What?" I ask.

"Nothing." His attention slides over my shoulder. "Hey, babe."

My shoulders slump as the scent of *Ashley* fills the kitchen.

She smacks the back of my head as she walks by. "I'm happy to see you too, Sparkles."

"I never get him all to myself anymore."

Ashley laughs as Maddox pulls her into his chest, cupping her ass cheeks in his hands, and kisses the shit out of her.

As much crap as I give them about their relationship, I love it for them. They are two of the best people I know. Maddox is loyal and responsible. Ashley is a best friend stealer but otherwise funny and sweet—which is why I went to jail for defending her a few weeks ago. She's family, whether I like it or not.

I do like it. *But I really do miss my brother*. It's so much more fun getting into trouble in pairs.

*"I'm over all of that now. I'm a newlywed, for fuck's sake. I want to spend time with my wife."*

He's over *all of that* now. Well, I'm over him being all over it.

"Did you ever do anything with your roommate ad?" Ashley asks. "I've been watching your Social account to see if you posted it."

"Nah, it needs a few tweaks." I settle my gaze on Maddox. "I need to add a line that I'm looking for a new best friend."

He throws up his hands with a sigh.

"I'm kidding." I down the rest of my drink and then toss the can in the trash. "But, no, I haven't done anything with it. Maybe I should, though. It worked for you and Brooke."

"And Pippa," she says.

"Yeah, and the Pipster," I say, remembering how Jess snagged his dream woman. "I'm thinking about just getting a dog."

Maddox's eyes widen. *"Don't do that."*

"Why?"

*"Banks.* You don't even know how to feed yourself. It would be reckless for you to take responsibility for another living thing that can't fend for itself."

"Ye of little faith."

Maddox's phone buzzes. His pointed look lingers before it switches to his phone. "I gotta go. I'll be home in a couple of hours. Love you, Ash."

Ashley kisses his cheek. "See you then."

"Bye," I say as my brother walks by.

"Later."

I lean against the counter. Ashley bebops around the kitchen, taking out various vegetables, a package of meat, and a few pots and pans.

"How was your day?" I ask, not really feeling like going home.

She smiles at me over her shoulder. "It was really good. I spent the day with your mom, actually. If I tell you something, you won't say a word to anyone, right?"

I nod.

"Say it. Promise me," she says.

"I promise you I won't repeat whatever top secret information you're about to tell me, super sleuth."

She rolls her eyes. "We went looking at couches."

I smack my forehead, making her laugh.

"Did you talk her out of whatever she was looking at?" I ask.

"Yes. You know I did."

"This couch situation is going to be the end of me. I feel like we're all sneaking around like double agents." I raise a brow. "I wasn't built for this level of stress, Ash. I just wasn't."

She laughs.

My phone vibrates, and I look down.

Maddox: NO TO THE SPIDERS.

Me: I noted your feelings on the situation.

Maddox: I mean it, Banks. And, for the love of all that's holy, don't do anything to Foxx. I can't save you from him. I'll have to live with that guilt for the rest of my life. You don't want to do that to me, do you?

Me: You shouldn't text and drive. It's unsafe.

Maddox: It's called voice-to-text.

Me: I refuse to participate in your attempts at self-harm. Come see me later.

*Ha.*

I put my phone in my pocket and ignore the series of vibrations afterward.

"What are you making for dinner?" I ask, peering over her shoulder.

"I'm roasting a chicken with some root veggies."

I step back, giving her room to work. "*Oh.*"

"Do you want to come for dinner?"

"I mean, yeah."

She tries not to smile.

"I aired your tire up this morning," I say, sitting at the bar. "It was low. Tell your husband to start checking that for you."

Ashley sets the veggies down and turns around, leaning against the counter. "That was very nice of you."

"Because I'm a nice guy. And I like when you're nice to me back. And when you invite me over for dinner. And when you tell me I can stay and watch a movie with you guys."

She laughs, grabbing a towel and drying her hands. Her phone begins to ring. "Hang on." She lifts her device. "Hello?"

I take my phone out and surf the interwebs. What did people do in situations like this before there were cell phones with the internet? Did they just sit and stare at the person on the phone? Did they carry books around with them as a diversion? How could you pretend not to listen to the conversation happening in front of you, because obviously, you are, if you have nowhere else to direct your attention?

I'll ask someone old. *I'll ask Foxx.*

My fingers fly across the screen.

> Me: Hey, what did you old people do before you had phones with internet and were in social situations where the other person was talking and you had to pretend not to listen?

*Foxx has silenced notifications.*

"No, Maddox can't," Ashley says. "He has a showing right now. Can it wait like two hours?" Her brows pinch together. "Oh. Crap."

*Sounds like someone is having a bad day.*

I click on my Social app and scroll through.

"Is Jess home yet?" Ashley asks.

"Nope. He and Dad are at an auction. They'll be gone until late," I say.

"He's not home," she tells whomever she's talking to. "Moss and Brooke are both still at work and we'll pretend Foxx doesn't exist."

*Smart girl.*

*A 1962 Ferrari 250 GTO? Nice.* I click the post and check out the pictures.

*"But Banks is here,"* Ashley says carefully.

It's the way she says it that stands the hair on the back of my neck on end. I don't have to look up to know she's looking at me.

The energy in the room shifts, and I know the change well enough to know she's going to ask me to do something I don't want to do.

I slip off the stool and start toward the door.

"Maybe," she says, her voice rising. "It won't be *that* bad." She pauses. "Beggars can't be choosers."

I try to get out of the door before she says another word. My pace quickens—but not enough.

"Hey, Banks," she says.

I stop in my tracks but don't turn around. Not making eye contact helps not to get roped into stuff. "Yeah?"

"Can you do me a teeny, tiny little favor? Pretty please?" she asks.

"Do *you* a favor, or whoever is on the phone a favor?"

"It would technically be doing me a favor either way."

*Fuck.* "So it's not for you."

It's for *her.*

My chin tips to the ceiling. A rough exhale drains from my body in the most dramatic fashion I can muster because I know who this is for … and I definitely don't want to do it.

She sighs. "Banks, please."

I turn around slowly as if it's killing me—because it kind of is—and narrow my eyes.

"She's in a bind," she says, frowning as if that's going to help.

*Which it will, but I'm going to hold strong until it kills me.*

"Is that … *Sara* on the phone?" I ask, curiously.

"Yes."

"Then no," I say, smiling and pivoting on my heel to leave.

"Banks!"

*"What?"* I groan and face her again. "Call someone else. Whatever it

is, call someone else to help her. I'll even pay for it. It'll be cheaper than the therapy I'll have to endure after seeing her."

"She needs help."

I cross my arms over my chest. "Oh, *I know that*. I rode with her all the way to Orlando and back to pick up *someone's* shit when they moved in with Maddox."

She sighs.

I sigh back at her.

We watch one another. Neither of us says a word. *But Sara?* Sara says *lots* of words, many of which can be heard through the phone dangling in Ashley's hand from across the room.

If Sara had called and asked for my help, I wouldn't answer. The woman is hell on wheels. She's headstrong and thinks she knows *everything*. Her aversion to physical labor is astounding.

If I'm water, she's oil—oil that hasn't been changed in a hundred-thousand miles. And I'm basically holy water, so it's a no-go.

But it's not *Sara* who's asking for my help. It's *Ashley*. And Ashley is family.

*Oh, fuck my life.*

I blow out a long, hasty breath.

"I'll let you come over for dinner tomorrow, too," Ashley says, luring me in with her fluttery lashes.

Still, I hold strong and think it through.

Even if I put up an argument and do my best to resist her pleas for help, I'll give in. Arguing will only delay the inevitable. At worst, Ashley will call Maddox, and he'll call me, asking me to go. And I can't say no to Maddox because he never says no to me.

*Except for the spiders.*

"*Three* dinners," I say. "And movie nights with you guys every Saturday for a month."

She grins and thrusts the phone my way.

I take it, glaring at her. It only makes her giggle.

I sigh again, just to set the stage. *Can't let Sara think I'm happy about this.*

"Hi, giant pain in the ass," I say.

"Thinking about my ass again, I see."
*This is gonna suck.*

# CHAPTER 2

*Sara*

"I'm not any happier about this than you are," I say, holding the door open for Banks.

My house fills with the scent of Luna Rossa Black—a sexy, masculine cologne with an energetic, almost sweet touch at the end. It's like a glass of expensive bourbon with a side of Pop Rocks.

*How do I know this?* I've had plenty of time to dissect it. I bought a bottle after our trip to Orlando. Not that I'd ever admit that to Banks … or anyone else, for that matter.

"What have you been doing today?" He smirks. "Or maybe I shouldn't ask you that since your vibrator is in the toilet."

"Shut up."

His smirk deepens, sinking the slight dimple in his right cheek that much further. "Where's the bathroom?"

"That way." I point toward the door down the hallway. "Did you bring tools?"

He whips a wrench out of his pocket. As he makes his way to the room in question, he holds it in the air.

*God, he's infuriating.*

The past two weeks have been the most frustrating of my life, and it's all my fault.

Screwing your boss is generally frowned upon for a reason. I get that. I accepted the risks. I crawled into Joshua Eubanks's bed with nothing but red lipstick and black heels—no regrets … *then*. I'm full of regret now—that and a shot of anger that doesn't make me feel great about myself. But if I'm one thing, it's honest.

*And I'm angry.*

"What color is the vibrator?" Banks yells from the bathroom, his voice barely above the sloshing of a plunger.

I groan and march my way to him. "What does it matter?"

"Unless you know anything about removing toilets, which I *highly doubt*, just answer my question."

I stop in the doorway and lean on the frame. "Purple."

"How big is it?"

*"Banks …"*

He grins. "What? I'm painting a picture of what I'm looking for."

"I'm not sure you have anything big enough to compare it to."

He looks me up and down, his eyes dragging over my body. "Okay."

*I hate him.*

Goose bumps spreading across my skin, I hop up onto the sink and watch him work. I don't know why God decided to shake a few extra shots of hot magic into the Banks mixture, but I'd like to talk to Him about it. It was an abysmal choice.

Banks is a conundrum—and stupidly handsome. An Ivy League haircut and grease-stained jeans. A wildly successful businessman who craves attention like a child. He has the kindest heart but will make you want to kill him despite it.

*What do you do with that?*

His back muscles flex under his thin white T-shirt. I bite my lip. *I know what I could do with that.*

"Do you even know what you're doing?" I ask, my feet dangling off the edge of the counter.

He peers up through his thick lashes. "Do you want to do this?"

"I could figure it out, but I have to be out of here by six."

"Why?"

"Because my landlord is a dick." I sigh as he turns back to the task at hand. "My ex-boss helped me arrange this place because the location is the bomb, and the rent was ... discounted."

"I bet."

I poke him with the tips of my pink-painted toes. "But now that my ex-boss and I aren't getting it on, I'm not getting a sweetheart deal anymore. And because I can't afford the actual rent for this area, I have to be out of here by six. *And* if I leave something stuck in the toilet, he's going to keep the baby-sized deposit I put down on the place, and I need it to survive."

"Maybe you should fuck the landlord."

"Ha, ha, ha."

Banks moves to the other side of the toilet with his wrench. "At least you'd have a place to stay. You cut the middleman out that way."

"I'd consider it, but I don't have enough money at this point to even pay what I *was* paying."

"Where'd your money go?" he asks.

"Muggers. Shade House. Concert tickets. The usual irresponsible places to spend your paycheck."

He glances over his shoulder.

"What?" I ask. "I'm terrible at managing money."

"Want a life hack?"

"Sure."

His arms flex as he works the wrench. *Damn.* "The key is to get others to pay for your stuff. I have tons of cash in the bank because I learned this at a young age." He picks up the two nuts that held the toilet to the studs. "If I liked you, I could be your sugar daddy."

"I'd rather panhandle, but thanks."

He stands, stretching his long frame out.

Banks's wide shoulders are offset by his narrow waist. His thick legs remind me that Ashley said he and Maddox wrestled all their lives. *I bet his cardio is spectacular.*

He positions himself just shy of being between my thighs. If he notices the proximity, he doesn't react. But I don't expect him to. He pulled this shit throughout the Orlando trip—touching my waist as he walked around me, guiding me into gas stations with his hand lightly against the small of my back, holding open every door we reached.

*Does he do it to screw with me? Is he playing a game? Or is he truly just a goofball with good manners who doesn't read the room?*

Beats me.

"If you're moving out, where are you going?" he asks, dropping the nuts into my palm.

"I'm staying with Ashley for a while."

His forehead pulls together. *"Excuse me?"*

"What?"

"Say that again."

"I'm staying with Maddox and Ashley. Why?"

He spins around and yanks his phone from his pocket. *Swipe, swipe, tap, tap.*

"Hey," Maddox says through the speakerphone almost imme-diately.

*What's he doing?*

"You're letting Sara stay with you?" Banks asks, staring at me.

I smile just to watch his annoyance grow. He narrows his eyes in a mischievous way that makes me laugh.

*"It's not funny,"* he whispers.

*"Yes, it is,"* I whisper back.

Maddox sighs. "It's just for a little while. A couple of days, max."

Banks frowns. "What about me?"

"What about you?"

"You kicked me out as soon as you got married because you needed alone time with your wife. I believed you and respected that. I don't come over nearly as often anymore. But now you're letting Sara *actually move in with you.* She's not even family. I'm … I'm … *insulted.*"

He looks up. It's my turn to smirk. His eyes narrow in what's prob-ably supposed to be a warning glare, but it's more of a smolder.

It's no secret that Banks and Maddox are very close—Ashley said he's the third wheel in her marriage. She also says it's a good thing she adores Banks because she can't get rid of him. It didn't hurt anything that he got into a bar brawl to save her from her piece-of-shit ex, Eton.

My stomach tightens as memories of that night shuffle through my mind.

He didn't hesitate to jump into the melee. When a punch was

thrown at his brother, Banks had his back. And when he noticed Ashley trapped in a booth with Eton, he did what had to be done to get her out.

He was a knight in work boots, switching from goofy sidekick to ultimate fighter in the span of two seconds. Watching him in that situation was impressive. He didn't flinch. He didn't even break a sweat—proverbially speaking. He was calm, cool, and a sexy badass.

Witnessing that moment is one of the reasons I can't just be annoyed at Banks. *He's actually one of the good ones.*

I look up as he sighs.

"I'm done with you," Banks says to his brother.

*And then there's this side of him.*

"Oh, you are not," Maddox says. "You'll be over here for dinner."

"I'm *really* mad."

"Ashley is making roasted chicken," Maddox says. "And I heard something about chocolate cake."

Banks sighs again, the fight in him waning.

"I'll be home in about an hour, and we'll eat. See you there," Maddox says.

"*Okay.*"

I giggle.

"Bye," Maddox says.

"Bye."

He ends the call and puts the phone back in his pocket.

"I don't think I've ever seen someone cave as quickly as you," I tease. "Is roasted chicken your weakness?"

"I don't *have* a weakness." He nods toward the nuts in my hand. "Don't lose those."

"There." I push them to the corner of the counter. "Secure."

Banks grabs the towel beside me, his knuckles brushing against my bare legs. If he notices the chill that snakes through me, he doesn't mention it.

He drops the towel on the floor. Then he waves me over to him.

I hop down, my feet smacking against the cold tile.

"Grab the other side of this and help me move it," he says.

I make a face. "Um ..."

He looks at the ceiling.

This is reminiscent of one of our—many—disagreements in Orlando. Banks couldn't get it through his head that I accompanied him on the trip for entertainment value and to run interference in case Ashley's jerkoff ex-fiancé showed up. *Ashley didn't want Banks going to jail over her twice in one week.* No, Banks expected me to help move heavy, dirty boxes in the sweltering sun in the oven that was the storage unit.

"It's … gross," I say, gesturing to the porcelain. "It's filthy. And … gross."

"You already said that."

My hands go to my hip. "Well, it's deserving of two grosses. It's a toilet."

"That your ass sits on every time you come in here. Now grab this thing and help me, or your landlord can handle your vibrator."

"This is not a gentlemanly thing to do," I say, gingerly touching the parts that feel dry. "Should we use gloves for this?"

He looks over the toilet bowl at me. "Do you have any?"

"No."

"Then we don't need gloves for this. Lift it up now."

The damn thing is heavier than I anticipated, and it takes a bit of muscle to get it off the floor and onto the towel. Water sloshes from the bowl onto the floor.

"Good thing I've been working out, huh?" I flex for him. "I think I did more than half of the work there."

He rolls his eyes.

"Now what, Mr. Fix It?" I ask.

He crouches down and uses the flashlight on his phone to peer into the back of the toilet.

"Do you see it?" I ask.

"How do I not? This thing is massive."

I swat his shoulder, making him chuckle.

He plucks the perpetrator from the depths and presents it to me on his palm.

The sight of my purple peach in Banks Carmichael's large,

calloused hand does something to me. Lots of things. To a lot of parts. *Dear lord.*

"Toss it in the trash," I say, unwilling to make contact with him and it at the same time.

"Are you sure? You went to a lot of trouble to rescue it."

"I went to a lot of trouble to get my deposit back."

He wraps his fingers over the silicone, dropping his hand to the side.

It's virtually impossible to think of many things other than the fact that *my vibrator is in Banks's hand.*

"How'd it get all the way back in there like that?" he asks nonchalantly.

*Put it in the trash, Banks.* "I don't know. I plunged it for almost an hour before I called Ashley. I couldn't get it to come up."

"You probably pushed it down."

His eyes lock with mine.

"That's funny," I say, holding his gaze. "I never have a problem getting things to go up."

He grins. "I bet you don't." He turns and tosses the device in the trash.

I blow out a breath in relief.

"How much do we care about this toilet?" he asks.

"In what way?"

"Technically speaking, we need to put a new wax ring down to make sure it doesn't leak all over the floor when I turn the water back on."

I wave a hand through the air. "I don't give a crap about that. Pun intended. Can we just set it back on there and call it a day?"

"Yup. Grab your side, muscle woman."

I groan as we get it lifted in the air and placed back over the hole. I'm not sure Banks really needs me for this because I don't think I'm doing much in terms of assistance, but I don't let go until he tells me to.

I hand him the nuts before I pick up the towel and toss it in the trash.

"You can wash that, you know?" Banks asks.

"Yeah, but where do I have to put it? Everything I own is in my dad's garage except the bag I'm taking to Ashley's."

He turns on the water to the toilet. "Why don't you just stay at your dad's?"

My heart pulls in my chest. I squirt enough soap on my hands to be overkill and then turn on the water in the sink.

"Because my dad doesn't live there," I say. "He passed away a few years ago. My stepmother lives there with my little sister."

Banks stands shoulder to shoulder with me. His eyes catch mine in the mirror. In his blue irises is a genuine sympathy that he doesn't try to hide. It's the counterpoint to his lackadaisical approach to just about everything else. He may not always act like he cares—but he cares.

It's the main reason you can't really dislike Banks Carmichael.

"I'm sorry," he says.

I take a quick breath and squirt some soap on his hands too. "Thank you. I have a good relationship with Sabrina, my stepmom. I mean, we aren't best friends by any stretch of the imagination, but we tolerate each other and get along pretty well."

"What about your sister?"

I grin. "She's the best. Bethany is funny and smart, and I love her to death."

Banks glances at me, grinning too. A rush of warmth floods my veins.

We finish washing our hands in silence. I want to ask him what he's thinking, but I don't. The last thing I want to do with two hours left in my apartment is get emotional.

I look up at Banks. *Or find more reasons to like him.*

He turns off the water, and we shake our hands dry.

"Guess that's it," he says.

"Whatever I owe you, charge Maddox."

He laughs. "I already got dinner and movies out of this. I pre-negotiated."

"And to think I thought you did this out of the kindness of your heart."

He looks over his shoulder as we head back to the foyer. A playful grin splits his cheeks. "It would take more than the kindness of my heart to do anything to help you."

"Fuck you, Banks."

"Considering the reason I'm here, it looks like you need to stop fucking and finish packing."

I open the door. "I hate you."

"Back at ya." His eyes crinkle at the corners as he walks by me and onto the porch. "Enjoy your night."

"I will … at Maddox and Ashley's."

He gasps. "You play dirty."

"You have *no idea*."

His brows lift to the sky just before I toss him a wink.

My lips twist as I close the door.

I wish I really did hate that sexy, badass, and delicious-smelling man. Life would be so much easier.

# CHAPTER 3

## *Sara*

"Have you ordered yet?" I ask, sliding into the booth across from one of my best friends, Rebecca.

"Nope. I was waiting on you."

La Pachanga, our favorite eatery in Kismet Beach, is slow for a Friday night. The parking lot had plenty of spots open. Usually, you have to squeeze your vehicle into precarious situations to get a margarita to kick off the weekend.

"Well, here I am," I say, inhaling the delicious aroma of Mexican food—my favorite. "Let's get this party started."

"Jenny said she'd be back around in a second to see what we wanted to drink. I told her we weren't in a hurry."

"Nope. We are not." *Because I have no place to go, for once.* "It's weird being this lame."

Rebecca just shakes her head, amused by my dramatics. My statement is true but dramatic, nonetheless.

My Friday nights are usually stacked with commitments. Becca, Ashley, and I generally meet for drinks at La Pachanga or Mega Pint. Occasionally, we'll do dinner at Shade House. Once I part ways with my friends, I meet up with the flavor of the moment. Lately, that had been Joshua for a little extracurricular work activity until that crashed. I still have The Businessman, aka Brock, a man I met picking out a watermelon at the grocery store, saved in my phone. *Why?* Because that boy gets down to business.

Aside from the move, tonight feels dull—just like last Friday. I don't know what it means, exactly. Am I hitting the wall? Am I getting old? My libido is still strong. I'm *very* attracted to men. I'm just … bored. Uninspired. Apathetic about men, really.

*Most of them, anyway.*

"You are not lame," Rebecca says. "You're dealing with a lot of crap right now. It makes sense that you want to press the brakes a little bit."

I lean forward, my chest pressing against the table, and look her in the eye. "But I'm not a brake presser. I'm a *gas smasher*."

She laughs. "I know. I'm not saying you're weak, so calm down. Even legends have to sit one out every now and then so they can refuel."

*Okay, true.* I grin, reclining against my seat once again, satisfied by her explanation.

"I know how you feel about emotions, so I won't harp on it," she says, her tone wrapped in sweetness. "But how are you? Really? It's okay if your day made you feel-y."

I stare at her.

"You can tell me. I won't tell anyone."

"Why do you think so little of me?"

"*Sara,*" she says, laughing. "*Come on.* You moved out of your apartment with a week's notice, and your new rental won't be ready for a few days. It's understandable if you feel out of whack."

I narrow my eyes. "Are you trying to get me to say I'm having big emotions and need consoling?"

She grins. "Yes."

"Too bad. I'm not."

Rebecca and Ashley understand me more than anyone else on the planet. Ashley and I have been friends since we were kids, and when Rebecca moved here a few years ago, she fit right in. But despite our close friendship, I don't think they really understand me.

No, *I know they don't.*

It's not their fault, though. It's not really mine, either.

That doesn't mean I don't appreciate their concern, thinking I secretly operate on the same playing field emotionally as they do. I'm not sure if they think I'm just a badass that views sharing too vulnerable or if they suspect I truly harbor feelings that I won't share with them.

Neither is the case.

I don't have them.

*Thank God.*

She clears her throat. "And you also quit your job unexpectedly."

"Because Joshua was a condescending asshole." I cross my arms over my chest. "I could've still worked with him if he would've just been like, *'Hey, we're done here. I fell in love with this chick, and I'm gonna marry her.'* Hell, I would've bought them a wedding present. A nice one, too, because I truly don't care. But the whole, *'What did you expect? You're not marriage material, and you know it'* bullshit was too much. Fuck that guy."

Jenny slides up to the table, placing a basket of chips and a dish of salsa between us. "Ooh, who are we fucking?"

"Currently, no one." I frown. "That sounds *so* unlike me."

Jenny laughs. "Yes. Yes, it does."

I sigh. "Can I get a chicken fajita, no beans, please, with a coconut-lime margarita? Maybe put an extra shot of tequila in there?"

"Same, but *with* beans and *without* the extra shot," Rebecca says.

"Sure. I'll be back with your drinks," Jenny says, waving at a new set of customers sitting down at a table across the room from us.

Rebecca dunks the corner of a chip into the salsa. "For the record, I agree with you on the Joshua thing. You both knew it was just a fling. I don't know why he had to flip the script like that."

"Because he could. And, honestly, I'm not super surprised. He can be a total dick—which is precisely why he was relegated to being a side piece."

"He can't be a side piece if you don't have a main piece."

I consider that. "All right. Good point. But if I were to have a main piece, he would never be a contender for the honor."

"Are you insinuating that someone would?"

"Absolutely not."

She smirks, chewing her chip while watching me with amusement.

I roll my eyes. "What about you? Who would be in contention for the honor of settling down with Rebecca?"

The smirk melts off her face. "I don't know."

"See? Don't act like I'm a maniac because I'm not into long-term relationships."

"I didn't say I wasn't into one. I just said I don't know who that person would be. I'm just ... picky. I've had my share of traumatic personal relationships."

I grab a chip and scoop up a healthy amount of salsa. A part of me wants to poke her about that, push her to share like she does me. But Rebecca closes, builds a wall, and hides when she's prodded for information. It's like it physically makes her ill. *Very different from me.* I have no interest in making her uncomfortable. *She'll talk when she's ready.*

"And I would like to avoid them," I say, watching salsa drip into the dish from the edge of the chip. "But, for once, I have bigger issues on my plate than men."

"How does that feel?"

"Odd yet refreshing."

She laughs, the severity clouding her features just moments ago now gone. "What can I help you with?"

"Nothing." I pause while Jenny places our drinks on the table and then scurries away. "I have to handle one thing at a time. Today, I was finishing up getting out of my apartment. Tomorrow, I will find a job. Next week, I'll settle into my new place and then continue my job hunt. And thank God for Maddox helping me find someone who will rent to an unemployed person—for cheap, at that."

"Have any job leads?"

"Actually, no. No one seems to need an accounts rep right now. I'm sure I'll find something but it's harder than I thought to find something decent."

*And that's not bothering me at all. Ugh.*

She takes a sip of her drink and sighs happily. "Damn, that's good."

I slide my margarita toward me.

"How did the move out go?" she asks. "Was that at least as simple as you thought it would be?"

My heart skips a beat.

Instead of answering her, I take a long slug of my drink and hope it cools my insides.

*"But Banks is here."*

I don't know what I expected to happen, but it wasn't him showing up at my door. The last time we saw one another, we were mid-argument about whether spending money on high-octane fuel for vehicles was worth it or a scam. To be honest, I don't know why I was even in that conversation. Not only am I not that concerned about which gas goes into my car, as long as it isn't diesel, I'm also unbothered about what anyone else, let alone Banks, thinks.

Yet there I was, standing on Maddox's front porch, holding down the line that it's just a way for gas companies to make more money from consumers. Why I chose that hill to die on, I'll never understand. All I know for sure is that I was smack dab in the middle of it, and I wasn't backing down—especially to him.

*Especially to him and that dimple.* I sigh.

"Sara?" Rebecca asks.

I flinch and mentally return to the table. "Yeah?"

Her brow furrows. "I asked how your move went, and you just checked out on me."

"Oh. Right. It went fine. Mostly."

"Mostly?"

I shift in my seat, swirling my long pink straw around my drink. "I had a very *Sara* moment today."

"Meaning ..."

Jenny drops off our plates and asks if we need anything else. Then she scoots off toward the table full of construction workers in the corner.

Our plates sizzle. Steaming peppers and onions fill the air, and I wonder why someone hasn't created a candle for kitchens that smells exactly like this. *Heaven.*

I remove the foil from my tortillas. "I was getting my last few things packed up—mostly bathroom stuff. I was able to get my extra clothes, kitchen crap, and all of that to Sabrina's earlier this week. The furniture came with the apartment, so all I really had left was the stuff I'm taking to Ashley's."

"Right."

"Do you remember that glass jar of macadamia nut oil you got me for Christmas?" I ask.

She nods.

"Well, I love that stuff very much, and I've been milking it for as long as I can."

Rebecca grins from ear to ear.

"I had it in one hand to carry to my bag and my vibrator in the other," I say, not making eye contact with her. "And, through a series of unfortunate events, the glass broke. The oil went all over the tile floor. I slipped, and the vibrator went down my toilet."

"*Sara.*"

"I'm fine, if that's what you're wondering," I say, generously slathering sour cream on my tortilla.

"Um, yeah. That's not really what I was wondering."

*Didn't think so.* I layer lettuce and pico de gallo on top of the sour cream. "I got the oil cleaned up. There wasn't that much left, so it wasn't a huge loss."

"And?"

"I used a coat hanger to try to fish the vibrator out, but it wasn't happening. So I borrowed a plunger from the neighbor and tried to use that. Also, a fail."

Rebecca's gaze doesn't stray from me. It nearly burns a hole in my forehead.

She and I have had many conversations about Banks and the rest of the Carmichaels over the years—more so now that Ashley is officially one of them.

The good genes run deep in that family. They're a loud, mischievous, chaotic bunch who values family over all else. They have striking eyes in various shades of green and blue. Every one of them is lean and built from years of sports and physical activity. There isn't one of them that doesn't belong on a magazine cover.

And then there's Banks—the hottest one of them all.

I don't know what it is about him that makes him so ridiculously attractive.

He sings old country songs too loudly in the truck. He seems to think things like knowing the location of your car fuses are downloaded into your brain at birth. Worst of all, getting him to take anything seriously takes a shield and sword, and he prioritizes things on his own scale. *It matters not what anyone else thinks. He runs on Banks time.*

But then his wild blue eyes with thick black lashes are an open book. He makes you laugh but never feel laughed at. He opens doors and overtips servers—he pulls over on the side of a busy highway to help a random old man with his car in a one-hundred-degree, hundred-percent humidity afternoon when he could just keep going.

I sigh and raise my eyes to Rebecca's. "So I called Ashley to see if Maddox was busy."

She leans back, her eyes widening and a slow smile spreading across her face.

"Blah, blah, blah," I say, getting to the part she's obviously expecting. "Banks shows up."

"*No.*"

"*Yes.*"

She leans forward like she's about to leap over the table.

"Easy, tiger," I say, laughing. "Don't attack me."

"Banks Carmichael showed up at your apartment to get your vibrator out of the toilet. Is that what you just told me?"

"Yup."

Her face flushes, and she sits back again. "My brain just blew up."

"Imagine what *my* brain did." *And my body.* "My vibe was in his hand—just lying there in his palm like it was a pile of candy or something."

"I don't think I could've handled that. Heck, I *can't* handle it, and it's not even mine, and I wasn't even there."

Laughing, I go back to my fajita creation.

Like me, Rebecca secretly drools over the Carmichael men. She prefers the quieter ones, though. Her preference has always been for Jess or Foxx. *Me?* Quiet is boring. Give me all the energy.

"It wasn't how I anticipated the afternoon going, that's for sure," I say.

"You know …" She swishes her margarita around in her glass. "You're going to be at Ashley's for a few days, and he lives across the street."

It's crossed my mind. *More than once.*

I'll undoubtedly be blessed with more than a few visuals of Banks Carmichael. But that will be all the blessings I'll be bestowed.

At the end of the day, we operate on some level of frenemies. We're not flat-out enemies, but I wouldn't say we're friends. Sometimes that kind of situation can result in the hottest sex imaginable—but it never ends well. There's a compatibility problem that shouldn't be ignored. And with Maddox being his brother and Ashley one of my closest friends, that's trouble with a capital *T*.

I'm a seasoned vet about this kind of thing, and Banks flies every red flag with the words *this will be complicated* printed on the side.

My life has enough complications to last a lifetime—most of which I don't give two cares about. But adding Banks to that list?

That would be the most foolish thing I could do.

# CHAPTER 4
## Banks

"WHAT ARE YOU DOING HERE?" I ASK.

Tasha looks up from her computer and leans back in her chair. "I had a few things I needed to catch up on, and you guys are so distracting during the day that I can't get to them during normal business hours."

"Sucks to be you."

She grins. "I brought you a coffee. It's on your desk."

"This is how you keep your job security, Tash. Bringing me treats."

"Huh. I thought it was that I'm the only one around here who knows how to do all the things that don't involve a wrench."

I grin too. "Well, and that."

Tasha has opened all the shades in the Carmichael Classics lobby, filling the room with bright early Saturday morning sunlight. The shop is officially closed on the weekends, but I'm here nearly every day. Dad always said to find a job that doesn't feel like work. The only thing that didn't feel like work was messing with cars. I've managed to assemble a pretty amazing group of people to help build my business into something I'm proud of—and Tasha is the person who makes sure that all pieces of the company operate smoothly.

I couldn't do this without her. I wouldn't know where to start.

"How long are you going to be here?" she asks. "I have a stack of parts invoices that I need you to approve. I tried to nail you down all week and couldn't."

"Where are they?"

She plops a folder on the edge of her desk. It hits with a thud.

"That's a lot," I say, eyeing it.

"Most of them are for the car Eddie's working on. The bump from *fun car* to *show car* hasn't been cheap."

I pick up the folder and sigh. "Well, I warned the guy about that and was even heavy on the numbers. It's probably going to double our man hours, let alone this." I shake the folder in the air. "But it's not my money he's spending, and it's gonna fatten my bank account, so whatever."

"Speaking of Eddie—you remember he's taking the next two weeks off, right?"

"*No.* Why is he doing that?"

"He's visiting family in Portugal," she says, laughing. "You literally had a conversation about this a month ago right here. You were standing in the same spot you're in now."

"How can you remember where I was standing a month ago, and I can't even remember the damn conversation?"

She shrugs. "I don't know."

I furrow my brow. "Did I work those two weeks into the project schedule?"

"You did."

"I knew it." I pump my fist in the air. "Why was I even worried? *Last month me* took care of *this month me.* He was a genius."

"Calling him a genius might be overkill."

I make my way to my office. "When was the last time you took a vacation?"

"The week before I started here."

"You deserve one."

She laughs. "I can't afford to take one, Banks. I'd come back, and this place would be out of control."

I stop in the doorway and flip on my light. "You have no faith in me."

"*Banks.* I took two days off over the winter with strep, and you guys acted like I was gone for a year. Can you imagine if I took a whole week off? Or two?"

I might seem calm on the outside, but I'm literally shaking on the inside. If Tash isn't here, I can't function. No one can function. We'd all sit around staring at each other.

*Please don't leave, Tash.*

"Well, for what it's worth, you deserve one." I look at her over my shoulder. "But, for the love of God, take your phone. Or better yet— just take me with you. I'm a great vacationer. I'll even plan the itinerary. How do you feel about roller coasters?"

"What kind of a vacation would that be? You and my husband talking cars and me trying to get both of you *and* the kids in line? Count me out."

"You're no fun."

She turns back to her desk. "You don't pay me to be fun."

*That's true.*

I toss her folder on the edge of my desk and then sit in my ripped office chair.

The tension in my shoulders eases as I breathe in the scents of grease and oil and the thing Tasha plugs in my outlet that smells like fresh linen. *Or that's what the label says, anyway.*

My office is my favorite spot in the world.

Pictures of the cars we've restored over the years hang on a bulletin board. Various awards hang on the walls next to plaques from baseball teams, volleyball clubs, and cheerleading programs that I've donated to or sponsored. *It makes me feel good.*

The door facing me looks across the lobby and Tasha's desk. The door to my left opens to the shop floor. Sometimes I just sit here and can't believe that this is all mine. I'm not sure that I imagined I could have something this big—that people from all over the country would send their cars to me to have them restored. That so many people would trust me. Respect me.

It's the best feeling in the world.

"Hey, Banks," Tasha says. "Check your email, if you can. I got copied on one from Bristbank Aftermarket, and I think you'll want to respond fairly quickly."

"The way you just said that makes me think I probably shouldn't read it at all."

She laughs. "Want me to log in to your email and pretend to be you?"

"Not unless you want to deal with about a hundred messages from the Golden Years Dating app." I scowl. "You know what? Fuck Jess."

Her laughter grows louder.

I must admit that Jess's prank was a good one—excellent, even. If it were directed at anyone else, I would've found more entertainment value in it. But being that it was *my* name—or Sparkles, actually, and my picture and contact info that he uploaded into the Golden Years Dating app, it isn't quite as hilarious.

But what *will* be hilarious is how I retaliate. I just haven't figured that out yet.

I click open my email and find the message in question. My jaw drops.

"They're charging me a thousand dollars as a rush fee?" I say, getting Tasha's attention. "Are they kidding?"

"That's what it says. I knew you'd want to see that before they ship the part."

I hit *reply all*. "I'll mine metal out of the earth and make my own part before I pay that."

Tasha grins.

My fingers fly over my keyboard. "Hey, Tash."

"What?"

I sit back in my chair. "Is it for fuck's sake or for fuck sakes?"

She rolls her chair around and faces me from across the building. "Why?"

"I'm replying to that email. I want to sound professional."

"You are ridiculous."

"So for fuck sakes then?"

She sighs. "Are you joking?"

"No. I really don't know. *For fuck's sake. For fuck sakes.*" I wrinkle my brow. "They sound the same."

She crosses her arms over her Carmichael Classics T-shirt and says both variations aloud. "Dammit. I'm not sure how you say it now."

*Right?* "Well …" I rub my chin. "Neither of them really makes sense."

"I'd go with *for fuck's sake*. But this is like adding brown sugar to your oatmeal—decide with your heart."

I grin. "Got it. Thanks, Tash."

"Any time, any time."

She mumbles something as I finish the email and hit send. It's probably good that I can't hear her.

"How's that response look?" I ask.

"Well, it's sent. So there's that."

I look down at my phone when it starts buzzing. I see who it is and pick it up.

"Hey, Golden Girl," I say to my new friend. "How are you this fine morning?"

"Oh, Sparkles, you stop that," she says, laughing. "Are you already on fire today? It's still early."

I glance at the clock. "It's almost lunchtime."

"And that's early when you're in retirement."

Gloria was one of the women who contacted me through the dating app. It turns out that she's a good friend of Brooke's grandma, Honey. It also turns out that she's hilarious, makes a great sandwich, and has taken me on as her pet project.

I hate to tell Jess, but Gloria is the best thing to happen to me in a long time. I get food, and attention, and she loves me. *If she were fifty years younger, we might have a thing.*

"I'm calling to see if you've done your photo shoot yet for the fundraiser," she says.

Laughing, I take her off speakerphone and ignore Tasha's amusement. "No, I haven't. I'm still picking out poses. I want to be original, you know? Really get my good side."

"Boy, you don't have a side that's not good."

I beam. "I've heard that before. But keep saying it. I like it."

Her cackling makes me grin.

"Well, I need them by next week," she says. "I'm going to have fliers made and hung up around the retirement center. I'm gonna wet these ladies' whistles."

"That's probably not all you're gonna wet with those pics, Gloria."

"You're damn right. We may be old, but we still got it. There's some of us that could still rock your world."

My cheeks ache. "I have no doubt. None at all." *But I would never want to find out for myself. Just … no.*

Foxx is old, but I don't think he'd even want to have his world "rocked" by Gloria or one of her friends.

*What if …* I grin.

"My Charlie was a satisfied man, I'll tell you. I was a belly dancer back in the day, and I learned how to work these hips."

"You know what? I wondered that when I saw you. I said, '*Self, I bet that woman was a belly dancer because look at how she sways those hips.*'"

She snorts. "You should see me when I don't have compression socks on."

I burst out laughing.

"All right," she says, snickering. "Enough messing around, you little flirt. Pictures by the end of the week, okay?"

"How many poses?"

"As many as you want. If we don't use them for the fundraiser, we'll use them in other ways."

I gasp. "Gloria, are you insinuating what I think you're insinuating?"

"Get your mind out of the gutter."

"Oh, like yours wasn't there," I say, laughing.

"You better be glad I'm not your grandma or I'd take you to church."

"Is that some kind of thinly veiled sexual reference?"

She sighs. "Are you coming to get me this week for lunch or what?"

"Yup. Text me whatever day you're free, and I'll make it happen."

"I'll see ya then, Sparkles."

"Bye, Golden Girl."

I end the call and lean back in my seat. Before I can get refocused on work, my phone chimes with the group family text. *And they say I'm annoying.*

Moss: We need a headcount on who is coming
for pizza tonight.

Maddox: Not us. Ashley made me go shopping
today and we're still at the outlet mall.
Someone help me.

Paige: I wish I was coming. I miss my brothers.

Maddox: We miss you too.

Jess: Pippa and I are already on the way to
Silver Springs. Miss you, Paige.

*Foxx has silenced notifications.*

Me: Guess that's a no on Foxx.

Jess:

Moss: Are you coming, Banksy?

Maddox: Are you really asking him that?

Me: Yes, he really asked me that.

Jess: WHY? You know he'll be there.

I start to answer, but another text pops up first.

Maddox: Hey, Moss. You guys don't care if
Sara comes, do you?

*Fucking hell.*
My stomach tightens, and I adjust myself behind my desk.
It has taken a lot more brainpower than I wanted to expend to keep

Sara and those little pink shorts out of my head over the last eighteen hours.

I don't understand how someone can be so hot and so … *not*, all at the same time.

She has this uncanny ability to sink her hooks into you whenever you're around. I swear, the woman has some kind of manual on how to drive men out of their minds. *Especially me.*

I've never had a female get so under my skin.

Her body is perfection with all curves and soft edges. She has a pair of green eyes that flash with energy and fierceness that I can't help but crave … and fear a little bit. Her smile would be sweet if it wasn't prepping to say something to annoy the piss out of you.

She doesn't know how to do anything. She's constantly talking about guys that treat her like shit. Worst of all, she's fine with it, and if you even try to chime in and offer that she should expect more out of a guy who says he likes her, she bites your head off.

*If a guy treated Paige like they do Sara, I'd throttle them with my bare hands.*

Moss: Yeah, sure. She can come. No problem.

Me: I might have something going on. I'll let you know later.

Jess:

Maddox:

Moss:

Paige: What might be going on?

Me: I'm keeping my options open.

Moss: Okay  Be here at seven, Banksy.

"Yeah, we'll see," I mutter, clicking the button on the side of the phone.

I stare at my computer screen for a long time, but my mind is elsewhere. *Namely, Sara.*

I can't help but wonder what happens to a woman like her. Does she ever find a guy who's not a jerk? Does she just drift around her whole life? It wouldn't be a bad life, but something in my gut tells me that might not be all she's looking for.

*If* I ever settle down, and that's a big *if*, I want to have the relationships that my parents have with one another. I want to take care of my girl like my dad does Mom. I want a house full of laughter and food and the door opening and closing all the time with people.

I want the life I had growing up. To get that, it would take a fun, lighthearted, family-centric woman. Someone like Mom. Or like Brooke, Ashley, or Pippa.

*Not* Sara.

*Why am I even thinking about this*? We hate each other. Sort of. I think.

I stare at my phone for a long moment and then pick it up again.

> Me: See you then.

I click off as fast as I can, before the comments roll in.

*"That's funny. I never have a problem getting things to go up."*

I shake my head and turn back to my computer.

## CHAPTER 5

*Sara*

"Hello," I say, poking my head through the front door of Moss and Brooke's house. Their text said to come on in and that they would be in the kitchen or the lanai. Despite my new friendship with Brooke, thanks to Ashley, it's still a *new friendship*.

I'm not entirely comfortable just waltzing into their private space unannounced.

"We're in the kitchen," Brooke says, her voice ringing through the foyer.

I step inside and shut the door behind me. *Wow.*

Their house is so well put together and gorgeous. It has very strong details and lots of metals and blacks. But the spattering of pinks and yellows softens it just enough to make it clear that a woman lives here too.

"Hey," I say, smiling at the two of them. "Thanks for inviting me over."

Moss leans against the counter and nods. *Man, he's handsome.* "No problem. We're glad you could come."

"I made brownies." I hold a tray for them to see. "I'm not saying these are the best things you'll ever eat in your life, but I did follow the instructions and they smell great."

Brooke laughs and takes the dessert from me. "Oh, they do smell great. And they look great too."

"Thanks. Speaking of smelling great—your house smells *amazing*."

"It's the pizza dough," Brooke says. "I love that smell too. It's so comforting."

I slide my hands down my sides, smoothing out the fabric of my blue sundress. My clothing options are limited, and this felt like the most *casual dinner with friends* outfit that I had on hand—even if I did have to wear a bikini underneath.

"You look very pretty," Brooke says. "I love that dress."

"Fifteen dollars at Brinkmann's. They also have it in a mint green color that I love, but it looked weird against my skin."

"Green can be hard to wear," Brooke says, adding balls of dough to small round pans. "Unless you're Moss. I love green on him."

Moss smirks and shrugs. "I'm going to go get the pizza oven warmed up."

Brooke smiles at him with little hearts in her eyes. *So cute.*

"Want me to help you?" I ask Brooke.

"Sure. I'm getting the dough ready so when Banks gets here, we can all make our own pizzas."

I turn toward the sink so she can't see the heat in my face.

I haven't been able to forget the image of Banks with my vibrator in his hand. The whole situation feels surreal, and I half wonder if I didn't imagine it. That whole day was a shit show. *Maybe I was stress-dreaming.*

"How have you been?" Brooke asks. "Ashley said you were staying with them until Wednesday."

"Yeah." I turn on the tap and squirt a shot of soap in my hands. "Maddox helped me find a rental. Those things are impossible to find in Kismet Beach right now. It's awful."

"I know. Pippa—do you know Jess's girlfriend?"

I shake my head and finish rinsing my hands.

"Well, she was renting a place before she moved in with him. She was saying it was horrible trying to find something—let alone something that wasn't overpriced."

I turn off the tap and dry my hands. "It's true. But it's still cheaper here than in the surrounding areas. I just hope I can find a job that lets me still live in Kismet Beach."

"You haven't found anything yet?"

"No. I sent my résumé out to a bunch of places this morning. So fingers crossed."

"Can you get out the sauce and toppings from the fridge?" she asks. "I forgot. I like to take the chill off them before we add them to the dough."

"You're a pizza expert, huh?"

She laughs. "No. Not at all. I'm a pizza hobbyist."

"You sound like my kind of person."

I dig around the refrigerator and find all the things she asks me to locate. My heartbeat settles. The nervousness that I had about coming over here magically melts away.

Originally, I told Brooke that I would pass on the whole pizza party thing and just grab a sandwich somewhere myself. But Maddox insisted that I not do that and instead walk across the street for dinner. I was worried it would be awkward. *But it's the Carmichaels. I should've known better. They're the nicest family I've ever known.*

I find the cooked sausage crumbles in the very back, behind Moss's beer. I'm turning around to put it on the island with the other things when Banks comes around the corner—nearly running into me.

"Damn you," I say, my hand smacking my chest.

He towers over me, his eyes twinkling.

My senses are overwhelmed with *Banks*. The scent of his cologne. The sound of his low chuckle. The slightest brushing on his fingertips against my side as he continues into the kitchen.

*Shit.* I blow out a long, quiet breath.

"There you are," Brooke says. "Someone told me you were thinking about not coming."

*Oh, really?* I lift a brow and watch Banks.

He's dressed in a pair of worn jeans. Unlike a lot of men who wear distressed denim, Banks's jeans are that way because they've actually been used. The material looks soft. There are dark stains spattered around and the pockets are frayed with threads hanging in the air.

*It's so damn hot.*

His shirt is black and faded. There's a slogan across the back that I think refers to wrestling, but I'm not totally sure. On the front, over his heart, is a logo for a sports club. *Maybe*. And on his head sits a backward Tennessee Arrows hat.

*Kill me now.*

"Yeah, I thought about it," he says. "For like five seconds. Then I remembered how good your pizza is and that if I didn't come here, I'd have to figure out dinner myself. And, I took pity on you, Brooke. I know you'd miss me if I didn't show up."

Brooke laughs. My shoulders slump in relief.

Banks picks up a pepperoni and tosses it in his mouth. His gaze lands on me. "What did you do today?"

I set the sausage on the counter. "I sent out a bunch of resumes. Fun, exciting times. What about you?"

"Went to the shop. Did some work. Did a little … oh, what would I call it? *Preparation*," he says, smirking.

Brooke puts her hands on the table and looks at him.

"*What*?" he asks like he's offended.

"What did you do?" she asks him.

"I have no idea what you're referring to," he says sweetly.

"Preparation? For what?" she asks.

"I did things today to get a head start on next week."

Brooke looks at me but points at Banks. "When he uses that tone, he's up to something. Probably something that's going to cause a whole lot of drama around here."

"No. Not here. You have nothing to worry about." Banks snickers. "But I've been working on a project for a while now, and it just came together today."

Brooke looks at the ceiling and groans.

"What's wrong?" Moss asks, coming back inside. "Hey, Sparkles."

"Hey," Banks says.

I look between them. "Sparkles?"

Banks rolls his eyes. Moss, however, looks all too pleased to explain.

"Jess set a trap of buckets of glitter all over Banks's house," he says.

"He deserved it. That's all I'm going to say. But Banks sparkled for weeks afterward. Sometimes he still glistens in the sunlight."

"Fuck off," Banks tells his brother.

I giggle. "I've noticed that. He came over to my old house yesterday, and I swore I saw a flurry of sparkles all over the bathroom floor."

As soon as I say it, I regret letting the words topple from my lips. Banks nods, biting his bottom lip like he's all too happy to jump on the *he came over to my house yesterday* train.

*Please, no.*

"Come over here and top your pizzas, everyone," Brooke says, oblivious to the standoff between her two dinner guests.

We all take a pan of dough and begin crafting our dinner. I make it a point to stand across the counter from Banks—just to be safe.

"Banks was at your place yesterday?" Brooke asks, adding a handful of shredded mozzarella cheese to her pizza.

I look up at the same time as Banks does. Our gazes collide.

A chill snakes up my spine at the heat in his eyes. But the playfulness in them—buried just under the fire—causes my heartbeat to quicken.

"Yeah," Banks says, smirking at me. "I had to swing by and help her out."

My face is hot. *Surely, he won't tell them why.* I glare at him, hoping it will dissuade him from saying anything else.

In return, I get a wink.

*Banks, no.* "He was very sweet and helped me out of a bind," I say, staring at him.

"Banks? Sweet?" Moss laughs. "What did you ask him to do in order to get that reaction?"

Brooke elbows him in the side. "Don't ask questions that you might not want the answers to."

"*Oh, no,*" I say, waving a hand in the air. "It was nothing like that."

Banks's jaw drops. "What are you saying, *Sara*?"

"I'm not saying anything, *Banks*. Only that you stopped by for platonic reasons."

He tosses a final pepperoni on his pizza and then grabs the edge of the counter.

*My God, his eyes are gorgeous*—even when they're trained on me, taunting me like this.

His dimple sinks in his cheek as he cocks his head to the side. "Maybe we should tell them why—just so they're clear."

My chest shakes as I hold back a chuckle. *"Don't you dare."*

"What if I do?" he asks, holding my stare. "What are you going to do about it?"

"The question you need to ask yourself is, are you prepared to handle what I'll do about it?"

He chuckles too. "Is this anything like the time I kept skipping your sucky-ass songs in the car on the way to Orlando?"

"That wasn't funny, Banks."

"You sure? Because I laughed. *A lot.*"

I try desperately not to smile at him, but it's so hard.

"Let's take our pizzas to the lanai and get them in the oven," Brooke says. "The sooner they get in there, the sooner we can eat and I'm starving."

"Sounds like a plan," I say, happy for the diversion.

We all take our pans and head to the sliding glass door. Banks walks behind me.

"You've already taken over Maddox and Ashley," he whispers. "You can't have Moss and Brooke too."

I slow my pace so he can walk beside me.

*"Too bad,"* I say, chiding him. "I can't help that your family welcomes me with open arms."

As we step into the lanai, he makes a face, making me laugh.

Moss helps Brooke get a couple of our pizzas into the oven. It doesn't take long.

"Okay, that's done," he says. "Do you guys want a drink? Beer? Water? Tea? A pop?"

"I'll have a beer," Banks says.

"We have wine, too," Ashley says. "Do you want a glass, Sara?"

"Please."

Moss and Brooke head into the house, leaving Banks and me alone.

We wander to the lounge chairs by the pool and sit. A fountain trickles water down a small cascade of rocks into the deep end. The sound is relaxing.

"I love this," I say, settling against the overstuffed pillows and pulling my feet up onto the cushion too. "I've never had a pool."

"Ever?" Banks asks.

I shake my head. "Sabrina was always worried that my little sister would fall in, so we never got one."

"How old were you when your dad married her?"

"Ten."

He nods like he's thinking about that. My chest tightens as the realization of talking about this with Banks is on the horizon. *Not what I want to do.*

I pull my phone out of my dress pocket and make a point to open my email. I'm sure Banks is watching me, curious. *But I won't be entertaining you, Sparkles.*

I scroll freely, not really worried about finding anything specific. This is simply a distraction from having to talk to Banks about my family. But when my gaze hits an email marked urgent, my finger slides off the screen and halts my pointless scroll.

*What the hell?*

I tap the email and read the contents, my blood pressure rising.

Dear Sara,

Mr. Eubanks informed me that you are no longer employed with Eubanks and Fields Distributing, and he said he would be unable to contact you about the Petterson Label Wines Gala this coming weekend. You wouldn't be able to attend.

You were personally an integral part of our growth last year, and we would be remiss if we didn't extend an invitation to you. Please come as my personal guest and network with some of the most important players in the industry.

The details are below. Please RSVP to my assistant, who is copied on this email, as soon as possible.

With regards,

Myles Petterson

President, Petterson Label Wines

I drop my phone in my lap, my mouth gaping. *"That jerk."*

"Who?" Banks asks.

"Joshua. My old boss."

He lifts a brow. "The ex-boss who provided you the nice little discount on rent for ... a little extra? *That* ex-boss?"

*He has a good memory.* "Yup. The one and only."

I sit tall, still wrapping my head around the email. *He could've contacted me. He could've had Human Resources contact me. Why be a dick?*

"What did he do?" Banks asks carefully.

"I did a bunch of work—almost exclusively, really—for a client called Petterson Label Wines. They throw this gala every year that's the place to be and everyone clamors for an invite. Apparently, *I* was given an invitation and Joshua told them I didn't work there anymore and would be unable to attend—even though I deserve to be there."

Banks sits back, his hands folded in his lap. His face is unreadable. Handsome but unreadable.

"Fuck him," I mutter, picking my phone up. I type out a succinct, professional response to his assistant, thanking them for the offer and accepting it. Then I shove it in my pocket. "The nerve of that guy."

"Are you going?" he asks.

"Where?"

He gestures toward my pocket. "To the party or gala or whatever."

"Yes, *I'm going*. I worked my ass off on that account. And, besides, I'm unemployed. Maybe I'll network with someone and get a job offer."

His lips twitch. "Will the *ex-boss* be there?"

*Crap. I didn't consider that.* "Probably. He goes every year. Only, this year he'll have his new fiancée with him."

"You don't care about that?"

"Nope. Not even a little. It was his parting shot that pissed me off. He told me that I wasn't wife material. Can you believe that?"

Banks smirks. "Yeah."

I pick up a pillow and throw it at him. He catches it easily and tucks it beside him in the chair.

"Just take someone with you," he says. "Make him think that you didn't lose any sleep over him. That you rebounded the next day. Guys hate it when they think they weren't memorable."

*Not a bad idea.* I whip out my phone once again and check the details of the invitation. *You and a plus-one.*

An idea percolates in my mind, slowly coalescing into one smooth, solid idea.

"I don't just need a rebound," I say, still working through the plan. "I need to make him eat his words—make him think he really screwed up. That he miscalculated."

"What do you want to do? Get married real quick?" Banks asks, laughing. "A little overkill, don't you think?"

A slow smile stretches across my face. "Yeah, but a fake fiancé isn't."

"A fake fiancé?" Brooke hands me a glass of wine and sits on the loveseat beside Moss. "Who is getting a fake fiancé?"

"Me. Maybe." I take a sip. "Oh, this is lovely."

Banks tips back his beer, watching me over the brim.

"Who is going to be your pretend husband?" Brooke asks.

"I don't know yet. I'm working that out."

Brooke rests her head on Moss's shoulder. She grins mischievously. "Are you going to tell us why you were at her apartment yesterday, Banks?"

My gaze snaps to his. As his smile grows in amusement, my brows lift in fear.

"*Banks* ..." I warn.

"Well, she—"

"*No,*" I shout, placing my wine on the table beside me. Laughing, I leap off the chair and toward him. I clamp my hand over his mouth. "Don't you dare."

Moss and Brooke laugh as Banks and I struggle.

He opens his mouth wide, licking my palm. I yelp in disgust but don't pull away. Eyes twinkling, he wraps his arm around my waist and pulls me onto his lap.

My heart races as my body temperature spikes. I pant, trying desperately to hold my hand against his mouth. *And not melt against him.*

Banks's body is as hard as I imagined. Sturdier than I dreamed. His hand on my hip is both as strong and tender as I anticipated.

*Dammit.*

He smiles under my efforts before reaching up and peeling my hands away from his face. Once he's free, he chuckles.

*"Don't,"* I say, looking him dead in the eye. Our faces are only inches apart. They're so close that I can feel the heat of his breath.

"What if I do?"

I pout. "I'll cry."

He smirks. "What if I don't?"

"I don't know." I catch my breath. "I'll be thankful."

"Not good enough."

"Of course, it's not," I say, unable to look away.

He slides my phone out of my pocket. The feeling of his hand only separated from my thigh by the thinnest piece of cotton ever made sends a rush of electricity through my body.

"What are you doing?" I ask, cognizant of the hardening of his cock beneath my ass.

He sets the phone beside him.

My heart races. "What are you doing, Banks?"

The words come out faster, higher than I expect. But that's what happens when you're filled with adrenaline and anticipation.

"I won't tell them on one condition," he says.

"What's that?"

Before I know what he's doing, he's standing with me in his arms. The movement is fluid and smooth—like I don't weigh an ounce more than a feather. My legs are scooped under one thick forearm. My back is supported by the other. Thank God—*for my sake*—his brother and Brooke can't see his front.

I hold on to his neck, squealing as he spins me around.

"Can you swim?" he asks me.

"What?" I look over my shoulder at the clear blue water. "Yeah. Why—*ah!*"

My body hits the pool surface with a splash.

As I return to the surface, a grinning Banks stands at the edge.

I tread water, running a hand over my face to clear off my hair and water. "You, Banks Carmichael, are a jerk."

"Just trying to make you feel at home." He holds my gaze for a moment until something flickers through his eyes. Then he turns. "Hey, Brooke. Can I take my pizza to go? I need to run by the shop."

"Sure," she says. "I guess. You need to go this late? Right now?"

"Tasha is going to kill me if I don't sign off on this stack of invoices, and I can't seem to get her to fake my signature."

Brooke laughs. "That's probably illegal."

"Yeah, but who is gonna turn her in? Not me," he says, following her to the oven.

I climb out of the pool and nod as Moss lays a towel onto a chair beside me. My dress clings to my body. *Thank God for my bikini underneath.*

Banks watches me while he waits for Brooke to get his pizza onto a plate.

His eyes are heated, warming me from across the room. *You want to mess with me? All right. Take this.*

Vaguely, I hear Moss and Brooke chatting away about the oven's temperature. I'm just trying not to combust under Banks's gaze.

I lift the edge of my dress. Water drips onto the decking, creating a little puddle around my feet. I lift it up and over my body, knowing damn good and well Banks hasn't looked away. As the fabric comes over my head and my eyes find his again, I'm proven right.

His pupils widen, and his bright blue eyes hood. *Good lord, I might combust on the spot.*

My core clenches as I toss the soaked material onto the ground next to me. I grin smugly, pulling my long hair to the side and twisting the water out of it.

His eyes drop, skimming the length of my body—down my chest, stomach, and thighs. A trail of heat is left in its wake as he draws his attention back the way it came.

I lift a brow, smirking.

Banks's gaze follows me to the towel and watches intently as I wrap it around my body. *Was your little prank funny now, buddy?*

"You know how I thought I hated you yesterday when you left my house?" I ask, wrapping the towel around me.

"Yeah."

"You outdid yourself today."

He runs his tongue around his lips and then turns to Brooke. He takes the pizza she hands him, and then looks at me over his shoulder as he leaves.

"Hey, Sara," he says.

"What?"

He gives me a parting wink. "Back at ya, babe."

Then he's gone.

# CHAPTER 6

## *Sara*

*I SHOULDN'T BE DOING THIS.*

"Yet here I go," I mutter, exiting Maddox's back door.

Birds chirp in the trees as I plod my way across the lawn. The late Sunday morning sunshine is bright but not as hot as it has been. *Or maybe my insides are still burning, and I don't notice the outside temperature.*

The only good thing about not being able to stop thinking about Banks's arms around me last night is that it confirmed one thing—I'm not fucked up. My era of being bored with men seems to have passed because I certainly wasn't apathetic last night. *Annoyed that my favorite vibrator is gone, but not apathetic.*

To celebrate the matter, or, at the very least, to test beyond Banks, I texted The Businessman to see if he was available this afternoon for *a meeting.*

"If everything goes right with Brock, he'll be my fake fiancé by nightfall."

My stomach twists, but I ignore it.

Banks's house is blue with crisp white trim and shutters. The porch has a white swing hanging from the rafters, and the garage attached to the side of the house is nearly as big as the living space.

Something about that makes me smile.

I take the five stairs and knock on the front door.

"Who is it?" Banks yells from the other side.

"It's Sara."

There's a pause. "Go away."

I chuckle and try the handle. It turns in my hand, so I push it open.

The house is open and airy as I step inside the foyer. A bookcase sits to my left next to an archway into the living room. A large clock sits on my right. There is a set of stairs in front of me, and beside them is a walkway leading to the kitchen.

Banks sits at the table in only a pair of shorts.

I gulp and close the door behind me.

His hair is wild, like he just got up, and as I grow closer, I notice his eyes are sleepy. It's a soft, gentle version of him—and I don't hate it.

"I'm pretty sure *go away* doesn't sound like *come in*," he says, grinning.

"No, but I knew what you meant."

He shakes his head but goes back to his cereal.

"What are you doing?" I ask him.

"Eating," he says as a dribble of milk falls from his lips into a bowl. "Want some?"

"No. Maddox made pancakes this morning."

He rolls his eyes.

I laugh. "I would bring you some, but then I remembered you threw me into the pool last night."

"Yeah," he says, licking a dot of milk off his bottom lip. "I did."

I shiver. To hide the movement, I sit at the table.

"Have a seat," he says after I'm already sitting.

I ignore him and look around.

The kitchen is a mess but not *dirty*. There's stuff piled on the other end of the table, on most of the counters, and a lopsided box by a door that I presume goes to the garage.

The trash can is overflowing with pizza boxes and paper towels, and a blanket is draped over a barstool.

"What?" he asks.

"Are you a hoarder?"

He lets the spoon clink against his bowl. "Are you always a pain in the ass?"

"I'm just saying that there are systems you can use that help you declutter."

"I like things the way they are."

"How do you find anything?"

"Because it's where I put it."

"Huh." I shrug and look at him again. "I'll cut to the chase. I need your help."

"Nope." He gets up and takes his bowl to the sink. "Not helping you ever again."

I sigh. "I don't need you *to do* anything. I just need to borrow something."

He leans his back against the cabinet. His abs are a freaking washboard, rippling as he moves. *Dear Lord.*

Banks stares at me like I'm an alien, like I showed up here and operate under a set of rules that don't make sense.

"*What?*" I ask.

"You realize that no one comes here to borrow my stuff, right?"

"That's not true because I'm here to borrow your stuff."

"No. That's not how this works."

"That's not how what works?"

He spreads his arms out. "This. My life. I'm the borrower, not the borrow-ee. I borrow everyone else's things. They don't borrow mine."

*A satisfied smirk looks very good on Banks Carmichael. A fact I wish I didn't know …*

I square my shoulders to his. "I'm not everyone else."

"No, you're not. You have less of a chance than they do to borrow my stuff." He cocks his head to the side. "You show up here, move in with my brother—"

"For a few days."

"Join us for pizza night—"

"I was invited."

"You walk in my front door uninvited—"

"*It wasn't locked.*"

He stands tall. "And now you think you can borrow my stuff?" His voice rises. "Who do you think you are?" He takes a deep breath. "*Me?*"

I roll my eyes, undeterred by his antics. "Obviously, I don't think I'm you. If I were you, I wouldn't need your help."

"Well, you're over here ignoring personal boundaries and thinking my things are community property. That's very *me* of you to think."

"I quite like your way of thinking when it benefits me." I narrow my eyes. "Like now."

He shakes his head. "I'm not helping you."

"Do you have a little thing you use to make sure your tires have enough air in them?"

He watches me like he's not sure what to do with me—which is precisely the reaction I wanted. The fucker practically blackmailed me, pulled me into his lap and set my libido on fire, and then threw me into the pool—*and then left*.

While I might not be exactly mad about it, if I must be frustrated, sexually or otherwise, he does, too. Period.

"A tire pressure gauge?" he asks.

I shrug. "There's a light on in my car about my tires. I assume that's what it means. Anyway, I don't have the thingy to check it."

"You know there's one built-in to the air pumps at gas stations, right?"

I lean forward. "No, I didn't know that. But I'd like to check it before I go."

He crosses his arms over his chest. "Where are you going?"

"That's none of your business."

"It is if you want my *tire pressure thingy*."

I glare at him. He finds it amusing.

For some reason, I don't want to tell him where I'm going. I'm not embarrassed that I'm meeting The Businessman, but the idea of telling Banks I'm meeting a guy for a quickie and then a fake fiancé proposal doesn't make me all warm and fuzzy inside.

"Forget it," I say, starting to stand.

"Stop." He groans, tilting his head to the ceiling. "Just … stop."

I lower myself back into the chair and try not to fix my gaze on his Adam's apple. The alternative is to look at his pecs, abs, and glorious arms. *Not. Helping.*

"You're really driving me nuts," he says, dropping his chin again and looking at me.

"Why?"

He sighs. "Are you going to tell me where you're going or not? Your tire pressure might not be good for going to the beach, but it might be okay to go to the grocery store."

*Good point.* "Okay, well, I'm going to Sunnydale."

He waits as if he expects me to expound on the topic. The longer he waits, the more irritated I get. *He wants to know? Fine.*

"I'm meeting a guy over there," I say.

His head nods slowly, but his face remains passive. "The asshole ex-boss?"

"Nope. Because even I have lines I won't cross and being engaged is one of them."

"Who is this one?"

"What's it to you?"

"Nothing. Just asking you a question."

I take a deep breath. "His name is Brock."

"What's he do for a living?"

I snort. "I don't know."

He screws up his face like he's confused.

"We don't talk about what we do for a living, Banks. I'm not into him because he's a banker or a used-car salesman, you know?"

"Is he nice to you?"

"*I don't know,*" I say, laughing. "I guess so. Why? What a weird question."

"You said that your boss was a dick. I'm just wondering if you only choose assholes or if that was a special occasion."

I stand. "Oh, no. They're usually dicks. Why? Do you want to join the harem?"

Banks keeps a side-eye trained on me as he moves across the kitchen. He opens a drawer under the microwave and rummages through it.

"Is there a reason he's not picking you up?" Banks asks.

*Huh?* "Because I have a car. When is the last time you picked up a woman for a date? Not that this is a date."

He slams the drawer shut and looks at me. "I pick up Gloria every Tuesday afternoon, thank you very much."

*Gloria. The old woman who Ashley was telling me about.*

I hold his gaze, grinning. He grins back. *His smile is blinding.*

"Where's your car?" he asks.

"In Maddox's driveway."

He walks by me. "Let's go."

*Okay.*

"Did you just pull that thingy out of your silverware drawer?" I ask, following him.

"No. I'm magic. It appeared out of thin air."

*What?* I have so many questions, but I don't know where to start.

He slides on a pair of sandals before we exit the house. I follow him across the lawn, taking the opportunity to appreciate his ass in those shorts and his shoulders in the sunlight.

He squats next to my back tire. "Which one do you think is low?"

"I have no idea. It just says *low tire.*"

"That one is fine," he says, moving to the front. "Maddox could've done this for you, you know."

"Yeah, but he was up pretty late." I blow out a breath. "They are *so loud.*"

Banks smirks.

"I mean, I get it," I say. "They're in the honeymoon phase of things. But still. I felt dirty listening to it."

He gets up and walks to the other side of my car.

"What do you do on Sundays?" I ask.

"Depends. We all have dinner at Mom's, though." He looks up at me. "Are you coming today?"

I shake my head. "Believe it or not, I don't want to disturb your entire family dynamics."

"As much as I love that for me, they wouldn't mind."

"Would *you* mind, Banks?"

He grins, getting up and going to the last tire. "I always mind when you're around."

I grin too. Because I think he's lying.

"Do you just not want me to see your girlfriend?" I ask, poking for information. I don't know why—it doesn't matter. Still, I'm curious. "Are you afraid I'll tell her you threw me into the pool like a barbarian?"

Surely, he wouldn't have messed with me so much if he had a girl-friend. *And looked at me like he wanted to do very dirty things to my body.* Even as I consider this possibility, I don't think it's true. That kind of game doesn't seem to be something that's in the Carmichael men's genetics.

He stands, dusting his hands off. "I don't have a girlfriend."

"Why not?"

"I don't know. Busy, I guess. I work a lot."

"That's a cop-out answer."

He leans forward and smiles. "That's the truth." He rocks back away from me. "What about you? Why do you have so many boyfriends?"

"I don't have *that many*," I say, scoffing. "And I wouldn't call any of them *my boyfriend.*"

"Why not?"

"I don't know. It's not like that between us."

He lifts his chin. "What's it like between you?"

I have half a notion to blow him off and tell him it's none of his business—because it's not. But he doesn't seem to be judging me at all, just curious. Concerned? I'm not sure. But whatever it is, it has me answering him.

"I don't want a boyfriend," I say. "But I want the benefits of having one."

"So you want to have sex."

"Right." I grin. "I want sex, but not the other crap that goes along with it. I just don't have the stomach for it."

"What kind of crap?"

"You know, the wanting to tell me what to do with my time. Expecting me to be a certain person. Thinking that it could end with marriage." I shrug. "I'm not into *that* kind of dating."

He hands me the gauge. He's ... angry, maybe. It's a look I don't think I've seen on Banks's face before. Yet I don't think he's angry with me.

"At least get the fuckers to pick you up," he says. "Make them show you a little respect."

My heart swells at the unexpected burst of kindness from Banks.

"What do you want me to do with this?" I ask, twiddling the gauge between my fingers.

"Put it in your glove box and keep it. Then you'll have one."

"I don't want to take yours."

He grins. "I have a hundred of them. It's fine. Trust me."

We exchange a soft smile.

"What's the verdict?" I ask. "Do I need a new tire? Just some air?"

"It's fine. You just need your computer reset."

I grimace. "That sounds expensive."

"It's not. Just bring your car by my shop this week, and I'll reset it for you."

I gasp. "Banks Carmichael, are you doing me *another* favor?" I swat his shoulder. "Look at you, being so sweet."

"*Hardly.* I'm saving myself a step because you'll mention it to Ashley, and she'll mention it to Maddox, and he'll mention it to me like he does every damn car issue." He pauses and stands tall. "Well, that makes sense since I am the resident car expert."

I giggle. *He's so adorable when he wants to be.*

He's about to speak when an engine starts, and a car comes down the road from the cul-de-sac. It slows when it gets to us.

"Hey, Banksy," a man who looks like an older Banks says. "You must be Sara."

I nod and wave. "I am."

"I'm Kixx, the father of this brood. This is Damaris." He juts a thumb toward a beautiful lady in the passenger's seat.

She's waving too. "Dinner is at three. You're welcome to come. We'd love to have you."

"Thank you for the invitation," I say.

Kixx looks at Banks. "Going to the grocery store. We'll be back shortly." He looks at me again. "Nice to meet you, Sara."

"You too," I say.

With a beep of their horn, they're gone.

Banks looks at me and shakes his head, a grumpy smile on his lips. "No, Sara. You cannot have my parents too. They're mine, dammit."

I laugh. I can't help it. He's a petulant child who's just had his favorite toy taken away. I can barely hold back a snort.

How this man goes from this to the sexy fucker at Moss's last night is beyond me. *I'm not mad about it, though. Not even a little bit.*

"Don't worry, Banks. I won't be there this afternoon."

"Good. When did you say you're moving again? I need all the attention back on me."

I laugh. "Tuesday."

"Great."

"Good," I say.

He watches me for a long moment, a playful smile on his lips. Instead of volleying with me anymore, he turns toward his house.

"Later," he says.

"Later."

I watch him go and assess the softness in my chest. It worries me. I'm not soft.

*But why do I feel like too much time with that man will make me that way?*

Better get my guard up and fast.

# CHAPTER 7

## *Banks*

Mom thrusts a package of toilet paper into my chest. "Here."

"Oof." I take them from her. "How did you know they were mine?"

"Because I didn't order them."

"Could've been Foxx."

She lifts a brow and sighs. "Everyone else in this family has their own Prime account except you."

I lift a brow right back at her. "Because I'm minimizing my environmental impact. There's no sense in all of us having an account when we all live right here and can share."

Mom shakes her head.

"What?" I ask. "If you didn't want us being so close, you shouldn't have bought us all houses on the same street. It's all your fault when you think about it."

Dad comes down the hallway, a kitchen towel over his shoulder. He stops when he sees me holding the package. "One question."

"Shoot."

"Why can't you just stop at the store on your way home from work and grab a package of toilet paper?"

"Easy," I say. "Two reasons. One is that you don't think about needing toilet paper until you need it. As in, when you're on the toilet.

So ordering it when it's on your mind is better than running out. You feel me?"

Dad just stares at me.

"Two, have you ever tried to get toilet paper and paper towels at the store? It takes up your whole damn cart. I either get food or I can get toilet paper and paper towels. There isn't an option for both."

"You could get smaller sizes," Dad suggests.

"Wait." Mom holds a hand in the air. "Back up. When did you start going to the store? You actually have food in your house?"

I set the package by the back door. "I went once and that was my experience. I'm trying not to repeat it."

Dad shakes his head.

"You go in thinking you're going to grab some lunch meat and call it a day," I say. "But no. There are forty-six-thousand kinds of turkey. Then there's the family reunion happening at the deli counter. Ten minutes in, and I'm ready to offer to tell Uncle Bob to fuck off myself and I don't even know the guy."

Mom laughs.

"People stink," I say. "Like, they haven't bathed stink. And they're touching everything in there like they're intentionally trying to spread the stink to the apples." I gag. "I can't. And there's the kids screaming. The people on speakerphone walking down the middle of the aisles. Yeah, it's a nope for me. I'm just going to have the essentials delivered and eat at your house from now on. I tried."

"Well, trying *is* more than I expected," Dad says.

I kiss Mom on the cheek. She pats my face like she used to do when I was a little boy. Even now, it makes me happy. *Sara can't take this away from me.*

"What's for dinner?" I ask as Dad rummages through the overflow pantry in the hallway.

"I made your favorite—pork chops, buttered potatoes, and green beans," Mom says.

"And cooked apples?" I ask.

"You know I didn't forget the apples."

I grin and walk by her. "You're the greatest, Mom."

"Don't forget your toilet paper," she says.

"I'll get it before I leave." *Maybe.*

Sunday Dinner is in full swing as I enter the kitchen. Pots boil on the stove, a timer beeps on the oven. My brothers sit around the table with glasses of tea in their hands.

I look forward to this every week—the one day that we all get together without question. Mom making food. Dad giving her hell. My brothers catching up from the previous week and making plans for the next.

I've worried my whole life that this would end. That Foxx would move and do whatever it is he does somewhere else. Moss would decide to try life elsewhere. That Maddox would want a break from all of us and start a life in a place without being *one of those Carmichael kids.*

*Me?* Being *one of those Carmichael kids* has been a part of who I am since the day I was born. There's never been a moment in my life that there haven't been four boys before me and Paige with me; it's all I know. My teachers compared me to them. My girlfriends' parents were aware of the antics of Jess and Moss. The wrestling teams remembered Maddox coming through the year before and were ready to tear me apart.

And I didn't mind. Actually, I kind of liked it. Paige liked it too.

I never felt alone in that scenario. I always felt like a part of something bigger, like I was a piece of a puzzle. There were people to come home to, that expected something of you, that would hunt you down if you were late on curfew. *And probably relished the chance to embarrass you in front of your friends. Thanks, Jess.*

The only thing I've been afraid of in my life is this ending. Every week when we show up at Mom and Dad's, it reminds me that it hasn't. And hopefully, it won't.

I pour myself a drink. "What are you guys arguing about?"

"Listen to this shit," Maddox says, rocking back in his chair. *Mom's going to be pissed about that.* "Jess thinks he can beat me in a race."

I take a sip of my tea and make my way to the table. "Race as in cars or feet?"

"Feet." Maddox laughs. "There's no fucking way."

"*Please,*" Jess says, shaking his head. "You'd have no chance against me in a forty-yard dash."

Foxx crosses his arms over his chest and tries not to laugh. He flicks a toothpick around between his lips.

"Moss," Maddox says. "Tell him the truth—that I'd beat his ass in forty yards."

Moss looks between the two of them. "I don't know."

"*What*?" Maddox says, mouth gaping.

"You both know I'd take you, right?" I say, sitting at the far end of the table.

Jess snorts. Maddox laughs. Moss shakes his head. Foxx just stares at me.

"I'm the youngest," I say. "Quickest. I'm in better shape than all of you. And although looks probably don't have much to do with it, I'm also the most handsome."

"I would've brought my boots if I'd had known the shit was gonna get this deep," Foxx says.

"Oh, what?" I turn to him. "You think *you* could beat me?"

There is no doubt that I would beat Foxx's ass in wrestling. As a matter of fact, I'd take all my brothers with little fanfare. And if it was a straight-up fair fight, Jess is the only one that I think has the potential to give me trouble. But if all rules were off the table and it was a life-or-death situation, something tells me that none of us would stand a chance. Call it a fighter's intuition.

Foxx would win before we even knew we were in trouble.

"Banksy," Foxx says, slipping the toothpick out of his mouth. "I applaud your self-confidence. But it would behoove you to remember that overconfident individuals are prone to making mistakes."

I look him in the eye, wondering if he'll flinch. He doesn't. *Awesome*. "Well, it's a damn good thing I'm not overconfident then, isn't it?"

"Banks versus Foxx," Moss says, resting his forearms on the table. "Didn't have this on my bingo card for today, but I'm here for it. Let's go."

"Can you even measure forty yards?" Foxx asks. "If I asked you to name something forty yards from you right now, could you give me a respectable answer?"

"Of course." *I think.* With my brothers' eyes on me, I start to sweat. "Forty yards from me right now is about to Mom's mailbox."

Foxx looks pleasantly surprised. I exhale. *Thank you, God.*

"Why is it always *Mom's* mailbox?" Dad asks, coming into the kitchen. "What about Dad's mailbox? I get mail there too, you know."

"Well, so do I, but I don't call it my mailbox," I say.

Jess snickers.

"Hey," Dad says, draining the potatoes. "Can one of you set up one of those apps on my phone that lets me send and request money?"

"Yeah," Maddox says. "Are you finally joining the rest of the world?"

"I finally have no choice. I needed to send some quick cash to a client today and I didn't have any of the apps. I had to go to the ATM and get cash."

"You know, Dad, that sounds a little suspicious," I say.

He looks up. "Very funny."

"Dammit," Maddox says, looking at his phone. "*Fucking hell.*"

"What's wrong?" Moss asks.

Maddox slams his phone on the table. "I just got a text that the guy occupying the house that Sara is supposed to rent on Wednesday won't leave. The landlord is going to have to evict him and that can take weeks."

My stomach falls to the floor.

This has nothing to do with me—not one little thing. I didn't set up Sara to live with my brother. I didn't help organize her new digs. Heck, I don't even know the landlord in question.

*Why do I feel like this is about to affect me?*

"What are you going to do?" Moss asks. "That kind of puts you in a pickle."

"Don't I know it," Maddox says. "I just got married. You can imagine what I want to be doing and what I can't be doing when there are houseguests."

Foxx shrugs. "Then why did you allow her to stay with you in the first place?"

"Because Sara is Ashley's best friend," Maddox says. "And a part of marriage is compromising and keeping your spouse happy."

"If Ashley isn't happier …" Jess looks around for Mom, making sure she's nowhere within earshot. "…fucking you than having Sara sleeping over for a week, then you got yourself a problem, brother."

Maddox holds his head in his hands. "I don't know what to do. I have to get her out of my house, but there's nothing available that she can afford. Trust me, I've scoured the market and called in favors from everyone I know. There's nothing."

Call me a soothsayer, but I can see the future. I know where this is going—where they're going to want it to go.

My chest burns as I quickly try to craft why Sara can't stay with me. *Because I know they're gonna ask.*

"Hey," Ashley says, coming into the room. Brooke and Pippa are on her heels. "Sorry that we're late. I found a bookstore and you know how that goes."

Maddox tips his head back. Ashley plants her hands on either side of his face and kisses him.

"I got bad news, babe," Maddox says, twisting in his seat to see Ashley.

"What?"

"Sara's rental fell through."

Ashley's face pales. "*No, it did not.*"

"Where is she now?" Maddox asks. "We need to get a plan together because I need you all to myself as soon as possible."

Ashley sits on Maddox's knee. "I just talked to her. She's with Becca at the beach."

A smile ghosts my lips. *With Becca at the beach, huh? Interesting development.*

Brooke bumps my shoulder as she walks by. "Hey, Honey said to remind you that they need your new pics this week." She grins as she drops into a chair beside me. "Apparently, all the women at the retirement center are chomping at the bit to see Sparkles in all his glory."

"They know they aren't getting dick pics, right?" I ask, my eyes widening.

Everyone laughs.

"I'm serious," I say. "I'm starting to get stage fright."

"Your last picture was a hit," Jess says, smirking.

I narrow my gaze at him. "You are my least favorite brother. I like you even less than Foxx."

"I'm wounded," Foxx deadpans, bored with the conversation.

"Foxx," I say, "let me ask you a question. How did we all get amazing personalities, and you got one that resembles a cardboard box? Did you have to sacrifice that for the rest of us? If so, thanks, big guy."

He's nonplussed. "I would like to apologize on behalf of all your siblings that we didn't leave any brain cells for you."

"How do you get through the day without someone trying to fight you?" I ask.

"I never said I get through a day without someone trying to fight me."

"What do you do all day, anyway?"

His lips twitch. "If I told you, I'd have to kill you."

"Tell him," Jess says, making everyone laugh. "Please."

I study Foxx across the table. *Yup. It's time you got roped into the family shenanigans.*

Mom calls everyone to the kitchen to make their plates of food.

My mind goes to Sara and her smart-mouth, sweet-ass, gorgeous self. The way she fell onto my lap last night. How easy it was to hold her there. *How much I liked it.*

But does it matter, really, how much I liked having her against me when I know *it's Sara,* for crying out loud? She's a player. A vixen.

*"I don't want a boyfriend. I want the benefits of having one. I want sex, but not the other crap that goes along with it. I just don't have the stomach for it."*

She's a woman who won't be tamed.

Not that I'd want to tame her, but I'm not in the market to spend time with a woman who bothers me as much as she turns me on.

Nah, fuck that.

She can stay Maddox's problem. God knows I don't need any more of those in my life.

# CHAPTER 8

## *Banks*

"Hey, Banks," Ashley says, smiling at me over the back of the sofa.

The floor lamps cast a warm glow over the living room. It's a stark contrast to the inky night sky through the windows. But as I make my way into the living room, I pause and take in the scene before me.

*This is suspicious.*

Ashley sits on one end of the couch with a smile a bit too wide—even for her. Maddox stands behind her, clutching a beer. I've seen this look on his face before. He's borderline pissed. *At least I didn't have anything to do with it for once.* But then my gaze swings to the other side of the room, to the chair and ottoman next to the fireplace, and *shit.*

My stomach drops and then twists so hard my abs flex.

Sara sits with her legs, muscled and tanned, stretched across the ottoman. A fingernail is between her teeth. She's edgy. It's as if she's ready to spring from the cushion and burst into one of her line of questions or mini rants that I can never quite keep up with.

*I shouldn't be here.*

"Hey," I say, staying in place. "I, um, just came over here to see if I can borrow the duct tape in the back of the junk drawer by the sink."

Ashley's brows pull together. "How do you know there's tape there?"

"Did you move it?" I ask.

"I didn't even know there was tape there, Banks."

"So it's still there then," I say, avoiding Sara's gaze and heading into the kitchen.

*I should've gone to Moss's.* My lips threaten to part into a smile. *Yeah, but Sara wasn't there.*

The woman has been on my mind all day like a virus, infecting all my thoughts. I went to extreme lengths to stop thinking about her— lengths that included taking apart a transmission, calling my sister, and making a stop at the farm supply store.

*Did Sara see the guy she told me she was meeting? Why was she with Becca? What is she going to do about a place to live?*

Not that it's my problem—none of it's my problem. *Still, I'm curious.*

I pull open the drawer and locate the tape.

"What do you need that tape for?" Maddox asks. "Also, I love how you know exactly where things are in my house."

"Photographic memory," I say.

"That's not really what I was getting at," Maddox says. "It was more the ridiculousness that you know where all the things are in my house, not the impressiveness of it."

I shut the drawer. "Well, you're obviously looking at things the wrong way."

My phone buzzes in my pocket. I pull it out.


**Jess: ARE YOU FUCKING KIDDING ME?**


I smirk. *This should be fun.*

"Guys, I gotta go," I say.

"Wait," Ashley says. "We wanted to talk to you."

I glance up as my phone buzzes again. "Now is a really bad time."

Jess: WHERE ARE YOU, YOU LITTLE RAT
BASTARD?

"Can you wait just a second?" Ashley asks.

Me: I'd keep rats away, given the current
circumstances.

*Fucker.*
My phone buzzes again, but this time, so do Maddox's and
Ashley's.
*Oh shit.*

Jess: Anyone seen Banksy?

"Hey," I say, looking up. "No one reply to Jess with—"
*Ding*!

Maddox: He's standing in my kitchen.

I gasp. "You traitor."

Jess: Keep him there.

"What did you do?" Maddox asks, grinning.
"You know what?" I ask, side-eyeing the door. "I'm going to stay
right here. Since you just sold me out, the blood can spill all over your

floor and you can clean it up."

Ashley shakes her head. "I told you he was plotting something, Sara."

"I wasn't *plotting something*," I say. "I was preparing to execute a— *fuck*."

Jess must have jogged from the front door to the kitchen because it takes him all of one second to appear. I hop around the island so it's between me and the doorway. *Shit's about to get real.*

"Hey," I say, smiling at him. "How was your evening?"

He narrows his eyes. "I'm going to kill you."

"What did he do?" Maddox asks.

Jess and I stare at each other. The longer it continues, the more amusing it gets. The more amused I become, the angrier he gets. *It's a vicious cycle.*

"What did I do?" I ask, smirking. "Jess wasn't a fan of the big cock."

Sara snorts.

"I got him a bunch of little cocks instead," I say.

Jess turns to Maddox. "He fucking bought a dozen baby chickens and put them in my bathtub."

Maddox and Ashley burst out laughing. Sara grabs a pillow and covers her face.

"Twelve?" I ask, my forehead wrinkling. "There should've been thirteen."

Jess's head whips back to me. "There are twelve. We counted."

I grimace. "So did I. I actually got a deal on a baker's dozen because the girl working at the farm supply store thought I was a cutie." I shrug. "Her words, not mine."

"What, *the actual fuck*, am I supposed to do with a dozen fucking chickens, Banks? What were you thinking?"

"I was thinking that you'd relate more to baby cocks. I was trying to do you a favor."

He leans forward, planting his hands on the island. "What's wrong with you?"

"Me? What's wrong with you? I gave you a perfectly good giant chicken, and you put my name on the Golden Years Dating app, and I still have women on retirement pensions calling my phone leaving me really filthy messages that make me uncomfortable."

Sara giggles.

I turn to her. "You—*hush.*"

She lifts her brows and points at me. "You have enough problems on your hands tonight. Don't start with me."

"Don't start *with you*?" I ask, unable to keep from bantering with her. *My God, she's gorgeous.* "How did your date go this afternoon?"

She smirks. "It went amazingly well."

"Oh, did you and Becca find some nice seashells or what?"

Her smirk twists into a grin. But before she can retort, Jess slams his hands on the countertop.

"Can we focus here?" he booms.

"I was," I whisper.

This only irritates him more. "Do you know what Pippa is doing right now?"

I pretend to think about it. "No. There's really no way for me to know, but if you want me to guess, I'd say—"

"She's sitting on the bathroom floor with chickens crawling all around designing a chicken coop and calling herself a chicken mom."

"I don't think chickens crawl," I say. "You're a chicken dad now. You better know these things."

He grits his teeth together.

"Baby chickens are cute," Ashley says.

"Then I'll bring them over here. They *peep*," Jess says. "Loud. A lot. And they shit. And stink."

"The girl at the farm supply store said that if you keep their nesting material clean, they wouldn't smell. I got some extra bedding for you. It's in the back of my truck."

Jess glares at me before heading for the door. "I'm going home to disinfect my bathtub and try to convince Pippa to find a nice home for twelve fucking chicks."

"You better find that thirteenth one," I shout before the door slams shut.

As soon as Jess is gone, the room erupts in laughter.

A deep gratification from Jess's annoyance ripples through me. *He thought he would have the last laugh? I think not.*

"Chicks, Banks?" Maddox asks, amused. "Where do you come up with this stuff?"

"It's a talent."

"Are you ever going to let this go with Jess?" Ashley asks.

"Well, Maddox said I couldn't put spiders in Foxx's car. I have to keep myself entertained somehow. Besides," I say, moving into the living room. "What would be worse than getting texts and calls throughout the day? I'll tell you what—something you can't just turn off. I can put my phone on my desk or turn off the ringer. What can he do with chickens?"

Sara grins. "He can give them to a farm."

"Not when Pippa loves them." My laughter sounds like a villain's, but I can't help it. "He'll have to keep them. *Forever.*"

Maddox sighs.

"What if he can't find the last one?" Ashley asks. "The poor little thing. Could it have hopped out of the tub? Can chicks fly?"

I shrug. "I don't know. But there were only twelve. I just want him to have to look for the thirteenth one for a while."

Sara laughs. The sound makes my dick hard.

"The dating app crossed a line," I say, finding myself staring at Sara. *I gotta get the hell out of here.* "On that note, I'm going to take my tape and go."

"Wait," Maddox says.

*Here we go …* "I really can't. I have something, you know, falling apart at my house, and I need the tape to put it back together." *Not bad for thinking on my feet.* "I'll see you tomorrow."

"Banks, *please*," Ashley says, standing. "We need a favor."

I cringe. *No. No, no, no.*

"Banks," Sara says, cooing my name like the sweet innocent angel she isn't. "I was hoping we could have a conversation."

"Well, I was hoping Jess wouldn't find the chickens until I was home so I wouldn't have to open the door. Tough luck for both of us."

She rolls her eyes. *There's the Sara I know.*

Maddox sets his beer down. "I'm going to cut the shit and get right to it."

"You do that," I say, steeling myself against whatever he's going to ask of me.

"The rental Sara was going to move into is having logistical issues," he says.

"You said that at dinner."

"The tenant won't move out, and the eviction will take anywhere from a week to three or four, probably." Maddox takes a deep breath. "We were hoping you had a place Sara could stay."

I hold my arms out and gesture around the house. "What's wrong with here?"

He stares at me.

I take a deep breath. "I don't know anything off the top of my head. I'll ask Tasha. Maybe she knows something." *Keep playing oblivious, Banksy. Walk away …*

Maddox doesn't blink.

Slowly, I turn to Ashley. She's staring at me too. Then I pivot to Sara. With one hand on her hip, she blows out a breath like I'm a fool.

"What? Why is everyone staring at me? *I* didn't kick her out." *I wasn't fucking her either. Sadly.* I shake my head and refocus. "I said I'll ask around."

"Banks," Maddox says, sighing.

"*What?*"

No one speaks. No one moves. Not one of them does anything other than stare at me.

I gulp. *They can't seriously be thinking she can stay with me. It's Sara.*

*Sara and Banks makes Sbanks, which is like Spanx, which means no one will be able to breathe because things will be so tight … No. Don't think of Sara and tight in the same sentence.*

*This can't happen.*

Sara slowly makes her way across the living room. I'm not sure if she's swinging her hips or if she always walks like that, but my eyes won't detach from her midsection.

"Come on, Sparkles," Sara says, smirking.

"Don't start with that shit."

She giggles.

*Lord, help me.*

My face heats as the reality of the situation bears down on me full force. Their stares. Their suppressed smiles. Their expectations.

No one has expectations of me. I work fucking hard to keep it that way. So why has that changed?

She grins, stopping just a few feet in front of me. "Breathe."

I glance down. It's impossible not to notice her cleavage pressed together by what looks like navy-blue lace beneath her shirt.

I suck in a breath. "You're out of your damn mind if you're going to do what I think you're going to do."

"What do you think I'm going to do?" she asks.

Pulling my bottom lip between my teeth, I settle my gaze on her face.

A spattering of freckles dusts the bridge of her nose. A mole sits just below her right eye. It's so tiny that it's barely noticeable. It all complements the roundness of her cheeks and the soft line of her jaw. *Dammit.*

"I have nowhere to go, Banks," she says.

"That sounds like a *you* problem to me."

I refuse to say it. I'm not opening this particular can of worms even though it's already cracked. If she wants to ask me, she'll have to say the words.

She rolls her eyes. "Can I?"

"Can you what?"

"It will only be for a couple of weeks."

"What will?"

"*Banks,*" she says, sighing. "Can I please stay at your house until the rental is vacant?"

"*No.*"

She throws up her hands and groans.

Maddox comes around the corner of the couch. I have half a notion to make a run for it—to jet across the lawn, dive into my house, and lock the door. But there is no privacy in this family—something I take advantage of daily. I've never looked at it from the position of being the one taken advantage of. *Man, this sucks.*

"Why won't you help us out?" Maddox says. "I've helped you out a million times over the years."

I cross my arms over my chest. "Like when?"

I could easily rattle off a million and a half times when he's helped me out over the course of my lifetime, but I need a second to think. To digest. To come up with a way out of this disaster—*because it would be a disaster*.

Sara and I barely got along long enough to get Ashley's stuff from Orlando to Kismet Beach. She's argumentative and headstrong. She's beautiful and sexy. My attraction to this little pain in the ass grows every time I'm around her, and I've had enough experience with women to know that when someone drives you bananas from the beginning, you just walk away.

In this case, I need to *run* away.

"Do you really want me to answer that?" Maddox says.

I groan. "She can't live with me."

"It's not *living with you*," Ashley says, coming to Maddox's side. "It's visiting you for a couple of weeks."

I glance at Sara. "It's the same thing."

Sara sighs. "I can't stay here, Banks. I'm making them miserable. That's making *me* miserable."

"So you want to spread the misery to me?"

Ashley looks sweetly at Sara. "You are *not* making us miserable."

"You're newlyweds and were being overly gracious to me in the first place," Sara says. "I can't extend this. It would be totally unfair, and I'd be a jerk, and despite what some people think, I'm not a jerk. Or I try not to be, anyway."

My heart pounds as I turn to my brother. He gives me the only look I didn't want to see—the one of disappointment.

I run my fingers through my hair and pace in a circle. Why did I come over here? Why couldn't I just stay at home and sign the invoices I brought back from the shop? Or something.

Anything besides this.

"What would I get out of it?" I say through clenched teeth.

"I'll clean your house," Sara offers.

I spin around. "No. See?" I point at her. "She'll come in and touch my stuff. Rearrange it. Move it."

"Oh, the irony," Maddox deadpans.

I narrow my eyes. "This isn't funny." Spinning around to Sara again, I shake my head. "You're *me-ing* me again. The world is only big enough for one me."

"Stop being dramatic," Sara says.

"Good luck with that," Maddox says, sighing.

Sara puts her hands on her hips. Her perfect little pout presses together, and she looks at me in exasperation. "I don't want this any more than you do."

"We've been here before. It seems to be a recurring theme."

"Shut up."

"That's not a very nice way to talk to your landlord."

She throws her hands in the air. "He's right. This will never work. I'll stay in a hotel."

"Good," I say as she storms off.

"Good," she yells back.

Maddox and Ashley watch, bewildered, as I march to the door. I let it slam shut moments before the door upstairs closes with a loud thud.

# CHAPTER 9

## *Banks*

I GLANCE AT THE CLOCK. *AGAIN.*

The day has gone by slowly, even for a Monday. It didn't help that I couldn't sleep last night. It also didn't help that when I got here, Tasha was saying the word *vacation* a lot. And it surely didn't make things go by faster as I kept checking the time.

*"Just bring your car by my shop this week, and I'll reset it for you."*

I didn't say to bring it by Monday. So why do I keep thinking she'll come by today?

I study my computer screen and try to decide between the white and blue options for the item in front of me. The white is crisper, but the blue would probably grab more attention.

I click the blue and stick it in my cart. *Done.*

Maddox hasn't called or texted me today either, and that's not helping things. Not that having a conversation with him about Sara would help, but it would make me feel better about it. Just knowing he wasn't mad—that he understood—would help tons.

Except he probably is mad, and he probably doesn't understand.

*Hell, I don't know if I understand myself.*

I stretch back, my chair squealing from the effort. I groan, feeling the pull of my muscles all the way to my toes. The relief is nice. It's needed. It's not *all* the relief I need, but it'll have to do until I get home.

*Home.*

"Dammit," I mutter and sit upright again.

As much as I don't want to—as much as it's against everything I stand for on a daily basis—I need to be an adult about this. I need to do the right thing. I need to stop being a pansy and help my brother.

*But, my God, what a mess this will make.*

There are no two ways about it. There's not a chance in hell that I get out of this unscathed. At best, she'll leave marks down my back when she goes. At worst, we'll be mortal enemies by the time her apartment is ready.

I say I hate her. *I want to hate her.* I want to be able to think of Sara and remember all the ways she gets under my skin and be happy she's not around.

But the trouble is that when I think of her, I remember all the ways I wish she'd get *under me,* and I'm irritated that's not happened yet. I'm annoyed I want it to happen. I'm disturbed that I know how that ends —what a disaster this will be for Maddox and Ashley when Sara and I do loathe one another—and I still want it. *Badly.*

"Fuck it," I say, giving in to the need that's festered inside me since I walked out of my brother's last night.

I pick up my phone, open my text app, and find Sara's name.

> **Me: Are you bringing your car in today or not?**

Her response comes immediately.

> Sara: No.

> **Me: We close in an hour.**

> Sara: Enjoy your evening.

I sigh, blowing out my breath hard.

> Me: Bring your damn car over here so I can reset the computer.

> Sara: I'm busy trying to find a place to stay.

> Me: Oh, okay. What are your options?

> Sara: Right now, I'm sitting at Mugger's and waiting on Brock to text me back.

*Brock? The guy she lied about meeting yesterday?* My fingers fly over the keyboard.

> Me: If you don't get your computer reset, your car might not make it to Brock's.

My insides twist, and I'm not sure if it's because the thought of her staying with Brock pisses me off or if it's that I just lied to her. Her car isn't going to do shit if she doesn't get it reset.

*And who cares if I don't know this Brock dude?* I do know men like him, and they're all assholes who shouldn't get to touch Sara. Period.

*Oh, well. Hard times call for desperate measures.* I adjust myself. *And I'm definitely hard.*

> Sara: That sucks for me. Although you said it would be fine to drive. So were you full of shit then or now?

"Stop being so difficult," I mutter, typing out a response.

"You okay, Banks?" Tasha calls from her desk. "Sounds like you need a vacation. But not with me. You need your own vacation."

*Stop talking about a vacation, Tasha.* "I'm fine."

"You're acting like a weirdo," she says just loud enough for me to hear.

I ignore her.

> Me: Muggers is a mile from my shop. Come here and let me help you.

I roll my eyes and send another text.

> Me: You'll be doing me a favor.

Sara: How?

> Me: Because I won't have to worry that you'll break down.

*Another lie, but I'm getting pretty good at this.*

Sara: 🙂

> Me: 😢

Sara: Fine, but I'm paying you.

> Me: Whatever. Just come over here.

There's a long pause.

> Sara: Can you make it cheap, though? I'm broke.

>> Me: JUST COME OVER HERE.

> Sara: Bossy you sometimes turns me on. I'm not going to lie. But today—it pisses me off.

*Motherfucking hell.*
My entire body tenses as I type furiously.

>> Me: Are you coming?

> Sara: Is that an innuendo or a real question?

>> Me: 😒

> Sara: I'll be there in five minutes. I was leaving Muggers anyway.

I drop my phone. It rattles on my desktop.

"You sure you're okay, Banks?" Tasha asks.

I look up to catch her standing in the doorway. She's studying me intently.

"I'm fine," I say. "Ashley's friend, Sara, will be in here in just a few minutes. Can you send her back here, please?"

"Sure," she says slyly. "But remember I'm leaving early today. I gotta get my daughter to her dentist appointment on time, or they won't see us anymore."

I nod.

She swallows, her chest rising and falling. "I also wanted to talk to you about something."

*Don't say vacation. Don't say vacation. Don't say vacation.* "Sure, what's up?"

"My husband and I were talking last night, and I told him how you said I should take a vacation."

Internally, I scream. "Yeah."

"He's going to an Illinois Legends meet-and-greet or something in Chicago. He won tickets somehow a while back. Anyway, he was thinking that it would be really cool if we could make it a family trip."

"When is it?" I ask.

"Friday," she says. "I told him it was probably too soon to take time off, but he insisted that I try. But if you don't think it's possible, then—"

"Go."

Her brows shoot to the ceiling. "Really?"

"When is he coming back?"

"He's staying a week," she says in a rush. "But I can be back Monday. The weekend is all I'm after, and oh, my gosh, Banks. I can't believe—"

Fuck it. "*Hey, Tash?*"

"Yeah?"

"Take the whole week off."

"*What*? Banks? *Really*?" she asks, her voice nearing squeal level.

This is not at all what I want to do, and I'm not sure how we'll function around here without her. But she's never asked me for a thing since the day she started, and if anyone deserves a week's break from this place, it's Tasha.

"Have fun with your family," I say, remembering Maddox's disappointment last night. "We might as well make one of our families happy."

She bounces on her toes. "Thank you, Banks. Honest. I could kiss your face right now."

"Don't let me interrupt." Sara stands next to Tasha, her eyes sparkling. "Should I wait in the lobby?"

Tasha's eyes go wide as a slow smile stretches across her lips. My heartbeat quickens.

"You're fine, Sara," I say, my eyes glued to hers. "I'll see you tomorrow, Tash."

"Have a good night, Banks," she says, smirking.

Sara enters my office, and Tasha shuts the door softly behind her.

The room fills with a warm, slightly sweet scent and an energy that I only feel when Sara is around.

My gaze drags up her bare legs capped in a pair of yellow shorts, over her thick thighs, across the curve of her hip, and over the round tits showcased in a tight white tank top.

"Hi," I say.

"Hi," she says, her tone as clipped as mine. She waits for me to respond, and when I don't, she rolls her eyes and sits in the chair across from me. "I looked up my tire alert, and the internet says it'll be fine and that the chances I'll break down are very, very small."

*Oh.* "There's a lot of misinformation online."

"Maybe." She lifts one leg and crosses it over the other. "My car is in the parking lot if you want to check it out. I'm not really sure why we're sitting in here."

I lean back and blow out a breath.

"Look," she says. "I found a place to live. You're off the hook."

My brows shoot to the ceiling. "You did?"

"Yeah. So if you can just clear my computer or whatever mechanic magic it requires, I can be on my way."

"Where are you moving to?" I ask.

"That's none of your business."

"With Brock?"

She grins. "Maybe."

I bend forward, resting my forearms on my desk, and look at her. She's so damn pretty and tries so hard to be tough. The persona she projects is a good one. She's a tough nut to crack. But underneath that strong-girl facade is a vulnerability she doesn't want the world to see.

I know because Paige had the same look in her eyes for a long time. It was only when she and I were alone, hanging out on the beach or riding around in my truck to escape the chaos of our brothers, did she explain it to me.

My sister grew up a Carmichael, but she was born a Hudson—to another family in another place. And even though she played it off like it didn't bother her that she was adopted, *it did.* She would have these bouts of feeling like she didn't fit in. And because of that, she had to be strong, tough, and indestructible. If she wasn't, it would only deepen the crack she perceived between her and our family.

It made her prone to destruction.

*Is that what's going on with you, Sara? Did you lose your whole family when your dad died? Do you feel alone in the world?*

My insides twist. *Whoa, get ahold of yourself here. She doesn't want you to know her deeply. She's told you that.*

"Well, that's too bad that you said yes to Brock," I say, shrugging.

She narrows her eyes. "Why?"

"Because I was going to let you stay with me. But since you've already committed to him and—"

"Wait."

*Got ya.* I grin. "Wait? Why?"

"Are you screwing with me?"

"Do you want me to be screwing with you?"

She fights a smirk.

This is a mistake—one I'll come to regret. But between needing to ease my guilt in regard to Maddox and needing to find a way to quell this pull I have to Sara, this is the only viable solution.

*Let's just hope I'm still viable after this is over.*

"If we could come up with some ground rules … I do have an extra bedroom."

"You do, do you?" She grins. "What kind of ground rules are you talking about?"

*Fuck if I know.* I grab the first piece of paper I can find—one of the invoices Tasha gave me to approve—and flip it over.

"First one is no touching my stuff," I say.

She tilts her head to the side. "Your stuff is everywhere, Banks."

"Because it's my house."

"I can't even walk through the house without touching your stuff. There's a car part on the kitchen table. You had a pair of boots turned upside down in the sink."

"I was working at the table, and the boots were drying."

She holds her hands out. *"You got the tire air thingy from your silver-ware drawer."*

"You could take a fork out and then close it. The tire pressure gauge didn't need to be moved."

She huffs. "Fine. What else?"

I scribble down the first rule on the invoice. "The second rule is that my room is off-limits."

"Easy. Deal."

"Third thing is don't leave your girly stuff all over my bathroom. And if you shed in the shower, pick it up."

"There's not a second bathroom?"

I add the two new rules to the paper. "There used to be. The second one is inoperable at the moment."

"Do I want to know why?"

"Probably not." I take a breath. "Fourth rule is no men who don't share my bloodline in my house. Period. Got it?"

She frowns. "What? You don't want to hear me and Brock getting it on?"

I narrow my eyes.

"Fine. No men in your house." She crosses her arms over her chest. "But I have rules of my own."

"I'm not done."

She narrows her eyes at me. "Go on."

"Five," I say. "Keep your vibrators in your room."

"Oh, you are so funny."

"I'm being serious." The thought of her lying in bed fucking herself is too much for this conversation. "Moving on … No touching Betsy. Don't even breathe on her."

"Who the hell is Betsy?"

"My car. She's in the garage under a dust cover." I narrow my eyes. "She's my baby."

"Fine. I don't want to touch your dumb car anyway. Rule seven," she says. "I can clean the house."

"*You can't make rules in my house*. That's not how this works."

She lifts a brow. "I won't move anything where you can't see it if you were looking for it in the original location, but—"

"I don't want you touching my stuff. Any of it. Hands off."

She groans. "We have to be able to sit at the table, Banks."

"Eat in bed. That's what I do."

She grips her arm rests like she's a second from lurching forward and walking out.

This isn't the hill I want to die on. I don't even really want to be on this hill, but I've already started climbing it and scaling back down without hitting the peak would be more awkward than suffering through the rest of the adventure.

"Fine," I say. "You can clean. But you can't throw anything away."

"*Fine.*"

"*Fine,*" I say again.

A slow smile spreads across her face, and she sinks back in her chair. "When do you want me to move in, roomie?"

I'm not sure whether to feel defeated or excited. Played or playing. Whether this is going to be hell … or heaven.

I shift in my seat in a futile attempt at relieving some of the energy coursing through my veins. "I'll be home in an hour and a half."

"Since I'm going to be there longer than a couple of days, I'm going to get a few more things from Sabrina's."

"Need help?" *Shut up, Banks. Help yourself for once, and shut the hell up.*

She grins softly. "No. But thanks."

The irritation riddling me begins to disappear as I absorb the relief in her eyes.

"I'll get out of your hair," she says, standing.

"I'll see you at home then?"

She smiles. "Yeah. I'll see you at home."

"Hey," I say as she gets to the door. "I still need to clear the code from your car."

She laughs and twists the knob. "We both know that's not necessary."

Then she winks and walks out.

*Played. I just got played.*

# CHAPTER 10

## *Sara*



It's so weird knocking on this door.

My knuckles rap against the purple-painted wood, a color I know my father would've hated. He let Sabrina do whatever she wanted, though, so he probably wouldn't have said a word.

The modest two-story house has seen better days. A crack runs along the edge of the porch. It gets bigger and deeper every time I see it. The garage door is dented in a perfect line of symmetry to Sabrina's car bumper and the hedges need trimmed as badly as my hair.

Dad would've had a meltdown at the sight of his castle in disarray. He kept things neat and tidy, a preference out of habit that hung around years after he left the Army. He was always so careful, so particular about everything in his life ... except me.

I knock again, the sound echoing inside the house. I stand on the stoop like I didn't live here for eighteen years—like this isn't my childhood home.

"Coming," Sabrina's voice rings from the other side of the door. When she pulls it open, it squeaks. "Hey. What brings you by for the second time in one week?"

She lets me inside.

"My plans changed," I tell her as she shuts the door behind me. "The rental I was getting is delayed, so I'm staying with a friend for a couple of weeks. I thought I'd grab a few more things from the garage, if you don't mind."

She leads me into the living room. "Of course, I don't mind. It's your stuff."

"Thank you for letting me store my things here. I'm sure it's a bit of a headache to walk around, but I really appreciate it."

"It's no trouble. So how are things?" She sits on the sofa. "You were a little scrambled when you were here before."

I sit in my father's recliner. It smells of cigars and Old Spice, and I find it hard to breathe for a moment. "I'm better. Calmer." I laugh to release some of the tension in my chest. "It's been a bit of a mess the last couple of weeks, but things are starting to settle."

*"If we could come up with some ground rules ... I do have an extra bedroom."*

A flood of warmth spreads through my veins as I recall Banks's words.

When Maddox told me the rental wasn't available, I panicked. There's no feeling quite like not having a home and being at the mercy of your friends—especially friends who are newly married. I knew Maddox and Ashley didn't want me there for an extended period. Why would they? And I knew I couldn't wear out my welcome. But the fact that I had nowhere to go was embarrassing.

I'm too old for this shit. *Shouldn't twentysomethings have a permanent place to stay?* I'm certain I should have a fat nest egg in the bank instead of walking the line of overdrawing it each month.

"You could always stay here, you know," she says politely. "Your room is still upstairs. Granted, I've made it into a hobby room for Bethany. But we could always pull out an air mattress for you."

Behind the words lie a caution not to take her up on the offer.

My heart squeezes, and I blink back a wash of red-hot tears. *Don't be emotional, dammit. Dad would be appalled that you don't feel welcome in his home.*

*Why does Sabrina pulling out an air mattress feel so temporary?* My breath catches. *Because that's all I am to her, to the life within these walls.*

I steady myself against the feelings welling up inside me—ones that I go out of my way to keep down. I can't focus on how alone I feel when I'm here. How this place reminds me of all I've lost … and can never get back. The loneliness that permeates my soul when I look around and everything I know, the things that made me who I am, are all distant memories. And the house, the people who are left—the stairs I raced down in the mornings and the wooden floor I mapped out to miss all of the squeaky boards when I came home late—it's all moved on. It's like I never existed. And that hurts so intensely that I grip the armrests to keep from keeling over in pain.

*Stop it, Sara. Stop allowing emotions into this moment. It's ridiculous.*

"Thank you," I say, widening my eyes so the tears absorb and don't overflow down my cheeks and humiliate me. "But I'm good."

She's relieved. "I'm sure you'll be happier there—or with Gretchen. How is Ashley's mother?"

Sabrina's words *sound* nice. They *are* nice. But they aren't *meant* to be nice.

Gretchen was my mother's best friend, and she promised my mom that she'd take care of me when Mom died. I was three, so I don't remember that. But Gretchen and my father both agreed that this conversation took place, and they both operated as if this were the law. By the time Dad married Sabrina when I was ten years old, Gretchen was my pseudo-mother, and it drove Sabrina out of her mind.

My new stepmother resented me; I was a stain on the perfect life she wanted to create. And I was unwilling to accept her role, pretend to enjoy her cold hugs, and I wasn't about to let her introduce me as her daughter in public.

"She's great," I say. "She's really happy Ashley is back in Kismet Beach."

"I bet she is. I can't imagine Bethany moving away. I'm not sure what I'd do with myself."

I give her my best smile. It's not much, but it's all I can muster.

"Speaking of your sister," Sabrina says. "She should be home soon. Want to stick around and say hello? I know she'd love to see you."

My spirits rise. "I'd love to see her too."

She smacks her palms off her thighs and stands. "Well, I'm going to get back to the kitchen and finish getting ready for a bake sale tomorrow. Bethany's choir group is selling goodies in front of Mugger's in the morning. You should come out and support the girls."

"I'll try."

She smiles, pausing like she wants to say something more but stops herself. "Great. Let me know before you leave, okay?"

"I will."

She nods and slips out of the room and down the hallway.

Baking trays rattle in the kitchen. It's the only sound in the house. I sit in Dad's chair and look around, rocking back and forth gently.

Our Christmas tree used to stand in the opposing corner. Dad would always let me put the angel on top. And on the mantel over the fireplace used to sit framed pictures of me with my mother and one of me with both of my parents. Those haven't been up in a long time.

I wonder vaguely where those things are. I've never asked. Questioning my stepmother while my father was still alive was out of the realm of possibility, and since he passed away, I haven't felt like dealing with Sabrina, the conversation, or the flurry of emotions that is likely to bring with it.

*Nah, it's just stuff. I can live without stuff.*

I stand and head toward the garage. There are no pictures of me—just images of Bethany with my dad and Sabrina hung in the places my elementary school pictures used to hang. The spot in the corner of the wall that I scribbled on when I was a toddler, right after Mom died, has been painted over. I pass the spot my high school graduation photo used to be—the one with me, Dad, and Sabrina. She took that down too.

It's like my mother and I never existed in this space at all. That this was never my home. Everything of my life here has been erased like none of it mattered.

The garage is hot and sticky. I open the door to the outside to get some air and light. My boxes are lined up along the back wall with labels such as *kitchen, bathroom,* and *who freaking knows?*

I find the one marked clothes and sort through until I find a few pairs of shorts and tops.

"Sara, what are you doing here?" Bethany asks, walking up the driveway. "I thought that was your car."

She has her mother's long legs and my plump lips. She has long, blond hair but the same birth mark that our father and I have in the bend of our arms. Unlike her mother, she races toward me with open arms and lets me pull her into a big hug. *This is the only thing that feels like coming home.*

"Hey, you," I say, letting her go. "Where have you been?"

She glances at the door to the house. "Don't tell Mom, okay?"

"Bethany ..."

"It's nothing bad," she says, the tone of her voice not matching the nonchalance of the words. "I was just at my friend's house and her parents weren't home. I know Mom will think the absolute worst and ground me for eternity."

"That's not cool, you know."

She rolls her eyes. "I know you were the black sheep of the family. I've heard stories about your wild days. So don't start lecturing me."

"Listen, I'm not lecturing you about anything. And, yeah, I've had some wild days. But I wasn't having them at fourteen and neither should you."

She looks unamused.

"Listen to your mother," I say, going back to the boxes. *What will I need for Banks's house?* A burst of excitement pulses through me. "If you ever get in trouble, you can call me. You know that, right?" I look at her over my shoulder. "You *should* call me."

"I'm not going to get in trouble. Relax."

"So you think ..."

I close the box with clothes and then open the bathroom box. *I doubt he has appropriate shampoo and conditioner. He probably doesn't even have a hairdryer. What about towels?*

"Did you get your new house?" Bethany asks, sitting on a tote full of kitchen equipment.

"No. Not yet. I'm staying with a friend."

"A friend that I know?"

I laugh. "I don't know."

"Ashley?"

"She's married now, remember? I told you that," I say, plucking a few towels out of my stash.

"Okay, so … Becca?"

I shake my head. "No, Becca was going back to Texas and let her lease expire. But then she changed her mind and lives in a one-bedroom cracker box. I'd be sleeping on the floor."

"So who then?"

I fight a smile as I close the box. "His name is Banks."

"Oooh. Okay. *His* name, huh?"

"You're reading too much into this, Bethany. He's Ashley's husband's brother and he lives right across the street from them. He's—"

*"Frigging hot."*

I spin on my heel to face her. She holds up her phone with the Social app on the screen. Smiling back at me is a picture of Banks, sans shirt, leaning against a car. *Wow.*

"*You* are moving in with *this guy*?" she asks, dipping her chin and raising her brows. "Is that what I just heard you say?"

I can't help but laugh. "That's what I said."

"Can I come over?"

My laughter grows louder. "I don't know. Maybe, but probably not. His house is a pigsty. You could get tetanus from stubbing your toe."

She looks at the phone, then back up at me. "Might be worth it."

"Stop it," I say, shaking my head. "You're too little to be looking at men like Banks."

*"Even his name is hot."*

"Help me gather this stuff and take it to my car," I say. "Stop thinking about bad boys who are way too old for you."

"Of course, he's a bad boy. Darn it, Sara. He's perfect."

I burst out laughing again. "I'm never letting you around him. His ego can't handle it."

I grab the towels and toiletries. Bethany gathers the clothes I pulled out of the boxes.

"What's your deal with this guy?" she asks. "Are you friends? More than friends? Are you engaging in activities that could lead to reproduction?"

My jaw drops. "Where do you get this stuff?"

"Health class." She opens the back door of my car. "That's how the teacher talks about sex. She makes it so weird. Like, just say *sex*. We all know what it is. Half my class has done it."

"Have you?"

She sighs. "No." She hands me the clothes. "I haven't met the right guy yet."

"I'm not making light of your teenage romances, but I assure you that you won't meet the right guy for many years, and if someone tries to convince you that they are the right guy—he's *really* not the right guy."

I shut my door, and we start the walk back to the garage.

"But how do you know?" she asks. "How do you know a guy is the right guy?"

*Didn't see this coming.*

I try to remember who I talked to about this kind of stuff because it definitely wasn't Sabrina. She would lose her cool. It would destroy her image of the perfect little family, and she would avoid that at all costs.

*Gretchen.* I smile. *I talked to Ashley's mom about this. Now I need to be this person for my sister.*

I slow my thoughts and try to come up with an honest but also safe response.

The first words that come to my brain are *hot* and *big dick energy*. I pause. *That's not the right response, and I could probably learn a lesson from that.*

My second thought is that you should have chemistry with the guy. But that's not really appropriate or clear for a fourteen-year-old.

I think about the men I've slept with over the years. *Which ones of them, if any, would I want my little sister sleeping with when she's of age?*

My pace slows, and a chill snakes up my spine. *None of them.*

"Have you talked to your mother about this?" I ask.

"I mean, sort of." She frowns. "She just tells me I'll know when the time is right and then moves on. That's super not helpful."

We sit on totes of my stuff and look at each other. I don't know what to say or what is my place to say at all. I definitely don't want to step on Sabrina's toes. But I have to say something so Bethany knows she can talk to me.

"Look, when you're ready to have sex, call me," I say. "And if you're in the throes of passion—"

She giggles.

"You should still stop and call me." I smile at her. "Sex can be wild and wonderful with the right person. But it can be a whole lot of headaches and hurt with the wrong one. So when you get to the place where you're considering it, let me know. We'll go have manicures and pizza and talk it out. Okay?"

Her face lights up. "You're seriously the best big sister in the world."

"I love you, kiddo."

"I love you, Sara," she says, wrapping her arms around my neck and holding me tight.

If only all emotions were this simple.

"There you are," Sabrina's voice rings out from the doorway leading into the house. "I didn't know you were home, Bethany."

"Just got here."

"Go get cleaned up. We're supposed to be at the Washburn's for dinner in an hour," Sabrina says.

Bethany turns to me. "Thank you."

I wink at her.

She gets up and goes into the house. Sabrina lingers in the doorway.

"I'm going too," I say, opening a wardrobe box and taking out the first dress I find. "I'll come back as soon as I can and get the rest of it."

"There's no hurry. It's not going anywhere."

"Thanks, Sabrina."

"Of course. See you soon."

As soon as I'm out of the garage, she pushes the button to make the door descend. It slams shut, sealing against the concrete.

I climb in my car with some of my possessions in the back, and buckle in. As I look down to grab the gear shifter, I notice my phone has a missed text.

Banks: Are you still coming?

A small grin tickles my lips.

Me: I'm on my way.

His response comes immediately.

Banks: Okay.

Me: Did you think I changed my mind?

Banks: After all the begging you did? No.

I laugh.

Me: I did not beg. I DO NOT BEG.

Banks: We'll see about that.

Goose bumps break out across my skin as I wait for another text. Nothing comes.

"Whew," I say, blowing out a breath and putting the car in drive. "This is going to be fun."

*Maybe more fun than I imagined.*

# CHAPTER 11

## *Sara*

Maybe I screwed up by not adding that he can't be shirtless at home *because* holy fuck. *I'll never get used to seeing him like this.*

Banks steps onto the porch as I climb out of the car. If I didn't know better, I would think he was intentionally trying to fuck with me.

His hair is unruly, like he just woke from a nap. A pair of gym shorts sit lopsided around his hips and highlight the sex lines that are a rarity in real life. They're usually only visible on Greek statues and Henry Cavill.

"I've never had a landlord meet me half-dressed before," I say, holding tight to the car door.

He smirks. "I'm not changing the way I live for you."

"I wouldn't dream of asking you to do that." *Especially when the perks are free porn.*

"Do you still have stuff at Maddox's?"

I shake my head. "No. I threw it all in the car before I went to Sabrina's."

He leans against a post by the steps leading down to the sidewalk and, without realizing it, I lean against my car.

A bubble of anticipation flutters in my stomach as reality sets in. I'm staying with Banks Carmichael.

*I'm. Staying. With. Banks. "Frigging hot." Carmichael.*

The idea was brought forth last night by Maddox and I only had five minutes to think about it before Banks walked in. But it was quickly put to bed after our little spat, and I began my search for temporary digs elsewhere.

His text this afternoon was a surprise—one that I didn't think he was serious about until he kept pressing the issue for me to come by. Even when I showed up, I never expected him to invite me to stay. And I expected even less that I would say yes and show up here this evening.

But here I am with my stuff in tow, ready to carry it into his home.

*Breathe, Sara.*

Banks's forehead wrinkles. "Are you all right?"

"Me? Yeah. I'm fine. Why?"

He shrugs it off, but my answer wasn't satisfying.

My phone rings, interrupting anything he's about to say. I reach into my middle console and grab it. The number on the screen is generic. *Probably a salesperson.* I click the button to send them to voicemail.

He jogs down the steps, and it takes every bit of self-restraint I can muster not to watch his muscles ripple in the sunlight.

"Let's get your stuff," he says. "I bought new sheets for the guest bedroom."

*He did?* "You did? That was very nice of you, and you didn't have to do that."

He grins. "Well, I shopped at Mom's. She has a closet full of clean linens that she never uses."

My phone rings again and the same number flashes on the screen. *What the heck?*

"Let me grab this real quick," I say. "They've called twice back to back and I don't know who it is."

"Go for it."

"Hello?" I say, walking toward the front of the car.

*"What are you doing, Sara?"*

The words are sarcastic, filled with exasperation and misplaced self-grandeur. *Joshua.*

A knot forms in the pit of my stomach. *How did I ever think this guy was fuckable?*

"Was that a real question or rhetorical?" I ask.

He scoffs. "I just got a call. Would you like to guess who from?"

"It doesn't interest me enough to guess who called you this afternoon. And, as a matter of fact, talking to you doesn't interest me enough to continue this conversation."

Banks watches me as I wander around the driveway and try to control my frustration.

*Why is Joshua calling me? Why does he think I care who called him? Why is it necessary that we ever talk again?*

Banks lifts a brow and folds his arms over his chest.

*Don't look at him. You'll get distracted.*

"Myles Petterson," Joshua says, spitting the words. "Myles Patterson called me this afternoon."

"I'm not sure why you think that pertains to me."

"Because he mentioned that you will be attending the gala this weekend."

*Oh, I see.* I grin. "I'm not sure what I do with my time warrants a call from you."

Banks's jaw sets in a firm line. *God, he's hot.*

"It warrants a call from me, *Sara*, because there's absolutely no reason for you to be there. You're no longer employed at Eubanks and Fields and therefore have no business at the gala. Period."

I laugh. "You're right, *Joshua*."

Banks's eyes blaze with the mention of Joshua's name.

"What? You're not going to fight with me about this?"

"I'm no longer employed by Eubanks and Fields," I say sweetly, aiming my face to the sky. The sun feels so good against my skin. "And I have no business at the gala. You're correct. Do we have anything else to discuss?"

He sighs. "I'm glad you came to your senses."

"Me too. But I can't help wondering if you were always such a prick or if this is a new quality of yours."

My attention switches from the sky back to Banks. His arms are dropped to his sides; his eyes are glued to me as I pace the edge of his lawn.

The feeling of his gaze on me fills me with a warmth that makes my insides wobble. But I can't think about that now. I have Joshua to deal with.

"Listen, sweetheart, I know you're upset that we ended things. I know you're jealous," he says.

"What?" I laugh out loud. "You think I'm *jealous*?"

"Of course you are. And I understand. I'm quite a catch and you're … well, you're you."

Steam rushes from the top of my head. "You're a catch and I'm … *me*? You got a part of that right but probably not the part that you think."

Banks walks slowly toward me like a predator stalking its prey. His posture makes me shiver.

"Try to manage without being bitter," Joshua says. "You'll be fine. You'll find someone who fits your life better than me."

Banks stops a few feet away, peering down with questions written all over his face. His cologne breezes through the air and his energy ripples across the lawn and dances around me—lifting me up. *God, the man is sexy.*

"It wasn't as hard as you might imagine," I say, licking my lips as I stare up at my new roommate. I don't know where I'm going with this, but I know I'm not letting Joshua think he got one over on me.

"What's that supposed to mean?"

"I reconnected with an old boyfriend a while back. Thank God I ended the extraneous fling with you because things are getting serious."

Banks makes a face like he's surprised. The look makes me giggle.

"*A month ago, you were with me,*" Joshua snarls.

I smirk. "A month ago, I was *fucking you*. I was never *with you*, Joshua." My words are met with a silence that turns my smirk into a smile. *Asshole.* "On that note, while it's been a pleasure chatting with you, I need to go. I'll see you at the gala."

"*What?*" He barks the word. "You said you weren't going."

"No, I said I have no business at the gala—and I don't. I'm going as a personal guest of Myles Petterson."

"*That's asinine.*"

"You'll have to take that up with him. Now, I must run. Have a great afternoon, Joshua."

I end the call with a flourish.

Banks narrows his eyes playfully and grins.

"What?" I ask, grinning back at him.

"Is there a new boyfriend in the mix that I didn't know about?"

I roll my eyes. "No. I'm building up to the fake fiancé thing—which I totally forgot about until now. *Shit.* I need to figure that out before Saturday night."

"You're really doing that?"

"*Yeah.* You heard Joshua. Well, you heard my side of the conversation. I'm not going to *not go* to the gala when it could be an amazing career move for me—and I desperately need an amazing career move for me."

He doesn't blink.

"This was your idea," I say, laughing. "A damn good one at that."

He rolls his tongue around his lips, his brows pinched together. I have no idea what he's thinking—*this was his plan to begin with.* Instead of standing in one spot staring at him, which isn't really a chore but kind of awkward, I head to my car.

He follows me. "I don't have groceries. I generally don't keep food to eat at my house because I hate to cook. So if you want food around here, we'll have to get some."

"I can go to the store tomorrow while you're at work. We'll just have to figure something out for dinner."

Banks groans.

"What?" I look over my shoulder and spot a large truck coming down the road. "Who is that?"

"Foxx."

The truck slows as it approaches Banks's house, and the window rolls down.

*My lord. What does this family have that others don't?*

I haven't seen Foxx in years—and only a handful of times at that.

He keeps to himself so much that I forget he even exists most of the time. But every time I see him, I'm gobsmacked with how delicious the man really is.

Foxx is close to ten years older than Banks and the old adage is true—men get hotter as they age. He's a mixture of his brothers in the best of ways. He's slightly taller than Jess with the same bright-green eyes. His hair is darker than his brothers. *Tall, dark, and handsome.*

As Foxx's truck gets closer, I shiver under his assessment. He does it quick, with a singular glance that somehow reads me deeper than anyone ever has. I must pass his inspection because he subtly nods his approval.

"What's up?" Banks asks as we reach his brother.

"Just seeing what was going on here," Foxx says.

Banks laughs. "You drove all the way down here for that? Want us to get you one of those scooters that people use when they break their legs? You can save gas that way."

I bite back a chuckle because Foxx doesn't seem entertained.

"Foxx, this is Sara. She's Ashley's friend. Sara, this is my brother, Foxx."

"Hi," I say, smiling at him.

He nods again, face blank, and then turns his attention back to Banks.

"I'm actually headed to the marina," Foxx says, his brow wrinkling. "I just got a call that I lost a key down there."

"When were you at the marina?" Banks asks.

"I wasn't."

"Then how did your key get there?"

"I have no idea, but it has to be mine. They described the labels that I put on my keys."

Banks glances at me. *"He labels his keys."*

"Seems smart," I say, looking back and forth between them. "I mean, under the circumstances and all ..."

"Are you staying here?" Foxx asks me.

"Yeah. How did you know that?"

He gestures over my shoulder with his chin. "Your car door is open and there are moving boxes in there."

*How did he notice that?* "Oh."

"Good luck," he says flatly. "I'll see you two later."

"Later," Banks says as Foxx steps on the gas and pulls away.

We turn toward the house, both of us walking slowly.

The early evening sun is still bright but softened by wispy clouds rolling through the sky. A light wind dances through the Carmichael neighborhood, detracting from the heat of the day.

"Let's get your stuff inside and figure out dinner," he says.

"You don't have to babysit me, you know. Like you said, don't change the way you live for me. I can handle myself."

He watches me out of the corner of his eye. "Well, the way I live includes eating dinner. And when my family isn't home, I order out. So I'm ordering out. Do you want to order out with me?"

I laugh and pull out a trash bag of my dirty laundry, handing it to him. "I'd love to order out with you."

He sets the bag on the driveway as I pull out the rest of my stuff. I notice he takes out his phone, looks at the screen, and then balks.

"What's wrong?" I ask.

"Come here and look at this."

I set a shoebox of toiletries on the ground and then peer over his shoulder.

Unknown: The term peacock only refers to male birds.

"What the hell?" I ask, laughing.

A slow smile splits his cheeks. "I'm not sure."

"Did you donate to an animal sanctuary or something?"

He scoffs. "Come on. Do I look like the kind of guy who donates to an animal sanctuary?"

"I don't know," I say, teasing him. "You did just buy a dozen baby chickens yesterday."

"Ha. Wanna know what I bought today?"

I grimace. "Do I?"

"I bought Jess a shirt that says Chicken Dad," he says, snickering.

"He's going to kill you," I say, laughing too.

His fingers swipe across his screen. "He'd have to catch me first."

I peer over his shoulder.

Banks: So, what's a girl peacock? A peavagina?

He chuckles and puts his phone in his pocket. The weight of the device tugs his waistband down a bit farther.

My body temperature skyrockets. I blame it on the sun. But, really, it's the proximity of the top of his shorts to the top of his pubic bone that has me panting.

I've sat on his lap, so I know just how muscled Banks is. He's all man, sex on a freaking stick, and how I'd love to trace my hands over his body.

Sex with him would be mind-blowing. I could imagine being on my knees, ready to take his—

"You ready to eat me?" he asks, picking up the box.

My head jerks up. *What*? I gasp. "Eat you?" *How could he read my mind?*

His brows pull together as he leans toward me. "*Are you ready to eat*?" He enunciates the words slowly. "Food. You know, dinner?"

"Oh, yes. Right. Yup. Ready to eat dinner. Let's go."

He looks at me over his muscled shoulder and smirks.

*Breathe, Sara. Breathe.*

# CHAPTER 12

## *Banks*



*I HATE SHEEP.*

Why do people say to count sheep when you can't sleep? Does that really work for anyone? I've started counting them a hundred times tonight. *That's what I should've counted—how many times I started counting.*

Every time I see the little white fluff balls hopping over a black fence, they smile at me. Then I smile back. Then I wonder what their names are, and why some of them have on bow ties and others little ribbons on their ears. *And then* I begin to wonder if they have a sexy-as-hell woman in a bed across the house from them …

*Fuck. Now I have to start all over.*

I punch the mattress with both hands and groan.

My elbow hits my phone, and the screen lights up. It's late, but not *that late.*

Not late enough that I can't text my sister.

Me: Hi.

It takes a couple of minutes before she replies.

Paige: Hi, Banksy. What are you doing up so late?

Me: Oh, just counting sheep. How far do you get before you get sidetracked?

Paige: 🤭 I haven't counted sheep since you and I slept in that blanket fort and counted them out loud. Do you remember that?

I grin.

Me: Yeah. Somehow that devolved into 99 Bottles of Beer on the Wall. 😅 Mom wasn't thrilled.

Paige: Where did you even hear that?

Me: Where do you think? JESS.

Paige: Sounds about right. How many sheep did you get to tonight?

Me: Seventeen. I made friends with number seventeen. His name was Rick. We got into a conversation about wool and then I had to restart.

Paige: 🤦 😅 What is wrong with you?

*Sara. That's what's wrong with me.*

I roll over onto my side and stare at the door.

Why do I want to fight with her and make her laugh at the same time? How is she in my house, in a bed I own, and I'm not touching her—yet, the thought of someone else touching her makes me want to hit something? *Hard.*

I know the answer. It hit me while we were eating ice cream from plastic cups—because I apparently don't have any bowls—and watching *Speed*. It was the only movie we could agree on. We're both big Keanu Reeves fans.

The issue at hand is that I don't mind her being here. Actually, *I kind of like it.*

I kind of like *her.*

She's entertaining and funny. The way she points out the smallest things in a movie is fascinating. Having her here made the night go faster, and it was definitely more exciting. *And she's so beautiful.*

It makes little sense on the surface that liking her makes it more difficult to fuck with her, but it's true.

*Thanks, Mom, for the conscience.*

A part of me doesn't want to play into her fucked-up views of men and relationships. Not all guys are jerks that want to treat her like she's a piece of ass. I'm not willing to do that. I won't.

Sara deserves someone to treat her nicely, to take their time, and earn her trust. To get to know her. To hear what she has to say and learn what she likes. *To make an effort.*

I know she tries to play the tough-girl role, and really, she does it well. And she gets away with it because no one sees past it. Do they want to? Do they try? Fuck if I know. But the longer she's around, the harder it's getting to toe the line and play along.

*"You're a catch, and I'm … me? You got a part of that right, but probably not the part that you think."*

Fuck that guy.

Me: Did you hear that I have a houseguest?

Paige: Maybe. Kinda. 😊 Wanna tell me about it?

Me: What do you want to know?

Paige: Whatever you want to tell me. This is really random for you, so I'm not sure what to even ask you to share.

> Me: It's Ash's friend, Sara.

> Paige: SHE'S PRETTY, BANKS. And hilarious.

> Me: 😊 Yeah, I know.

> Paige: Is there something going on between you?

I type *no* and then backspace over it.

There isn't anything between the two of us. We made it through burgers from Shade House and our ice cream without strangling one another. It was actually pretty calm, considering it was the two of us.

But saying no feels like a lie because when Sara looks at me—whether she's telling me a story or giving me shit—there's a twinkle in her eye that reminds me a whole hell of a lot like the feeling in my chest.

*Bossy you sometimes turns me on. I'm not going to lie.*

"But it's you," I whisper into the darkness. "It's always just about sex."

> Me: I think I'm too sensitive.

> Paige: 🤣 😭

> Me: I MEAN IT.

> Paige: I'm sorry. Why do you think you're too sensitive?

> Me: Because I don't just want to fuck someone for the hell of it. I mean, sometimes I do. Sometimes that's the whole damn point. But … I don't know what I'm even saying. Forget it.

It takes Paige forever to respond.

Paige: For all of your goofiness, you're a great person, Banksy.

Me: That's it? 😕 You took that long to answer me, and I get one sentence?

Paige: 🥺 You have a big heart. Maybe the biggest heart of anyone I know. When you care about someone, you take care of them. You never give them a chance to doubt your presence in their life.

Me: Is that a Jess-type joke about how I won't stay away?

Paige: 😌 What I'm saying is that we all give you crap about that because it's the only thing we can give you crap for. It's your most annoying trait but your most lovable too. Double-edged sword.

Me: Double-edged sword is that Sara is asleep in my house and I'm lying here in my bed thinking about her when I know that if anything happens between us that, one, it's just sex to her, two, I'm not sure it's just sex for me because I'm over here thinking about this way too much, and three, it'll end and then it'll make things really weird for all of us. Maybe that's like a triple-edged sword.

I roll onto my back and sigh.

Paige: Do you want advice?

Me: Only if it's good advice and not advice I'll hate.

Paige: 😊 Be you. I have learned in my life that when you're unapologetically you, you attract all the things that are meant to come your way. It works. I promise.

> Me: That sounds like a weak answer. That's some talk-show shit written to get good ratings.

> Paige: You asked.

> Me: I'm sorry I did. 😔

> Paige: Go to bed. Nate's working for Landry Security tonight, and Ryder has a fever, so I'm lying on the couch with him. I'm going to try to get some sleep too.

> Me: Tell the little rascal I hope he feels better. Love you, Paige.

> Paige: Love you, Banksy.

"I gotta piss."

I rip the blankets off and toss my phone on the bedside table. The floor is nice and cool against my bare feet. Yawning, I open the door.

Stretching overhead, I round the corner to the bathroom when a shriek makes me jump.

"Ah!" Sara slaps her hand to her chest. "You scared the shit out of me."

*Wow. You did not scare the shit out of me.*

Her hair falls across her shoulders in thick, messy waves. There's not a stitch of makeup on her face, and in the glow of the hallway night-light, she's motherfucking gorgeous.

She tugs the end of her shirt, and I look down.

My cock gets hard immediately. It presses against the fabric of my boxer briefs, the head of it starting to peek above the waistband. I start to cover it, to turn toward my bedroom—*but fuck it. This is my house.*

*And she's wearing my shirt.*

Her eyes widen, and her lips part as she stares at me.

"Did you forget to pack pajamas or what?" I smirk. "Because that looks a hell of a lot like my shirt."

She pulls the end down again. "It's a long story."

"Well, I have a lot of time."

She groans. "I spilled an entire bottle of nail polish remover on my sleeping clothes. The rest of my stuff is either dirty or not sleep-worthy. I found this shirt in the closet. It was either this or sleep naked."

I adjust my cock. "At least tell me you have something on under that."

"What if I don't?"

*This woman.* I narrow my eyes. "We're going to have to establish new ground rules around here."

"What? That we should wear underwear?" She drags her gaze up and down my body mercilessly. "No offense, but your boxer briefs aren't really doing you much good."

My body temperature soars. Every muscle inside me flexes and pulses. I want to bend her over the sink two feet away and fuck her until she's exploding on my cock. Would that feel good? *Fuck, yeah.* But would it feel good later? *Hell, no.*

I haven't tasted her. I haven't touched her, felt her mouth on me, or experienced her body wrapped around mine. Yet ... I'm already having a hard time getting my mind off her.

*How bad would it be if I did know these things?*

She might be able to check out after sex, but I know that if I gave in to her, checking out won't be an option. I'm not built that way. I don't want to be that guy.

*I'm not that guy.*

I'm sure she knows lots of guys who will give her sex if that's what she wants. How they look at her like she's only a piece of ass is beyond me.

She's so much more than that ... even if I want to throttle her some of the time. Most of the time. *Maybe it's a part of her charm?*

"Can I ask you something?" she asks.

I hum.

"Are you attracted to me, Banks?"

She bats her long lashes as she looks up at me, sucking her bottom lip between her teeth.

"Is that a real question?" I ask, chuckling.

"I asked it, didn't I?"

"Are you being funny?" I grip my package and squeeze it, giving it a little shake. The contact, even though it's my hand, sends shots of electricity buzzing through my body. "Does it look like I'm attracted to you?"

She leans against the wall, her shoulders touching the paint. "Then why did you not want me to stay here?"

"You didn't want to stay here either."

"Yeah, but that's not what we're talking about," she says, smiling.

That smile—part sleepy, part sex kitten—melts me.

"Where are you going with this?" I ask her, my voice rough from the late hour.

She sighs. "I overthink things at night."

"Join the club."

Her smile softens. "I hate that I let things that people say bother me. I wish I could let them go in one ear and out the other."

*"You're a catch, and I'm ... me? You got a part of that right, but probably not the part that you think."*

I stand in front of her. "I know what you're overthinking."

"You do?"

I don't know how to tell her what I'm thinking. I'm so bad at this shit. My brothers are all so good at putting their thoughts together in cohesive sentences. Me? I just sputter shit and wind up looking like a fool.

But as I take in Sara's face and, for the first time, see her without her defenses up, I know I have to say something. *Even if I fall on my face and she stays up the rest of the night laughing at me.*

"If someone's a catch, they don't have to say it," I say. "You don't have to point out the obvious."

Her eyes widen, and then a slow, genuine smile stretches across her pretty face.

"Take me, for example," I say. "I don't have to tell you to look at my abs—you just do. They're great. It's unnecessary to point it out."

She giggles, shaking her head. Relief is evident in her shoulders. I feel it in mine, too.

"And anyone that you let around you is a lucky man," I say, my voice low. "That's obvious too."

Her smile eases, almost turning shy. I need to pull her to me and wrap her in a hug … but I don't.

"I don't know your ex-fuckhead, but he sounds like he's compensating for something. He probably knows he would lose you eventually, so he's trying to play mind games with you to make you feel inferior."

"Do you do that? Do you play mind games?"

"I do not. I don't have time. I spend all my time playing real games … like buying chickens."

She laughs softly. "Why do you do that stuff to your brothers? It's hilarious, but isn't it a lot of work?"

"Because it reminds everyone not to take life too seriously. It makes us engage with each other."

"That's really sweet, Banks."

"That's me. I'm a sweet guy."

Her eyes darken, and she takes a step toward me. "You're also a *hard* guy."

*Because you're so fucking hot and being vulnerable, being real. That's the biggest turn-on of all.*

*My God, I want her.*

My cock throbs, precum dotting the head. Heat radiates from my body. But as I look at Sara and see the little sexy smirk on her lips, I'm reminded of her declaration that she only wants sex.

And that's fine. Except we'll wake up in the morning, and we'll just be fuck buddies. She'll place me in a category with her fuckhead ex-boss.

*And I'm not that guy.*

My stomach tightens as I look at her pretty face.

*I like her. I like the frustrating pain-in-my-ass.*

"You know what the problem is?" I ask.

"What's that?"

I lower my face to hers, every cell in my body screaming for attention.

She hiccups a breath, her eyes wild, and watches me get closer.

*Kiss her.*

*Don't kiss her.*

*Go for it.*

*Be smart, asshole. For once in your freaking life, be smart, Banks.*

I pause inches away and give myself one last chance to change my mind.

"What's the problem?" she whispers, her breath hot on my skin.

I smile. "I'm not your type."

*"What?"*

"I'm not an asshole, Sara. And that's a problem."

She exhales harshly as I pull away and head for my room. I must put some distance between us before I regret it.

"What the fuck was that?" she shouts.

"It's called self-restraint, and I hate it." I slam the bedroom door.

She slams the bathroom door.

*Wonder-fucking-ful.*

# CHAPTER 13

*Sara*

I DANCE AROUND THE KITCHEN, SURPRISINGLY UPBEAT FOR NINE IN THE morning. *And after getting turned down by Banks.*

*"I'm not your type."*

*What the hell did that mean?*

I purposely waited until I heard his truck start and pull down the driveway before I ventured out of my room. The house was scented by a freshly showered Banks. It's as if he used extra body wash and added a second squirt of cologne just so it would linger behind and torment me all day.

I made a cup of coffee, double-checked the creamer's expiration date in the fridge before committing to it, and then threw a load of laundry in the washer. Thank God I grabbed my detergent at Sabrina's. Banks was out … if he ever had any to start with.

Last night has messed with me all morning. *Why does he think he's not my type?*

*He's absolutely my type.*

He admitted he's attracted to me. I didn't need him to say it out loud to know. His gaze melts my skin every time he looks at me. But I thought getting him to voice it would be the icebreaker we needed to get things going.

*Because seeing him in those boxer briefs got me going.*

I have never seen a man so unbelievably gifted in my entire life—and I've seen a lot of men. His shoulders, his waist, his thighs—his bulging cock. I *really* missed that purple vibrator last night.

"Why didn't you want to be with me last night, Banks?" I say aloud, picking up a pillow shaped like candy corn and tossing it on the couch.

The odd thing about this situation is that I don't feel embarrassed. I didn't wake up scouring myself for some deficiency or flaw. It's a relief. It's even more confusing when I realize I almost feel *prettier* this morning.

It makes no sense at all.

*"If someone's a catch, they don't have to say it. You don't have to point out the obvious. Take me, for example. I don't have to tell you to look at my abs—you just do. They're great. It's unnecessary to point it out."*

Banks doesn't play games. He just speaks the truth. That's so rare … and attractive.

Yet another reason I don't need to like Banks Carmichael any more than I already do.

I venture into my bedroom, listening to the whirl of the washing machine as I go, and take the silver dress with a black tie around the midsection out of the closet. The closet where I found Banks's shirt.

I grin.

"Okay," I say, laying the dress on the bed. "Let's figure out this gala attire and then the date issue."

This color isn't my favorite, and this dress isn't in my top five things I love to wear either. But it was the first acceptable thing I found at Sabrina's. I sort through my things to see which heels I grab when my phone buzzes on the nightstand.

Banks: Hey.

I grin and type out my response.

Me: Hey.

Banks: Did you sleep okay?

Me: Like a baby.

Laughing, *because I did not sleep like a baby,* I sit on the bed and await his response.

Banks: Good for you because I didn't. 😔

Me: Poor you. 😜

Banks: Tasha is being mean today, and I don't
want to be here.

Me: She seemed nice to me.

Banks: Oh, she is. But she won't leave me
alone. She keeps giving me all this work, and
I'm not feeling very work-y today.

Me: 😏 Aren't you the boss?

Banks: I really don't need your negativity
right now.

I laugh again, enjoying the easiness of this conversation. *Thank God things aren't weird between us.*

Banks: Do you have any plans today?

Me: Aren't you supposed to be working?

Banks: 😒 Stop reminding me.

Me: 😊 I'm doing laundry so I don't have to
sleep in your shirt again, since that really
seemed to bother you.

Banks: Really—it didn't.

My stomach burns so hot that I shift on the bed.

Me: Seemed like it did ... in a couple of different ways.

I'm poking the bear. I'm doing it, and I'm not even sure I want to take it there—to why he essentially walked away from me.

Banks: So I take it you're pissy about last night?

Me: Pissy? No.

Banks: 🙂

Me: I'm just making damn sure I don't put us in that situation again. Your shirt will be washed, dried, and in the laundry room when you get home. 😌

Banks: That's a shame.

*What?*
I type furiously.

Me: I thought you said you don't play games, Mr. Carmichael?

Banks: I don't.

Me: 🖕

Banks: If I were playing games with you, you would've lost that shirt and been on your back in the hallway.

Me: Sounds like a fun game.

Banks: It would be. It could be.

Me: It should be.

Banks: Except you would've woken up this morning thinking I'm just like the other guys you hang out with.

Me: So?

Banks: So that's offensive.

"Offensive?" I mutter, typing my response three times before I get it right.

Me: I wasn't pissy about last night, but now I am.

Banks: Good for you. My mom might stop by today. She threatened to go through all my cabinets if I didn't return her yellow bowl. But I don't have it. So if she comes and starts poking around, laugh at her.

"Ugh," I groan.

Me: WHY DO YOU HATE ME?

Banks: WHY ARE YOU SO DRAMATIC?

Me: My dramatics are not new information.

> Banks: I gotta go. I have work to do.

> Me: I thought you weren't feeling work-y.

> Banks: I wasn't. See you tonight.

> Me: I might not be here.

> Banks: Yeah, you will be. 😊

"You are such a …"

The front door opening catches my attention. I get up slowly and poke my head around the corner. Damaris waves as she comes toward me. *Thank God I'm dressed.*

"Hi, Sara. Good morning," she says.

"Hi. Good morning to you, too."

"I hope you don't judge my parenting by the state of this house." She looks around and shakes her head. "This child has many strengths, but tidiness is not one of them."

The pride in her eyes over her son despite the state of his house warms my heart. *What a good mom.*

"I've been picking up all morning," I say. "I know you probably can't tell. But Banks put me on a strict list of rules, and I'm not allowed to throw anything away. I can't go in his room. I can't move anything to a place that he can't see it immediately if he looks where it was. Even if there's a transmission in the kitchen."

She laughs. "Oh, that boy. He gets it from his father. Don't tell Kixx I ever told you this, but the man is a disaster on legs. He's gotten better as the years have gone on, but he wasn't that far off from Banks when we first got married."

I go into my room, and she follows me.

"You all have the neatest names," I say. "How did you come up with them?"

She sits on the arm of a chair in the corner. "Well, Foxx was my grandfather's name—but it only had one x at the end. I wanted to name my first little boy that since I was a little girl, and luckily, Kixx agreed. And because his mother put two x's at the end for reasons I'll never know, we put two at the end of Foxx's."

"That's kind of cool."

She beams. "Moss was named after Kixx's grandfather. And then we got pregnant with Jess and realized that our names had the same ending sound—x's and s's. So we wanted to keep that trend."

"I love that," I say, grinning. "I never noticed that about your names, but it's a fun little fact."

"So then we had Jess. He was named after my brother. And then we had Maddox—who only got one x because someone at the health department screwed it up on his birth certificate and forgot the other x at the end. But I didn't want to go to all the trouble of having it changed, so we just left it." She sighs. "And then we had Banks. Our sweet, little cherub baby Banks."

I giggle at the smile on her face.

"He was a handful from the start. And poor Maddox—Banks attached himself to his brother the first time he ever saw him. It was really adorable, to be honest. And then we brought Paige home and those two ..." She laughs. "Banks got into more fights over his sister than he did on his own accord. Always defending her, even when she probably didn't need defending."

"I love that," I say, my cheeks aching.

"He's a good boy. He's filthy, as you can see. He's always on the go, always riling up someone in the family. He doesn't listen to a word he doesn't want to hear." She chuckles. "But out of all of my kids, and I have six of them, Banks is the one I know will come see me in the nursing home someday. And that says a lot."

My insides melt. "Yes, it does."

She pats her hands on her knees and looks around the room. "Oh, that's a pretty dress. What's it for? Do you have something special happening?"

I exhale a breath I didn't realize I was holding and turn to the bed. I pick the dress up by the hanger and hold it out to the side.

"There's a gala on Saturday night," I say. "It's a long and complicated and kind of ridiculous story, but I'm going. And this ..." I sigh.

"Well, it's not my prettiest dress, but it'll do. Just trying to figure out where the shoes are I brought to wear with it."

I set it back on the bed, certain she got a good look at it.

"It's lovely. I'm sure you'll look beautiful." She smiles. "You aren't talking about the Petterson Label Gala, are you?"

"Yes, actually, I am."

"I only know about it because our company, Laguna Homes, redid a house for the owner's daughter earlier this year."

"Are you going?" I ask.

"Oh, no." She laughs. "We aren't that fancy."

"I'm not either. But I got an invite from Myles Petterson himself, and I kind of have to go because a guy is going to be there that I used to work for …" My face heats. "You don't care. Ignore me."

She gasps and gets to her feet. "I do care. I love tea. Spill it."

*Who is this woman?* I chuckle. "Well, I worked with a guy who basically told me I'm not good enough to marry."

Damaris tries to hide her shock.

"Which is fine," I say. "I wouldn't have ever married him anyway. It wasn't like that. At all. But that same man told Mr. Petterson that I wasn't able to attend the gala. So, Mr. Petterson reached out and personally invited me as his guest."

"That's an outstanding invitation."

I smile. "So I'm going but the jerk will also be there with his fiancée. And maybe it's pride or petty, I don't know, but I really want to make a good showing for myself. I'm sure you can understand."

"I do." She presses her thumb to her lips and looks at my dress. "That dress is gorgeous, but—maybe you don't want my input here."

"Give it to me." I laugh. "I'll take all the help I can get."

She turns to me. "Are we out to make him jealous? What's our goal here?"

"Honestly? He said some nasty things to me, and I want him to eat his words. That's all. I don't care if he's jealous. I just want him to know he's wrong."

"Okay. In that case, with your skin tone and hair, you need to wear red. Be bold. You are a gorgeous girl, sweetheart. Steal the show."

I frown. "I have a great red dress. I'll see if I can get it."

"Where is it?"

"Oh, it's at my stepmom's. I'm storing my stuff over there until I get into my rental house. She's great and all, but also … not. And I don't want to go over there too much and rock the boat."

"Bring your things to my house."

"What? No. No, that's not necessary. Thank you, though."

She studies me for a long moment. "I don't mean this in any way, and you can say no, and you won't hurt my feeling. Honest. I have five sons. I don't think you *can* hurt my feelings."

I laugh.

"But I have a closet full of dresses I've worn once or twice. There's one red one in there with a red slit up the leg. It makes your cleavage look great." She winks. "You may hate it, and that's fine. But I'm happy to bring it over and let you take a look at it."

"Oh, Damaris, you don't have to do that."

"I don't do anything I don't want to do."

I stutter, unsure what to say to her kindness. *It's so … authentic.* She's not just saying nice things. She's offering herself sincerely.

*Nope. No emotions, Sara.*

I can see why the Carmichael family is as generous as they are. *But* … "I'm already putting your family out. I was staying with Maddox and now Banks and then—"

"*You are not putting us out.* We all have the room and the space to help a friend out. Get that out of your head."

I press my lips together to try to dispel the tears gathering in my eyes.

She starts to talk but stops. Then she moves toward the door and turns back to me. "I'm going to look for my bowl that I know is in the kitchen, and then I'll bring that dress over. You are under no obligation whatsoever to use it. But I'd love to give you another option if you aren't offended."

"How could I be offended, Damaris? You are being way too kind to me."

"I've never walked in this house and heard the washing machine running. I think I owe you one."

I laugh.

She puts a hand in the air. "I'll be back."

"Okay."

She disappears around the corner, and I sit on the bed. My heart races. *What is happening here?*

This family is unreal. *How are they all so nice? And sweet? And thoughtful?*

It makes sense that Ashley married into this family without a second thought. Damaris reminds me of Gretchen in the very best of ways.

I grin. And then there's Banks. Kind, sexy Banks.

*I'm not an asshole.* No, Banks, you aren't. *And that's a bigger problem than I think I realized.*

My palms sweat.

"I found the bowl," Damaris shouts from the kitchen. "If you talk to Banks, tell him he owes me a day of lawn work for lying to me."

I laugh. "Okay."

The back door snaps closed.

# CHAPTER 14
## Banks

"DON'T YOU LOOK GORGEOUS TODAY." I KISS GLORIA ON THE CHEEK AND then sit across from her. "Sorry I'm running late and couldn't pick you up. Eddie is on vacation this week, and I didn't remember. It's been a bit of a madhouse."

*And I've been distracted as fuck.*

She pats my hand. "I would sit here all day if there was a chance that you would show up. It's not common that an old lady like me gets a young stud to take her out to lunch once a week."

I chuckle. "Stop calling yourself old. It makes me feel weird."

She cackles.

The windows are open at Muggers, letting the sea breeze flow through. It's Gloria's favorite place for lunch when the weather isn't too hot, and we can avoid the peak rush time. She usually likes to sit at the bar that points toward the ocean. But today she's chosen a seat in the dining area.

*Whatever floats her boat.*

"Have you ordered?" I ask her.

"Just a lemonade. I was waiting for you."

"Such a lady."

She pats my hand again before withdrawing hers.

Our friendship is slightly odd, and I'm sure half the people who see us think either she's my grandma or I'm dating her for her money. Neither are true. She's just an ornery lady who answered the Golden Years Dating ad. *I can be a squirrel and help you bust a nut.*

I snort.

"What?" she asks.

"I was just thinking about the message you sent me through the app."

She laughs. "That was a good one, wasn't it?"

"Has that ever worked on someone?"

"Oh, hell no. Men my age don't know what to do with women who know what they want. But I'm not on that app to really find myself someone, you know? I'm just on there to entertain, to break up the day. And it's good for a few laughs too."

Becca comes to the table with a notepad in her hand. "Hey, you two. How are you?"

"We're good," Gloria says. "I'll have a BLT with no mayo." She looks at me. "The stuff tastes like puss mixed with paint."

"Ew," Becca says, wrinkling her nose.

"Well, mayo is out of the question now," I say. "I'll have a chicken sandwich with pickles. And a sweet tea."

"Fries good for you both?" she asks.

We nod.

Instead of going to the kitchen, Becca lingers.

"You okay, Bec?" I ask.

"Just wondering how you've been." She grins. "Innocently, of course."

"Uh-huh." I laugh. "Things have been tense, but we're both still alive."

Her grin turns into a smile as she walks away.

Gloria taps on the tabletop. "What was that about?"

I sit back in my chair and stretch my legs. I'm not sure if they ache from crouching under a car all morning or from the sexual energy stored up from last night.

*Dammit anyway.*

Gloria waits impatiently for me to explain myself.

"Becca's friend, Sara, is staying at my house for a little while," I say.

Her painted-on brows lift to the ceiling. "Is that so?"

"That is so."

"Oh, well—tell me about her. Is she a little hottie?"

I laugh. "Yes, she is a little hottie. Not nearly as hot as you, but she's okay."

She puffs her hair with her right hand. "Of course she's not as hot as I am."

My smile grows.

"Are you banging her?" she asks.

I shake my head and chuckle.

"Well, are ya? I need to know."

"Why do you need to know?" I ask.

"Because it'll mess up my fantasies at night." She winks. "I'm kidding. I don't need to know, but I want to know. I want you to find a nice girl. You deserve one."

"Damn right, I deserve one. But I don't know if this is *the one.*"

She flinches. "Why not? What's wrong with her?"

"Gloria, believe it or not, I'm not sure she wants me."

"Rubbish."

I laugh and take my drink from Becca. I wait for her to leave before resuming my conversation with my friend. Becca's not one to gossip, but it would be hard to resist telling Sara that the great Banks Carmichael is getting dating advice from a senior citizen.

"How could any hot-blooded woman not want you, Banks? You're handsome. You're built like a brick shithouse. You have your own business and you work hard. And you take old women out to lunch once a week. That's pretty perfect in my eyes."

"I don't take old women to lunch. I take you. Only you."

She beams, making me laugh again.

"Why can't you just be my girlfriend?" I ask, teasing her. "You see all my good qualities and none of the bad, and you have your own pension."

Gloria chuckles. "Because you gotta have kids with those genes, my boy. And this baby factory has been closed for decades—probably since around the time you were born, if not before."

*That puts things in perspective.*

"So what's wrong with this woman?" she asks. "Go on. Tell me."

"I'm not sure. It's kind of a mindfuck."

"Let me help you unfuck it."

I stare at her.

"I'm the best person around for advice," she says. "I've seen it all, and I'm too old to care enough to lie to you."

"Excellent points."

"Spill your guts. Your life is infinitely more interesting than mine."

I tap my fingers on the table. "She says she doesn't want a relationship—not just with me, but anyone. She just wants sex."

"I like her," Gloria says, impressed.

I chuckle.

"Tell me about her," she says.

"She's beautiful," I say. "Funny. Witty as hell. She's argumentative, and we bicker just about as much as we don't, if not more. She's hard-headed and doesn't take instructions well. I can guarantee she's at my house right now fucking with my shit even though I told her not to."

Gloria smirks.

"What?" I ask.

"All of that and you don't want to have sex with her?"

"Oh no. I do. I really, *really* do."

"And she's staying at your house and you haven't done anything?"

I shake my head.

She sighs, grinning. "She's scared of falling for you. She thinks if she can make it just about sex that it will put boundaries up and keep her safe."

I nod, letting that sink in.

"And you, my boy, know you could fall for her. You know that if you have sex with her, those boundaries will become obsolete. Because when you love, *you love*—hence, our standing weekly lunch date."

*Oof.* I sit back in my chair and feel the room spin around me.

Although I kind of suspected something along these lines, I hadn't thought about it in those words. But Gloria makes sense … but could I really fall for Sara? Haven't I already worked out that she's not the right fit for me?

*You know that if you have sex with her, those boundaries will become obsolete.*

I am afraid of that.

My phone buzzes on the table. Grateful for the interruption, I slide it to me.

"I'm going to use the little girl's room," Gloria says, getting up.

One of my money transfer apps lights up on the screen.

"That's weird," I say, picking up the phone.

Request from *KixxDaddy for the amount of $50.00 for T-ball registration fee, glove, and practice pants.

"What the fuck is this?" I reread it and then pull up my texts.

> Me: Did you just request $50 from me?

> Dad: It worked!

> Me: Were you just experimenting or what?

> Dad: No.

> Me: I'm confused. I played T-ball twenty years ago.

> Dad: I know. I'll get to the more recent stuff. Had to pick a starting point.

> Me: ARE YOU OUT OF YOUR MIND?

> Dad: Geez, settle down. I'm not adjusting for inflation.

I switch text chains.

> Me: Who taught Dad how to request money?

Jess: Me. Why?

*Foxx has silenced notifications.*

> Me: Because he just requested $50 from me for T-ball fees.

Moss: 🤣

> Me: It's funny now. How expensive was hockey that year you wanted to play? Mom still bitches about that.

Maddox: He just requested $100 from me for wrestling in 3rd grade. 🫠

Jess: Oops.

Paige: Sucks to be you guys. I don't have a money app thing.

Moss: $150 for youth hockey. He can't be serious.

I switch back to Dad.

> Me: I'm not paying that. I refuse.

Dad: There's a 30-day grace period before I start charging interest.

> Me: Have you been drinking?

Dad: Rude.

> Me: Where's Mom?

Dad: Do you really want to know? 😏

I switch chats again.

Me: I think something is wrong with Dad.

Moss: Clearly.

Jess: He has to be joking.

Maddox: He can suck it. I'm not paying this.

Me: He told me we have 30 days or he's charging interest.

Moss: What the hell?

Me: I'm telling Mom.

Jess: That's the most Banks thing you've ever said.

Me:

Gloria sits down with an oomph. "They need better hand soap in there. That smells like shit."

I side-eye my phone but lock the screen. *I can't deal with them right now.*

"So the ladies and I were talking," she says, "and we think a picture of you, topless, with a rose between your teeth. It's kind of cheesy, I know, but we're old, and that's a classic pose. It should appeal to our targeted demographic for the bachelor auction."

"How much do you think I'm going to bring in?"

"You? With those abs? I'd say we can get a good $500 out of ya. Maybe even a grand if some of the wealthier women come."

I narrow my eyes. "Who is my competition?"

"Competition? For what?"

"I'm not going up there and not having the top bid. This is for my ego as much as it is for your charity."

She cackles. "Well, we got Shawn Daze."

"The surf instructor?"

She nods.

*Shit. He's pretty good-looking.* "Who else?"

"Miguel from La Pachanga."

*Dammit. He practically has a fan club.* "Who else?"

"Let's see …" She sighs. "I forgot the list at home. There are about fifteen of you."

"I'm going to have to go home and do some push-ups or something. Just to be sure."

She wiggles her eyebrows. "Can you film it? We could use that as a promo?"

I laugh. "I'm gonna take you the best pictures you've ever seen. Because I'm going to have them foaming at the mouth for me, Glo."

She bursts out laughing, patting tears from beneath her eyes.

My phone dings again.

> Jess: I just want you all to know that I ran five miles today and I still got it. So whenever any of you are ready to race, let's go.

> Maddox: Name the time and place.

> Me: Don't leave me out of this. I'm the most talented out of us all.

> Moss: Sighs.

"My brothers have lost their marbles," I say. "Hang on."

"I'm hanging."

> Me: You want to time us, Moss?

> Jess: He could cheat.

Moss: Excuse me?

Maddox: Ouch.

Paige: 👩 You guys make it hard to get work done.

Moss: I'm on lunch.

Me: Me too.

Jess: Me too.

Maddox: I'm waiting for a client to arrive.

Paige: Must be nice.

I look up. "What is the most clear-cut way to time someone running? Where no one could cheat?"

"Well ..." She narrows her eyes, thinking. "You could go out on the highway toward Sunset Shores. They have one of those signs that clock cars. I bet it would clock you if you ran real fast, wouldn't it?"

I gasp. "You're a genius."

Me: Tomorrow night. 8pm. Sign on the highway on the way to Sunset Shores.

Moss: Huh?

Me: We race. The sign will clock us. No one can cheat.

Jess: I like it.

Maddox: I'm in.

Moss: All right. Let's do it.

Me: You're going down, fuckers.

Paige: Someone video this. I beg you. 🙏

> Me: Of course, I'm videoing it. I'm not letting my victory be forgotten. 🏆

Jess: 😶

"So what are you going to do about your roommate?" Gloria asks.

I look up to see that our plates have been delivered. *When did that happen?*

I set my phone down as a knot forms in my stomach again. "What do you mean?"

"It's gonna come to a head between the two of you. What's your plan?"

Shrugging, I pick up a fry. "I don't know. I almost gave in last night but was an adult for the first time in my life. And you know what, Gloria? I hated it. I've regretted adulting all day."

She laughs. "You'll be fine. You're a smart, kind man. Just tell her that if she scoops you up—as she should—I'm not giving up my weekly lunch dates. I had you first."

"No one is taking me away from you, babe."

She winks. "That's right."

We eat our lunches. Gloria chats with a lady next to her that's holding a baby. I gaze out the window and wonder what awaits me at home.

*That's hours from now. I have a lot to do before then.*

But Gloria's right. I need a plan because this thing with Sara isn't going to go away.

*So how am I going to handle it? Handle her?*

Hmm …

# CHAPTER 15
## *Banks*

"I GOT THIS. I JUST NEED TO STAY COOL AND STICK TO MY GUNS," I SAY, staring at my house. "You're a big boy, Banks. You're in control."

Holding my breath, I wait for the words to sink in. *For me to believe them.* Eventually, my lungs start to hurt.

"Oh, fuck it. I'm not in control," I say, swinging my door open and exiting the truck.

*"She's scared of falling for you. She thinks if she can make it just about sex that it will put boundaries up and keep her safe."*

I take the step to the porch. My heartbeat quickens as I open the door.

I'm never particularly excited to come home from work. I'm generally not torn up about how to handle a woman, either. It's a day of new experiences.

I step inside the house and immediately stop.

The pillows are on the couch. The box of car parts on the floor by the television is gone. A stack of magazines that weren't necessarily stacked but more leaning and toppling on the floor are now in three neat little rows on the coffee table.

*What the hell?*

*Have I been robbed? Reverse robbed? Did they come in, take some stuff, and then tidy up as a form of appreciation for having nice things they can hijack?*

I pull my gaze to the hallway as a blur of red comes at me.

*Oh my God.*

Sara walks toward me in a cherry-red dress. There's a slit that goes mid-thigh, and the top drapes along her chest, dipping just low enough to give you a hint of what's beneath.

*She's a fucking centerfold.*

"Hey," she says, smiling and brushing her hair off one shoulder. "I thought I heard you come in."

I don't know where to start. *Well, I would know where to start, but that's not happening.*

"Holy fucking hell," I say, jaw hanging open. It takes effort and intention to pick it back up. "What are you doing?"

I *should* bring up the car parts; that seems like a logical, neutral topic. But, unfortunately for me, that's not what comes out.

She looks down, running her hands over her stomach. "Getting my ducks in a row for the gala."

"You're wearing *that*?"

"Maybe." She lifts her gaze to mine, a wash of uncertainty on her features. "Your mom brought it over, which was so nice of her. You have the sweetest mother."

"Yeah. She's great. *You're wearing that*?" I ask again.

Her brows pinch together. "Do you want to see my other option?"

She's missing the point. *Or am I missing the point*? Hell if I know.

"I am a little worried that this hangs too low." She glances at her chest. "What do you think?"

"Sara," I say, struggling for words. "You look *incredible*."

She stills before focusing on me. When she does, a hand goes to her hip. I watch the change behind her eyes—the shift from vulnerability to guarded.

"Is this like the shirt thing?" she asks, deflecting the conversation to something easier for her to navigate. "You obviously like it but want to torture us both?"

*I see what you're doing, Sara.* The corners of my lips tilt to the ceiling.

She points at me. "That smirk is not an answer."

"It's gonna have to be."

I head to the kitchen, my brain spinning and body pulsing.

She follows me. The dress swishes across the floor with every step. "Walk slower. Walking in a dress slows a girl down."

"Or maybe just don't follow me."

"Or maybe just don't be a dick."

I pull out a glass—*I have this many clean glasses?*—and scoop some ice in it. Then I add some water.

*Okay, Banksy. Let's get it together.*

This is the moment Gloria was talking about—the moment it comes to a head. Sara isn't going to back away from this conversation, and I can't hide from her forever.

Still, I don't know what to say.

*I can give you so much more than sex.*

That sounds stupid in my head. *Who am I? Jess?*

I lean against the counter and sigh. "Is there a damn thing in this house that hasn't been touched since I've been gone?"

She smirks, her eyes filling with mischief. "Yeah. One thing. Wanna know what it is?"

"Not really."

"You are way less fun than I thought you were going to be."

"Well, there's one thing I've never heard before."

She glares at me. It's adorable.

"Who is going with you to the gala?" I ask.

Her lips press together. "It's not been confirmed."

"Have you asked anyone?"

She swallows, her confidence waning.

I'm not sure what to say here, whether I press her or leave her to do her own thing. But Paige's words echo through my mind, and I grasp them.

*Be you. I have learned in my life that when you're unapologetically you, you attract all the things meant to come your way. It works. I promise.*

"Why didn't you ask me to go to the gala with you?" I ask, holding her gaze.

"I've already taken so much from your family. From you. And

Maddox. And now your mom. I'd rather not be remembered as a leech."

I grin. "It's a little late for that."

She swats at my arm, the contact as strong as a lightning bolt. I feel it all the way to my cock.

Her eyes light up as if she feels it too, and her lips part as she sucks in a breath.

I step toward her. She grins and takes one back. I smirk and take another. She lifts her chin and takes another back.

"Do you want to go to the gala with me?" she asks, her voice flirty.

"And have you, in that dress, on my arm all night? I might be able to manage."

She grins. "You would be going as my fake fiancé, you know."

"I don't have to take any vows, do I?"

Her eyes widen as her back hits the wall. "Maybe a few."

I plant my hands on either side of her, caging her in. "Like what?"

"You might have to vow to hold my hands."

I press off the wall, reaching down and taking her hands in mine. Then I draw them up, over her head, and hold them against the wall.

Her chest rises and falls at a quickened pace. Her big blue eyes are wide.

"What else?" I ask.

She lifts her chin. "You might have to kiss me."

Every muscle in my body pulls taut as I lower my lips to hers. Blood races through my body so fast that I can hear it rush over my ears.

She sags as I cover her mouth with mine—gently, at first. I pull back when she tries to deepen it, making her slow down.

Her lips are soft and warm, her mouth hot and wet. I slide my tongue past her lips and roll mine around hers. She moans in my mouth and arches her back, her body craving contact like mine.

But if we're going to do this, we're going to do it my way. And I have no desire to hurry.

I release her hands as I break the kiss, resting my forehead against hers. We struggle together to catch our breath and put the frazzled pieces of our brains back together.

"That'll work," she says, chuckling.

I stand and step back. My body buzzes with need and energy—nearly bursting with anticipation of what's to come. *Hopefully.*

She smiles brightly, eager to continue. But again, I have to slow her down.

"Are you sure this is what you want?" I ask her.

"Hell yes, I am."

"What if one of us falls for the other?" I ask. "Then what?"

I stand before her, ready to peel her out of that dress. Somehow, I find a shred of self-restraint and hold on to it for dear life.

She smirks. "I'm not going to fall for you, Banks."

I smile back at her. "*I was talking about me.*"

She sucks in a breath, her shoulder blades digging into the wall.

"I'm not going to apologize for wanting you when this is over," I say.

"You don't know you'll still want me."

"Oh, baby, I do."

Her cheeks turn a pretty shade of pink. "You see, that's the beauty of an orgasm, Banks. It drains all of that desire right out of you, and you can go on with your life."

"But, you see, *Sara*—it's not that easy for me. Not with you."

"I ... I don't understand what you're saying."

I grin. "You know what? I don't, either. I can't believe these words are coming out of my mouth. Trust me, it takes a lot to surprise me when it comes to words I say because I say a lot of stupid shit without thinking about it."

She laughs, her defenses crumbling.

"But I don't know. There's just something about you," I say. "It makes absolutely no sense because you clearly don't want anything more than my cock."

She giggles, the sound warming my heart.

She searches my face for something to go off, something to hold on to. She's looking for a chink in my armor that she can use to finagle her way out of this. I'm not giving her the opportunity.

I take a step back again to give her room to think.

"I don't want this to be it between us. I want this to be *a part* of it," I say.

A grin settles on her face. "I'm not sure what to do with that."

"You don't have to do anything with it. I'm not pushing you for anything. I mean, I'll be your fake fiancé, but that's it."

She laughs.

"But know that when tomorrow rolls around, I'm going to be very, *very* interested in you. More than I am now."

She runs her fingers over the scruff dusting my cheeks.

*Why isn't she answering me? Why is she silent? Is she laughing at me, thinking this is a prank? A joke?*

"Don't get me wrong—I'm so *interested in you* right now that it hurts." I press myself against her so she can feel how hard I am. "Like it *actually hurts.*"

She peers up into my eyes. "It's a good thing I know how to make it stop hurting."

*My God.*

She fumbles with the button on my jeans.

Is this what I want? Wasn't I trying to avoid this, knowing I'd possibly fall for her?

My skin feels too tight, like I might burst out of it from anticipation. *She's making me weak.* Her fingers brushing over my cock is enough to make me almost lose it. *It's been too fucking long.* The sight of the tops of her tits rising from the silky fabric of the dress inches me another notch closer to being unable to contain myself. *And she's so fucking hot.*

*Screw it. I'm only a man.*

"I need to lock the doors," I say, groaning at the impending delay.

Her fingers pause. Her knuckles rest against my groin. "Why?"

"Because I've interrupted my brothers so many times that it's karma that one of them will walk in here. It's how the world works. Don't ask me why."

"Well, can you hurry?"

I smile. "I'll lock the front; you lock the back."

She turns and races down the hallway. "Get your ass moving, Sparkles."

I laugh, a smile planted on my face, and head to the front door.

# CHAPTER 16

*Sara*



*"But you should just know that when we're done, I'm going to be very, very interested in you. More than I am now."*

The lock turns with a *click*.

My insides burn, a chaotic mess of thoughts, possibilities, and feelings crashing together to create a dizzying experience. *The only kind of feelings I like.*

Banks's words tumble through my head as I gather the bottom of Damaris's dress so it doesn't drag on the ground. I don't know what he really means by that.

*"I don't want this to be it between us. I want this to be a part of it."*

The intensity in his eyes make me believe that he means it in a non-sexual kind of way—like he wants to start building something that looks very un-friends-with-benefits-like.

The anticipation swells in my stomach, perspiration dotting my skin despite the air-conditioning blowing from the vent in the floor.

*Don't overthink it yet, Sara. Enjoy it first.*

Banks comes around the corner. His dimple settles deep in his cheek.

*I'm so gonna enjoy this.*

He crooks his finger. "Come here."

I don't know whether it's the words, the fire in his eyes, or the coy smile on his lips, but it causes the tangle in my stomach to explode. His grin gets wider as I move quicker and, by the time I'm in front of him, I'm panting.

He grips my hips as soon as I reach him. Like a choreographed dance that we've done before, I jump as he lifts me. My legs wrap around his waist. The dress bunches at my hips, the thin straps sliding down my arms. *The dress wants off me too.*

My anticipation melts into excitement, and I giggle as his mouth crashes against mine. My fingers comb through his messy hair before cupping his face. His stubble scratches against my palms as I hold his face to me.

He groans as I nibble his bottom lip moments before he turns toward the living room. His fingers dig into my ass as he holds me, pressing me against him.

"I should've grabbed a shower," Banks says between kisses. He drops to the couch, bringing me with him. "I didn't plan this very well."

I straddle his lap, rocking my opening against his crotch. Between the hardness and the scratching of the denim against my swollen flesh, I could come from this alone.

"Do you plan anything very well?" I ask, laughing.

He cinches my waist with his hands as I grind against him. "Yes, I do, actually. I can plan the hell out of avoiding moving furniture."

"I call bullshit."

He groans, flexing against me as I slip my arms out of the dress straps. The top stays up and barely covers my chest.

"You were quick to jump when Ashley needed your help," I say, pulling my hair to the top of my head and securing it with a tie from my wrist.

He rests his head on the cushion and looks up at me with his blue eyes blazing. "That was a special situation."

I stop moving. "Is that so?"

He guides my hips in a circle. "Someone was already attached to that particular furniture-moving adventure."

"I thought you hated that particular someone."

He grins, and it obliterates anything not melted in my core. *How can a man be equal parts sexy and adorable?*

Banks slides his hands against my clavicle and then up the sides of my neck. His thumbs press just behind my ears and his calloused hands wrap around the back of my head. He grins as I raise onto my knees to kiss him.

I hold his shoulders, feeling the thick muscles under my palms. He kisses me lazily, sweetly—as if each stroke of his tongue or pressing of his lips is intentional. It's as if he's trying to tell me that this isn't about the result as much as it's about the moment. The experience. The act of whatever it is that we're doing.

Because this isn't fucking. This is something else entirely, and the terrifying thing is that I don't hate it. *At all.*

He drags his fingertips down my arms, leaving a trail of goose bumps behind. He lifts the dress and slides his hands under the fabric. I hold my breath as his tongue pulls across my bottom lip, and he grabs my ass cheeks again.

"*Fuck,*" he mutters against my lips. He pulls away, his eyes wild. "Tell me. Did you have anything on under my shirt last night or were you like this?" He squeezes me again.

I look down at him, grinning mischievously. "Wouldn't you like to know?"

He chuckles. "I'm not sure if not knowing last night was a good thing or a bad thing."

"Depends on the outcome you wanted, I suppose," I say, running my hands through his hair. "After listening to you last night, I think you got the one you wanted. So it was a good thing, I think. For you, anyway."

He rolls his eyes. "Why is everything that's good for you always kinda painful?"

I giggle, leaning back.

His hands slide around my thighs until his thumbs are on either side of my slit.

The room wobbles, and I hold on tight to his shoulders to keep steady. "Like what?"

"Oh, like when you order pizza and the cheese is really goopy and melty. That's when it's the best, but it'll also burn the hell out of you."

I laugh as he spreads my thighs farther apart. "You could have patience and wait."

"Waiting is overrated."

My heart pounds. "You seem to have tons of patience tonight."

"Patience is a virtue."

"An annoying one."

He smirks. "I'll be honest, I don't know how in the hell I have this much patience when your pussy is so close to my face."

*Fuck. Me.*

I can barely register that when his finger slides through my wetness.

"*Ooh,*" I say, hissing a breath and spreading my legs so far apart that they burn. "Now we're getting somewhere."

His grin is slow and oh-so sexy. "Okay. Tell me. How fast do you want to get *there*?"

"Now would be great—*ah,*" I say, as one finger dips into me and another finds my clit. "Yes. Now."

He chuckles, massaging slow, small circles against my swollen bud. "Do you know what I *really* like?"

I hum, my eyes falling closed at the pleasure rolling through me in soft waves.

"Watching your face turn pink and wondering if it matches the color of your pussy," he says.

*Dear God.* "There's only one way to find out."

He withdraws his touch. But before I can protest, he's pulling the top of my dress down. Seams crack at the quick and harsh movement.

"Don't break it," I cry as he pulls a breast into his mouth. "This is your mom's."

He holds a nipple between his teeth and looks up at me, grinning. "It's fine. She never expects anything to come back without it being broken. Trust me. Years of experience."

I laugh, but it instantly changes to a hiss. "*Banks.*"

He flicks my nipple with his tongue while rolling the other around in his fingers. I'm dripping wetness down my legs, my thighs sticky.

*He's. Barely. Touched. Me.*

*How can he do that?*

My thoughts are going a mile a minute, but I can't land on any one of them in particular. This is new territory—unhurried ... and sweet. We've been at this for however long, and it's been all about *me*.

*How wonderfully strange.*

I tip my head back, pushing my chest toward Banks. He licks, nips, and squeezes harder and faster—his hips raising up as if they, too, are dying for relief.

He pulls back and gathers my dress. The look he gives me is pure heat.

A filthy smile stretches across his face as he scoots around and lies on the couch. My brows pull together, unsure of what's happening until I'm not unsure anymore.

I gasp a quick breath as he urges me forward—toward his face. I'm still straddling him and it takes little effort to move from his waist *to over his head*.

He lines his mouth up to my pussy. *Oh. My. God.*

Banks holds my dress at my hip with one hand, but I do him a favor—*me a favor?*—and relinquish him of his duties. He smirks.

My heart thunders so hard that I can feel the pulses in my sex. Banks urges me toward him. I comply.

He holds my gaze, dragging a finger slowly through my slit. It's so wet, so ready for him.

"Whatever you want me to do, all you have to do is ask," he says, his voice gruff. "You never have to just take what you're given. Do you know that?"

Everything tightens—my chest, my core, *my heart*.

The juxtaposition of the moment steals my breath. The sweet, vulnerable look in his eye. The rough, raw timbre to his words. The feel of his fingers strumming slowly in and out of my body. *And all of this with his lips inches from my opening.*

This man is nothing like I expected. He's more in every way.

And that's a little terrifying.

"If a man doesn't understand how lucky he is to be able to touch you, don't let him," he says, twisting his finger as he withdraws it from me. "But I know, so let me."

I laugh, my chest so constricted that it hurts to breathe.

"But you're lucky too," he says, winking.

*Don't I know it—oof.*

My body sags against his face as he flicks his tongue against my clit. He circles the pulsing bud before sucking it into his mouth.

"Banks!"

The room blurs as wave after wave of intensity rips me from reality.

"Do you like that?" he asks, flicking it again.

"Yes," I say through clenched teeth.

He adds a finger, then two, stroking me slowly, then quicker—hard, soft, and rough. I grind against his hand and use my free hand to press his face deeper against me. Urging him to keep going. *Begging him for more.*

Banks understands the assignment.

He works me over without finding a rhythm. It keeps me on the edge and frenzied, ready to fall apart. What never stops is the constant contact of his mouth against my pussy. The noises filling the air as his mouth sucks and kisses could make me come on its own.

I regrip my dress, clenching it in my sweaty palm. My thighs ache. My core pulls so tight that I wince.

I look down to see him staring at me, his eyes filled with so much unadulterated lust that I whimper.

"You," he says before kissing my clit. "Are." He kisses it again. "Beautiful."

My eyes squeeze shut in a futile attempt to hold it together.

His fingers slide in and out smoothly, deeply, twisting and hitting every spot that triggers a physical reaction. My head swims with too many feelings, unable to register everything happening simultaneously.

Finally, he plunges into me and gently presses his teeth against my nub. *Oh fuck.*

I cry out, my head falling back and my eyes shutting against the searing intensity of the orgasm.

My legs shake, my body trembles. And every time I remember that Banks's face is between my legs, another surge of pleasure rattles me.

"I can't," I say, dropping the fabric. It shrouds him. I place my hands on the armrest and press back, whimpering. *"Please.* I can't anymore."

He removes his fingers and pulls away, knocking the dress away from his head.

His face glistens, coated with my climax. The smile on his swollen lips couldn't be more satisfied if it were him coming with the force of a thousand suns.

I laugh in full contentment as life pours back into me, scooting back to his hips again.

"The right thing, because you should never assume, is to ask if you liked it." He smirks. "But I'm pretty sure you did."

My chest shakes as I chuckle. "It's a good thing your brothers can't see you right now."

He lifts a brow. "Why?"

"Because this gives a whole new definition to Sparkles."

He laughs, sitting up. I scoot off him, but the lack of contact only lasts a moment. He scoops me up and stands.

"Where are we going?" I ask, my body suddenly heavy and tired.

"I need a shower, and you need cleaned up."

We start down the hall.

"But I need to repay the favor," I say, smiling at him.

He stops in the doorway and grins. "Don't worry. You will."

It's not the words that get to me. It's not even his grin. It's the way he says it—the way Banks seems to do everything. There's a playfulness in his tone, but also something else. Confidence. Honesty. A mixture of sexy and fun.

Typical Banks. You get more than you bargain for.

"I can't wait," I say, giving in and letting my reservations go.

He winks and carries me to the tub.

# CHAPTER 17
## *Banks*



"Here you go, my lady," I say, holding a towel open for Sara.

She laughs as she steps into my extended arms, and I swallow her up in the towel.

The red dress that will forever be burnt into my mind is on a hanger by the door. My work clothes are scattered on the floor, and my boots are mixed up with my jeans. Water puddles dot the tile floor from being splashed out over the past hour.

I take another towel from the linen closet and cover her hair. She giggles as I try to get it right but epically fail.

"Well," I say, stepping back. "You kind of look like Mother Teresa with that thing over your head, but you won't drip all over the floor."

She grins. "Your handiwork is appreciated."

I narrow my eyes.

"*All* of your handiwork," she says, winking. "You're quite impressive, Sparkles."

I groan. "Not you too."

She pushes an elbow into my stomach. I flex at the last moment to ensure I continue making a good impression. "Yeah, but at least mine doesn't refer to glitter."

"You can sparkle me anytime."

She snickers and follows me into the hallway. I start toward my bedroom but notice she doesn't follow me. When I stop in the doorway and look over my shoulder, my stomach tenses.

Her bottom lip is between her teeth. Her eyes are filled with hesitation.

"What are you doing?" I ask her. Although I know what she's doing.

*"I want sex, but not the other crap that goes along with it. I just don't have the stomach for it."*

"Come on," I say, going into my room.

"I'll see you later."

I poke my head around the corner. She hasn't moved, which tells me she wants to come. She's just nervous.

"Yeah, in like the three seconds it's going to take you to get in here," I say.

I rifle through my dresser for a clean pair of shorts.

"My pajamas are in my room," she says. "I need something to put on."

I rip a shirt out of a stack—ignoring the ones that I got from Jess the night he and Pippa were apart—and take it to the hallway. I toss it at her.

She catches it, holding it in her hands like it's a bomb. "What's this?"

"A shirt."

"For what?"

I roll my eyes. "For you to sleep in."

She tries not to smile. Luckily for her, the towel on her head wobbles, and it hides her face long enough for her to wipe the grin off her cheeks.

*Be you. I have learned in my life that when you're unapologetically you, you attract all the things meant to come your way. It works. I promise.*

Okay ... *what would I do normally?*

I sigh. Here's the problem. *There is no normal.* I haven't had a girlfriend in ... a while. I fool around here and there, have some fun, but worrying about them finding a shirt to hang in? Have I done *that* before?

This is Sara, and I *want* her to be comfortable. *Happy.* So ...

"We're going to have to order dinner out," I say. "Unless you want to sneak into Jess's. He keeps extra heat-up pizzas in the freezer in the garage. I took the last pepperoni last weekend, so unless they've been to the store, we're probably stuck with sausage and mushroom."

She laughs. "We can't keep eating out."

"Why?"

"It's expensive, and I'm broke. You know this. Hence, why I'm here."

I smirk. "I thought you were here for oral, but okay."

She just shakes her head, amused.

"Anyway, Shade House burgers again?" I ask.

She sighs. "You're paying."

"Of course."

I drop my towel and slide on my shorts. Her gaze holds tight to mine as I get them situated on my hips. There's something on her mind, something I'm probably not going to like. I can tell. I get that a lot.

"I really don't want to complicate things, Banks."

"Good. I'm not a complicated guy."

She presses her lips together. "I don't ask to stay with men."

"Good. Because I don't ask women to stay with me."

A light slowly appears in her eyes. *Sweet girl.*

I start toward the kitchen, pausing only to kiss the top of her head as I go. "Want a drink?"

She sighs in defeat. *Whew.*

"I'm going to grab my phone so we can call in our order," I say over my shoulder. "Be in my bed and in my shirt when I get back."

"And what if I'm not?"

I don't miss a step. "Then I'll come find you and carry you back there. Why don't you just keep it simple for both of us?"

She scoffs to save face. But the sound of her feet slapping quickly against the floor gets more faint, which means she's headed to my room.

I blow out a breath and find my phone. Then I grab two waters and a bag of cookies I borrowed from Mom's on Sunday, then head back.

I hope I'm projecting confidence and not the wobble in my gut. I'm not usually so assertive. *Live and let live.* But if I'm not super clear and give her too much wiggle room to get out of it, I know she'll revert to what she knows. And that's evading any possibility of depth in a relationship. Well … evading a relationship altogether.

Leaving.

If she really wanted to go, of course, I'd let her. I'd help her. But I don't think that's true.

I think she likes being wanted.

"Here you go," I say, tossing the bag of cookies on the bed beside her. "Consider it an appetizer."

I try not to stare or make a big deal out of how my heart thumps seeing her in the middle of my bed with the blankets just covering her chest. I just set the drinks on the bedside table and lie on top of the blankets next to her.

She offers me a cookie. "It's weird lying in your bed."

"Why?"

"I don't know."

I take the cookie. "Well, I'm your fake fiancé now. You should get comfortable here."

Her smile is soft. I love it on her face.

"Do you really want to go with me?" she asks, nibbling on the edge of a chocolate chip.

"Yeah. Especially if you're going in that dress."

She giggles. "I need to either wear the other one or have that one cleaned first. I'm going to have it dry-cleaned either way."

"Can I ask you something?"

"Sure. I guess. I mean, I might not answer, but you can ask."

*Fair enough.* I settle in against the pillows. "Why did what's-his-face saying that to you bother you that much?"

"What do you mean?"

I shrug. "I don't know. Maddox said I shouldn't get a dog the other day because I can barely keep myself alive."

She laughs.

"Although true, he said that because he knew it wouldn't hurt my feelings. And he knows that because he knows me."

"Okay …"

I blow out a breath. "So what was it about 'not being wife material' that bothered you?"

"What does it matter?"

"Because I want to understand you and that seems like a good place to start."

I hold my breath, positive that she's going to either get up and leave or tell me to fuck off. But, much to my surprise, neither happens.

She takes small bites of her cookie and stares across the room.

"You don't have to answer that if you don't want to," I say. "I was just curious."

"You know what's curious to me?"

"What's that?"

She turns her head my way. "That I've never really thought about it. It pissed me off on a gut level, but I've never thought about why."

I'm curious and want to press, but I give her space to get her thoughts together. My typical tactic of hounding people until I get what I want won't work here. And, strangely, I don't want them to.

Finally, she heaves a breath. "I think it's because it was a dickish thing to say, first of all."

"Agreed."

"But also …" She frowns. "I guess it makes me really mad, because Joshua doesn't know anything about me, but he was able to needle me. He struck a real fear, and I don't know if he did it on purpose or if he got lucky."

She looks so alone. *Is she really withdrawing from me? Is it intentional? Or is it habit?*

I lay my palm next to hers and bump her pinkie finger with mine. She holds it out to the side, and I lace mine over it. *That's better.*

"What are you afraid of?" I know I'm pushing my luck, but it's now or never.

She takes a long, deep breath. "I'm afraid that maybe he's right."

"What do you mean?"

She smiles sadly at me. "I don't really know how to talk about this."

"You just open your mouth and let the words flow. I do it all the time. Sometimes it works out for you and sometimes not." I wink. "I wouldn't recommend ordering a dozen chickens without thinking it through, though."

Her laughter is light and small, but it's there. And that's good enough.

She blows out her breath. "For someone who talks a lot of shit, I'm pretty uncertain about a lot of things—most things, really."

"Like what?"

"Like … I can't believe I'm talking about this," she mumbles.

I stroke her pinkie finger with mine. She stares at them as if the sight of them gives her strength.

"I don't know how to connect with people," she says softly. "I don't know if I connected with my mother or not and it drives me nuts every day. I have no memories of her, no stories to tell at parties when people share their favorite mom tales."

*Oh, Sara.* I want to hold her and kiss her, but if I do, she'll stop talking. And as much as I want to heal her wounds, I want her to have the chance to unload them. *Give them to me. I'll carry them for you.*

"My dad was great," she says. "But he was military, and there wasn't a ton of hugging or words of affection. And that's fine. It comes with the territory. But then he married Sabrina, and suddenly, he had the ability to do both."

She frowns and looks so … sad. She looks down at our fingers again, and I just wait, because I feel there's more.

"With Sabrina, and then with Bethany, he was warm, and you would even have thought he was cuddly. But he never did that with me."

And there it is. *Shit.*

I wrap my arm over her shoulders and pull her closer to me. She lays a hand on my chest and doesn't even try to pull away.

My parents are huggers. My family, except Foxx, are warm and tactile—sometimes too much. But Sara has never had the level of affection I have taken for granted.

My chest stings for her. I wish I knew how to fix it. I would.

"I love my friends," she says. "And Ashley's mother, Gretchen. I don't know what would've happened to me without her. At least she tried to rope me in." She chuckles. "She'd come to a party at two in the morning in her nightgown and find me if I hadn't checked in or come to her house."

*Thank God for Gretchen.*

She swallows against me. "I guess I'm scared that I'll never have a family or a connection with someone else because I've never had it. But I'm too scared to try to have it too because what if I fail? What if it proves that my fears are right, and I don't know how to …" She looks up at me. "Be *wife material*, I guess. And what if everyone else already knows?"

I press a kiss on the top of her head. "Well, for what it's worth, you're doing an excellent job as my fake soon-to-be wife."

Her entire body relaxes. She rests her cheek against me once again.

I don't know what to say. I'm so bad at this. When things get murky, I distract myself by walking across the street and seeing what everyone else is doing. But Sara doesn't have that option.

*So it's just been her all this time? How fucking lonely.*

"Why don't you talk to anyone about this?" I ask. "Have you talked to Ashley or Becca?"

She shakes her head. "No. I know they love me—they're the best. But it's just hard to imagine that anyone really cares."

"They care. I promise you they do." I squeeze her shoulder. "And I care too."

She laughs as if she's dismissing me.

"And my mom will care," I say, groaning. "Don't ever tell her any of this if you don't want her in the middle of your life trying to fix it all. This is a huge warning."

She sits up, holding the blanket to her chest. Her eyes are bright. "Oh, your mom said to tell you that you owe her a lot of lawn care for having her yellow bowl."

I push my head back on the pillows and groan. "I really didn't think I had that."

"You really did have it."

"Ugh. Okay." I breathe out and rest my eyes on Sara again. "But you have to help me."

"Me? *Why?*"

"Because you let her in."

She laughs. "She would've gotten in either way. And I didn't let her in. She just came in."

*I'm really not enjoying this open-door policy anymore.*

"Are we ordering food or what?" she asks.

I toss her my phone. "I'll have a burger and fries."

"That's what you had last night."

"That's what I like."

Her eyes hood. "So you like what you like, and you like it often?"

*"Often."*

She hums. "Well, that's good since you're my fake fiancé now."

"And you're my new best friend."

The words tumble out of my mouth before I think about it. *Again.*

*Dammit, I have to stop doing this.*

But the more I think about it, the more I like it. The more it makes sense. Not only do I need a new best friend—*thank you, Ashley*—it'll help me build trust with Sara.

She blinks once. Then twice.

"It's a trade," I say. "Take it or leave it."

A mischievous grin tickles her lips. "Friends with benefits?"

I grab her and pull her onto me. "As many benefits as you want."

"Deal."

I swallow her laughter with kisses and forget all about dinner.

# CHAPTER 18
## Sara







I walk around the Carmichael Classics building and find Banks standing at the door. His bright smile, happy to see me, makes my smile stretch from ear to ear.

This whole thing between him and me is bananas. I woke up this morning after getting three hours of sleep because we stayed up all night watching old movies, eating cold pizza that he stole out of Jess's garage around midnight, and replaying our couch activities.

It's the most fun I think I've ever had in my life. That's a high in and of itself—but it's also a little scary. At least, it's scary until I see him. Then the wobbliness inside me is kicked to the curb.

"Today has taken forever," he says, pouting.

But as soon as I reach him, the frown leaves his face, and he presses his mouth roughly, yet tenderly, against mine.

I place a hand on his chest and wad his dirty shirt in my fist. I could let him kiss me forever.

Finally, he pulls back.

"So we're just kissing like that now, huh?" I ask, grinning. "Out it public for the world to see?"

He grins right back. "Do you want me to stop kissing you, bestie?"

*No, no, I do not.*

"How was your day?" I ask. "Is Tasha ready for her vacation?"

Banks groans. "Stop saying *vacation*. It's my new least favorite word."

I laugh. "You'll be fine without her."

He makes a face like he's not convinced. But I am. I'm pretty sure Banks would be fine in any situation if he wanted to be.

I follow him inside the shop and through a little archway onto the actual floor. The room is expansive and bright with clean, white walls and big overhead lights. Cars line the room, some on the ground and others raised on lifts. It's surprisingly clean and organized—very much not like his house.

"You need to have whoever cleans this place come to your house," I say, laughing. "You could eat off the floor here, and I worry about eating off plates in your kitchen."

He gasps. "I'll have you know that I clean up here."

I gasp back at him.

"I do," he says. "I mean, the guys all help take care of their shit and keep whatever area they're working in clean. But I always stay late and go through and make sure it's all where it's supposed to be."

He walks over to a display. A plethora of glass jars sit in a red holder, and each is filled with different screws and bolts. On the front of every jar is a white label with black writing, denoting what's inside.

"I did that," he says proudly. "Doesn't it make you feel good to see it?"

"Um, no. But I'm glad it does you."

He flashes me a disapproving look. "Sometimes I come early on Sunday mornings before dinner at Mom's and sweep or wipe down all the heavy traffic areas."

"I don't …" My brows pull together. "How are you this person here and not at home?"

He shrugs. "I don't know. This place feels like home to me. My work family is here. We have a monthly dinner together here. We stay late and work on deadlines, yell, almost cry …" He chuckles. "At home, it's just me."

*Interesting.*

I know absolutely nothing about cars, but I need to show some interest because this is important to him. Even though his questions yesterday made me uncomfortable, he did it because he suspected I needed to answer them. *I know that's true. He wouldn't have done it otherwise.*

That's one of the things I'm learning about Banks. He's way more observant than anyone gives him credit for.

I mosey down the shop. *What can I ask about that would make sense?* My sights finally settle on an emerald-green car up on a lift.

"What kind of car is this?" I ask, pointing up.

Banks smiles. "That is a Camaro. It's one of my favorite body styles of all time." He grimaces. "I hate saying that because it feels like I'm betraying Betsy."

"Your car?" I ask, amused.

"She's my baby. Never tell her I talked about a Camaro. She'll be crushed."

"I promise. Your secret of loving Camaros more than Betsy is safe with me."

He grabs me and brings me into his chest. His hands lock at the small of my back. My heart flutters like a teenager with her first boyfriend, and if I think about it too much, I might be disgusted with myself.

*It's too bad I'm too focused on him.* And that I came here with a purpose.

"Am I taking your picture or what?" I ask, drawing a line down his jaw. "Because if you keep holding me like this, I'll lose my interest in photography."

"And gain an interest in …"

I snicker. "Pornography."

He bursts out laughing and steps away, pulling his phone out of his pocket. He scans the screen.

"I don't get it," he says. "Look at this."

I peer over his shoulder.

Unknown: Peahens prefer peacocks with the longest trains and biggest displays. They are most attracted to peacocks with the most perfect train, number of iridescent "eyes," and even their symmetry.

"Who is sending those?" I ask.

He shrugs. "My brothers get them too. Of course, I got a peacock when Moss got a flamingo."

I snort.

"I wanted a lion or a tiger," he says. "Something badass. Instead, I get a bird with iridescent feathers."

Our eyes snap together.

"A *sparkly* bird?" I ask, raising my brows.

"That can't be a coincidence. But the sparkles thing would make me lean toward Jess, but he gets the texts. No one else knows about the sparkles thing except my brothers, and they all get them."

"Even Foxx?"

Banks's eyes narrow. "But this isn't a Foxx kind of thing to do. It's too ... fun."

I laugh.

Banks shakes his head. "But maybe it is. He did lose his key at the marina, and that's very not Foxx-like. Maybe he's breaking down in his old age."

"It's the easiest explanation."

He grins like the cat that caught the canary. "I'm gonna get that bastard. I've been thinking of different ways to do it. I have one in mind, and it's a little ... over the top, even for me. But this whole peacock thing just sealed his fate."

"What is it?"

"Can't tell you."

I gasp. "And why not?"

"Because it's good. Really, really good. Like *he might actually kill me* good. I'll need an escape route pre-planned. Maybe up my life insurance."

I giggle. "Then is it worth it?"

His eyes sparkle. "Totally. Want to be my beneficiary? I have a great policy. Dad made me get one when I turned eighteen. Something about me not making it very long if I didn't straighten up."

"I don't want your money." I lean closer. "I want to know what you'll do to Foxx."

He cackles.

"Tell me. *Please.*"

He shakes his head. "Can't risk it. It's going to take a lot of work to get it to come together."

"Did you just say *come together*?"

He smacks my ass as he walks away, making me yelp. "Let's get these pictures over with so I can get you home."

*Home.* Not his home. Just … home.

There's something about how he says it so freely that burrows itself inside my soul. Like I'm welcome. Wanted. He says it like I have a place there.

I'm not sure what this is between Banks and me. I can't quite wrap my head around it. But I can't deny that it's a wonderful thing to feel this at ease with someone. To feel like we are friends and also lovers. That he wants me to be here, in his space—his favorite space, and in his home.

And in his bed.

He strips his shirt off and tosses it on a stool.

"Who was your photographer last time?" I ask, pulling my phone from my pocket.

"Tasha."

My insides tighten.

He grins. "Don't be jealous. She's happily married and thinks of me like her child, I'm pretty sure."

"I'm not jealous."

He walks to me and kisses me roughly and loudly. "You have no reason to be."

*What?* My brain scrambles as he disappears into his office. *I have no reason to be? Why? What does that mean?* While my head might be unsure, the rest of me doesn't care.

Banks comes back with a rose. "Okay, Gloria suggested one with a rose in my mouth."

I burst out laughing.

"I know, I know," he says. "But I have to give the fans what they want."

"There's something really weird about you having a fan club of geriatric women."

He shrugs. "They bake pies and bring me homemade lunches. They tell me I'm handsome. And, before you, they were clamoring to set me up with their granddaughters."

"Before me?"

"Yeah. Before you." He winks. "We're fake married, and I'm real monogamous."

*We're fake* married *now?*

*My heart. I grin so hard it hurts.*

"I considered bringing oil to give my muscles a little extra sheen, but I have a sparkles complex at this point," he says.

I snort. "I'm pretty good with filters. I can make you sparkle without sparkling in real life."

His eyes heat. "The way you make me sparkle is my favorite."

A rip of excitement tears through me at high velocity.

"You look a little nervous and inexperienced at this," he says. "So I'm just going to move around in the way I know the ladies love, and you just snap all the pictures."

"Okay," I say, laughing.

"Get my good side. And if you find an angle you really like, just tell me to work it."

"Got it."

He puts the flower between his teeth and widens his stance. He looks to the side, giving me a great view of his hard jawline. His chin lifts, drops, moves in a slow, dramatic circle while I click away.

"Oh, right there," I say, egging him on. "Work it. Make love to the camera."

He rips the flower out of his mouth and sends it sailing across the room. I can barely hold the phone still from laughing so hard.

"I should really charge them for these shots," he says. "This is like premium material."

"I should charge you for the photography. You're getting my best work."

He stops. "I got your best work last night."

A blush creeps up my cheeks. "That's what you think."

"Keep it up and the old women will get more than they requested." He grabs his cock through his jeans. "You make me so hard, Sara."

"I won't tell you what you do to me because we need to get this over with." *And I don't want to get wet while taking photos of this man.*

He poses with a wrench. Then he lies on a creeper and has me stand over him from a different angle. He squats in front of a car and puts his shirt back on, leaving the chest hanging open and the top button of his jeans undone.

We laugh as he slides down a pole like a fireman. I swoon as he gets serious and stares into the camera. My knees go weak as he licks his lips and looks just above the lens—right into my eyes.

"I think we got enough," I say, my body humming. "How many do you need to send them?"

"I don't know. Ten?"

"Well, I hate to tell you, but I'm keeping the rest as payment."

I turn to pick up the flower he chucked earlier when his hands grip my waist. My core tightens at the contact, craving him yet again.

"If you're going to touch me like that, you better be ready to follow through," I say, staring at the wall ahead of me.

He brushes my hair off one shoulder and then presses a kiss just behind my ear. "Do you object to getting fucked right here?"

My pussy clenches. "I do not."

He spins me around with urgency, and as soon as we're facing each other, *it's on.*

Hands rush over each other, lips touch, and tongues lick. *It's carnal.* It's hot as hell.

I shove his shirt over his shoulders. He makes quick work of ridding me of mine. Our breaths are quick, our kisses heady. He shoves my shorts down my legs and sucks in a hasty breath when he realizes I'm panty-less. I barely have time to step out of my flip-flops and my bottoms before he's lifting me.

My legs lock around his middle, my wetness slick against his stomach. His tongue slides across my lips before plunging into my mouth.

I gasp for air as he carries me across the shop. My fingers tug against his soft hair, pulling his head back to give me better access to him.

My back settles against something cold and hard. I look over my shoulder to see the yellow paint of a Volkswagen.

He pins me to the metal with one hand and undoes his zipper with the other. I'm panting so hard, needing to be filled so desperately, that I can't concern myself with what this might do to the machine.

Banks reaches into his pocket and brings a condom to his teeth. Tearing it open, his eyes are glued to mine.

I laugh. "Looks like you were a little confident."

"Optimistic." He rolls the rubber over his shaft. "You seemed to enjoy it last night."

"Just a little—*ah!*"

He plunges into me with no warning. The thickness of his cock stretching me is deliriously good. I rest my head against the car and tilt my hips toward him.

Something bites against my back, something hard and sharp. But there's little time to focus on that when my body already threatens to explode around Banks.

"I've thought about this all day," he says, finding a rhythm that suits us both. "You are impossible to forget."

I smile as he slides into me. My back squeaks against the car, mixing with the sound of his cock moving through my wetness.

"That was the plan," I tease. "Make sure Banks can't forget me."

"Mission accomplished."

I moan as he hits the spot I love. "What was your plan?"

"I have a few."

Humming, I close my eyes and soak up the pleasure. "Like what?"

He adjusts his grip on my hips. "To make you feel good."

"Done."

"To make you know you're beautiful."

I grin. "In progress."

"To make you want to be with me."

My heart swells. I don't have time to process his last objective because my body begins to shudder. I plant both hands against the car to help hold myself steady as Banks drives himself into my body.

I will never get over the sight of him between my legs. This tall, gorgeous, sweet man acting like I'm the most interesting part of his day? It doesn't get much better than this.

"I'm going to come," I say, my legs shaking.

"Good. I've been thinking about peacocks so I don't."

My laughter is loud and free. It's stopped as the first licks of orgasm tear through me.

I squeeze my eyes closed and enjoy the rupture of bliss that fills my veins.

"So good, Banks," I say, falling apart around him.

His fingertips bite into my skin as his hips pound into mine.

The sound of his groan, followed by a quick hiss of breath.

The taste of his kiss lingering on my lips.

The sight of him losing himself because of me.

It's hard to find my breath.

*"I've thought about this all day. You are impossible to forget."*

This is different. This is a moment to remember. It's fucking ... *but it's also not.*

My heart swells so big I fear it'll burst.

*You'll be impossible to forget too, Banks.*

*I hope I survive.*

# CHAPTER 19

## Banks

"Catch." I let an orange fly across the banana display. Sara turns just in time and catches it. "Oof. I thought that was going to end badly."

She drops it in the cart.

"I don't want that," I say, walking to the cart and plucking the fruit out.

She takes it from my hand, looking at me sternly, and puts it back in the cart. "You have to buy it now. You can't just bruise the fruit and let them sell it to someone else."

"Ugh. You are no fun. You're like shopping with my mom."

She rolls her eyes and pushes the cart down the produce section. I walk behind her so that I can watch her ass.

I've given my brothers a lot—*a lot*—of shit about discarding me for their women. I stand by my objections. Because I didn't know any better. But now … I get it.

Maddox is cool and all, but being with Sara … I whistle through my teeth.

She looks over her shoulder and grins. "What are you doing?"

I pick up a cucumber. "Just thinking about how I'd like to be inside you right now." I look at the vegetable. "I've never realized how sexual a grocery store really is."

She shakes her head and keeps pushing.

"Want to take this home?" I ask. "I can think of really good uses for this."

"Put it down, Banks."

I sigh. "You are so much more fun at home."

She stops at the tomatoes. "Because when you're in public, you have to behave."

"That's what's wrong with society. Everyone is worried about behaving. What about having fun?" I nestle my face in the crook of her neck. "What about kissing your girl in the fruits and veggies?"

She leans her head to the side. "I can get down with that."

I press a kiss in the spot where her neck meets her shoulder. "So you're also going to get down with me calling you my girl?"

"Don't push it."

She tries to walk fast so I don't see her smile, but she fails. I see it. I see it and it makes me hard as a rock.

The grocery store isn't as busy as it was the last time I was here. The apples didn't need a traffic light and the cheese case wasn't the setting for a PTA meeting. Really, when there's no one here, it's kind of nice.

"So what are we going to eat?" she asks, turning down the meat aisle.

"Aw, look. It's Jess's chickens' cousins."

She smacks me. "You're awful."

"It's funny. Admit it."

"*It's not funny.* I have a hard time eating meat if I think about it."

*Fuck.* I frown, thinking back to the cute little chirps in the box. "Well, we're not eating chicken."

She giggles.

My phone goes off as Sara digs through the bacon. I answer it instead of paying too much attention to what she's doing. I love bacon too much to think about it. I can't quit bacon.

**Foxx: Mom said you were at the grocery store.**

Me: Yup.

Foxx: If I call there, will you pick up a key
for me?

*What?* My fingers fly across the screen.

Me: You lost another key? 😊 That's highly
irresponsible of you. You really need to get
your shit together.

Foxx: Is that a yes?

Me: I'm going to need you to promise me that
you'll do better. I can't keep cleaning up your
mistakes, Foxx. Some of us have a life too—
lives a little more transparent than yours—but
lives anyway.

Foxx: Never mind.

Me: I'LL GET IT. Damn. 😒

Foxx: Thank you.

*Foxx has silenced notifications.*

"Well, isn't that interesting," I say as we enter the cheese section. I take packages of Muenster, Cheddar, Provolone Unsmoked, Colby Jack, and Havarti off the shelf and dump them in the cart. "Foxx lost another key."

"Another one?"

"That's what he said. Make sure I get it before we leave, okay?"

She nods. "Yeah. But do you need all that cheese? What on earth will you do with all of it?"

"Eat it."

"On what?"

I look at her like she's dense. "Usually my hand around two in the morning, but sometimes I put it on bread with a little ham." I make a face. "Not turkey. Do you know how many kinds of turkey there are?"

Something hits me and I gasp.

"What?" she asks, stopping the cart.

"Turkey is an actual cousin to chicken. *Fuck.* I can't eat that now either."

She shakes her head again.

"I thought I was fucking Jess by getting those little shits, but I think I was fucking me," I say.

"No, *I* was fucking you. You screwed yourself over."

I smile wickedly at her. "I like this side of you."

"From behind?" She looks at me over her shoulder. "I like it too."

I growl, making her laugh.

We go through the frozen foods and grab the essentials. Toaster strudels, pizzas, and tater tots all get added to the pile of cheese. Sara gets things like salmon, broccoli florets, and gelato.

We are not the same.

"This is where all your money goes," I say.

"Where?"

"All this food. Did you even look at the price of that shit? Tater tots are way cheaper."

"In the short term. Blood pressure meds and hospital bills are more expensive than salmon."

I scoff. "We're going to have to do something about this."

"What do you mean?"

"I mean you've ruined chicken for me tonight. Now I'm thinking negatively about tater tots. Could you please not ruin anything else for me?" I look ahead. "Caramel popcorn? Yes please." I add two bags to the cart. "Hush. I don't want to hear about diabetes."

She laughs. "You're a mess."

We walk quietly through the store, each of us in our own

thoughts. I don't know what Sara is thinking, but it doesn't seem to bother her. Actually, she looks really happy just walking around with me.

*And I love that.*

I snap a picture of chicken feed on an end cap as we go by. I upload it into a text to Jess.

Me: Do your babies need any food?

Jess: Come over tomorrow.

Me: I'm busy.

Jess: No, come over tomorrow. See what you've done.

Me: Can't you send me a picture?

It takes a few minutes for it to load. But when it does, I start laughing.

A coop large enough to fit a three-person family has been placed in Jess's backyard. Fencing and posts are on the ground as if he's not done.

Me: I knew you'd love them.

Another picture loads of a sign. It reads What a Fuster Cluck.

I snort.

Jess: I should nail this to your front door.

Me: I'd rock with it.

Jess: 😊 Pippa got that today. She's naming these chickens.

Me: Make sure one is after me.

Jess: We did. We call him Glitter. He keeps pecking the walls.

Me: He probably shines too bright that he's annoying himself. I can relate.

"Do you know how to make lasagna?" I ask.

"Yeah. It's not hard."

"Think we could make some this week?"

She grins. "You mean do I think *I* can make some this week?"

"I'll help."

"I think I'd rather you not."

Jess: Where are you?

Me: Grocery store. Need anything?

Jess: The pizzas you took out of my freezer.

Me: YOU KNOW ABOUT THAT?

Jess: It's hard not to know when you had ten because there was a sale and you go to get one and there's two.

Me: Oh.

I look up at Sara. "We need to grab Jess some pizzas."

She points in the cart.

Me: Well, lucky you, we already have pizzas in the cart for you.

Jess: Tell Sara thanks.

Me: I will.

"I need to get a tie for the gala," I say.

"That's out of left field."

"Which dress do you think you'll wear? I think I'm supposed to match you."

She thinks about it. "I dropped your mom's dress off at the cleaner's today before I came to the shop. So I could wear that one or the silver one I brought. What do you think?"

"I think you should try the silver one on for me tonight and then I'll see." I wiggle my brows. "Then we'll go off which one results in the best sex."

"If that's the case, I'll wear what I have on because I'm not sure you can beat today."

*Challenge accepted.*

We add water and Coke to the cart. Sara makes sure to grab the lasagna noodles and jarred sauce. She sends me to grab a package of hamburger. I avert my eyes from the chicken and get in and out of that department as fast as possible.

*Those poor little chickies.*

"What do you like for breakfast?" Sara asks as I return with the meat. "Are you a cereal guy? Muffin guy? Pancakes guy?"

"I usually don't eat too early. I have to caffeinate before I can eat and that takes at least three cups of coffee to do it properly. What about you?"

"My favorite are blueberry muffins. But I grabbed some in the bakery. I just wanted to make sure we didn't miss getting what you need."

I smack her ass. "You got what I need."

She stands on her tiptoes to reach for a bottle of agave syrup. I pluck it off the shelf and hand it to her.

"That's why you like me, isn't it?" I ask.

"Because you're tall? No. Sorry."

I scroll through my texts until I find the one I'm looking for. "No. Not that. It's because I have a *long train* and *huge display*."

She laughs. "I am attracted to your iridescence."

"I'm very symmetrical." I lift my chin and move my face from shoulder to shoulder. "See that? Almost identical."

"You're basically a peacock."

"Not just a peacock—*the peacock*. I'm the one that attracts all the peahens." I pause. "It has to be Foxx."

I take my phone out again.

> Me: Good call on the peacocks.

> Me: I was just thinking about it, and I really do have a lot of peacock qualities. Thanks for the compliments.

> Me: Do you want to hang out sometime? You seem nice.

> Me: I'm at the store now getting my brother's key. He's so irresponsible. He's supposed to be the older, more mature brother, but it's all a facade.

> Me: Let me know about hanging out. I'm free tomorrow after work.

"What are you doing?" Sara asks, getting in line for the cashier.

"Waiting to see if Foxx slips up and turns off his notifications. He hates texting and always shuts our group chats down. So I'm blowing up the peacock number just to fuck with him back."

The cashier turns on the conveyor belt. "Did you find everything okay?"

I start unloading our groceries. "We did. How are you this evening?"

"Tired. Ready to go home. I've been here since nine this morning."

Sara scoots me over. "Go bag these and help her out. I'll put the stuff up there."

*God, I love her.*

"Aren't you sweet?" the cashier says as I start bagging up our stuff. "Thank you so much. I really appreciate the help."

"It was my wife's idea."

Sara stops, her jaw hanging open.

I grin. "She's such a sweetheart."

*Did I really just think I love her? Oh fuck.*

"You two are the cutest couple," the cashier says. "I had a couple in here a little while ago, and they were fighting like cats and dogs. I mean, they were at each other's throats, and I wondered why they were even together. Wouldn't it be terrible to be stuck with someone you hated? And they obviously hated each other."

I nod. "I can't imagine. But I found the love of my life, so that's not a problem."

Sara laughs under her breath. "It's gonna be a problem if you keep it up," she says loud enough for only me to hear.

"Did you two date long?" the cashier asks.

"What was it, Sara? Three months?"

She stares at me. "What are you doing?"

"I'm sharing our love story, babe. It's inspiring." *Not to mention, I had better get a story together for the night of the gala.*

The lady checking us out goes into a ramble about her ex-boyfriend and how she thought he was the love of her life. Sara and I exchange glances while we finish getting everything sorted. She's amused but also thrown off a little.

*Good. It'll keep her on her toes. Can't let our fake engagement get stale.*

I slide my card through the reader, ignoring Sara's stare, and take the receipt.

"Don't forget Foxx's key," Sara says.

We stop at the customer service desk and retrieve it. This one is labeled *File Cabinet* with his phone number.

"You didn't have to buy all of that," she says as we walk to the truck. "Now I feel bad for getting all those things for myself."

I smirk. "Guess you'll have to figure out how to pay me back, *bestie*."

Her gaze heats. "I bet we can work something out."

Yes, I bet we can.

# CHAPTER 20
## Sara

"Are you nervous about tonight?" Becca looks over the empty chair between us, one hand stuck in the hand dryer. "I'm not going to lie. I'm kind of nervous for you."

"Yes, that one. The nude. Thank you," I say to the nail tech before returning my attention to Becca. "You know what's weird?"

"What?"

I do a quick internal check. *Am I nervous?* I wait to see if my stomach will curl or my blood pressure will increase. But all that happens is an excitement that bubbles from inside me. *I get to wear a gorgeous dress and be with Banks all night.*

"I'm not even a little nervous." I shrug. "When I think about the gala, I figure I should be a little nervous. I'll be meeting so many people who could really help me job-wise since I've gotten exactly zero bites on my résumé and applications. But I'm just not."

Becca lifts a brow. "And Joshua will be there."

"Meh."

She flinches, surprised by my apathetic attitude about my ex-asshole. I'm kind of surprised too.

But I haven't even thought about Joshua being there for a few days. He was the original reason I wanted to attend. I was so aggravated, so desperate not to be seen in a weak light. Now? I don't care what he thinks of me. I don't think of him at all.

A week ago, I was at one of the lowest points I've ever been. Discarded by Joshua, jobless, homeless—depending on friends to help me through the destruction. It shook me. I felt like I was grasping at straws to maintain some sort of semblance of order to my life.

That's been a consistent theme since I've been an adult and essentially on my own. There's never solid ground. I never have a footing from which to grow. I catch my breath only to have it knocked out of me as soon as I turn around.

A lot of it is my own fault. I try to fill the holes in my life, the loneliness in my soul—and the hours that go by—with people, places, and things. Anything besides taking a moment to breathe. Because if I take a moment to breathe, all of my feelings and thoughts and fears might rise up and overwhelm me. And who will be there to catch me if I collapse? *No one.*

But I feel more even-keeled than I have in a long damn time. It's odd because nothing in my life is any sturdier than it was, and I haven't fixed any of the problems plaguing me. But there's a little more sunshine when I wake up in the morning these days. I'll take it.

"Meh?" Becca says. "That's all you have to say about him? What about the rants and tirades? Where'd all of that go?"

"What shape?" the nail tech asks.

"Almond, please," I say.

"Almond. Okay."

I smile at her before looking at Becca again. "You know, I'm not exactly sure."

Becca's lips twitch. "I think I know."

"Do you now?"

"It's probably buried in the middle of Banks Carmichael's bed."

I laugh. "He's been a pretty great distraction."

Becca pauses to inspect her plum-colored nails. "These look great. Perfect. Thank you." Then she scoots over to the empty chair between us. "So tell me all about it. I've been working so much that I haven't had time to ask you how it's been going over there."

I smirk. "It's been … going."

Her eyes twinkle. "That good, huh?"

"You have seriously no idea, Becca. *None.*"

She glances at the nail tech. "So is it everything we used to sit around with margaritas and imagine it would be?"

"It's more than that. Better than that." I swoon, thinking of Banks's patience and sweetness—and how the switch can change to dirty in one hot second. "It's different too, though."

"How?"

I give the tech my other hand. "I don't know. It's like he makes you forget about everything else."

*"Oh, I bet he does."*

I laugh. "Yes, like that. But also in other ways." *How do I explain what I mean? How do you explain Banks Carmichael?* "Do you know how sometimes you can have dinner with someone, and it's you having dinner and them having dinner? You're at the same place, at the same table, and sitting across from each other. But it's very much you having your pasta and them having their steak or whatever."

"Yeah. And that's a great way to put it, actually. I watch so many people come in at Smokey's and they don't even say a word to each other. Or every time I stop at their table, they're talking about the same thing. Or the topics are always something really superficial—the weather, whether we're getting a Cane's chicken restaurant or not, how bad the traffic is."

"It's not that way with Banks. Whatever you do with him, *you're doing it with him.* I swear he's up your ass all the time."

Her brows shoot to the ceiling.

"Not like that," I say, laughing. "Just like, if you're making dinner, he's right there asking to chop things. If you're folding laundry, he sits down and fucks up the towels so you have to redo them when he's not looking. I've been filling out applications, right? Rather than doing it alone, he sat in the living room and turned on a movie. He's just ... *there*, I guess."

"Don't move," the tech says.

"I'm sorry."

"It's okay."

I turn back to Becca. "His little quirks used to drive me nuts, and I thought he did things to pester me. And the pranks that he does to his family? He actually admitted that he does them so they don't take life too seriously. So they can laugh and do things together." My heart warms. "I think it's just his way of letting you know he's there. He genuinely wants to be a part of people's days, of their lives." *Of my life.*

"That's so damn sweet."

"I know." My grin turns mischievous. "And then he strips down, and suddenly, it's not so sweet anymore."

She shifts in her seat. "Well, on another note so this doesn't get too R-rated, I decided not to go back to Texas."

"You did?" I squeal. "Becca! Yay!"

"I'm just not ready to go. I want to be ready—I'm just not there yet."

"Do you want to talk about it?"

She shakes her head. "No. I don't. Thanks though."

"I'm always here. Don't count on me to cry with you or anything, but I'll listen. And I'm always willing to throw clams in someone's car or bury a body."

"Not with these nails," the tech says. "Let them dry first."

Becca and I laugh.

———

Banks

Me: Hey, just checking in.

Me: Did a little investigating. You've really piqued my interest.

Me: Did you know that the peacock's train is what inspired Charles Darwin to think about how "sexual selection" might work?

Me: Really makes sense you chose the peacock for me. Good work.

. . .

I wait. No response.

"Come on, Foxx. Get pissed," I say before sliding my phone back in my pocket. I pick up my fudge fork and take another bite of pistachio fudge.

"What are you doing here?" Mom comes into the kitchen. "I thought you had the gala tonight?"

"I do. But I need a tie."

"What color?"

"What color do you suggest with your red dress?"

Mom beams. "She's wearing it?"

"She is. And she looks hot in it."

Mom rolls her eyes, but she can't wipe the smile off her face. She loves to *mom* everyone. Not only her own kids. *Sara is right. She really is the sweetest mom.*

"I was just telling Paige this morning that I wondered if she would wear it. She has such a cute figure. I bet she fills it out perfectly."

I smirk.

Mom points at me. "Whatever you're thinking, I don't want to know. Hey!" She plucks the fork out of my hand. "I've been looking for that. Where did you get it?"

"That's my fudge fork."

"Your what?"

I snap it back out of her hand. "I keep this fork over here so I don't have to go over there every time I want fudge."

"Get another fudge fork. That's real silver."

"Then why is it just hanging out in circulation?" I look at the utensil. "This is like fifty bucks."

"Because I use it on occasion. I didn't think my son was going to squirrel it away to eat fudge with it."

I scoff. "It's like you don't even know me."

She motions for me to follow her toward her bedroom. I slip the fork back in the drawer where I keep it. *If she wants it, she can look for it.*

I've never been excited for an event that required a tie. Actually,

I've avoided many events that called for me to dress up. It's just not my thing. But it's my thing if Sara wants me to.

I'm beginning to feel like a wimp. *This is what Jess must feel like.* But the more time I spend with Sara, the more I want with her.

Sara laughs at my jokes. She plays along with my antics. She doesn't always understand what or why I do what I do, but she doesn't try to change me. She just accepts that a carburetor might be on the table or my boots might be in the sink.

I'm already regretting the day she'll move out.

"Did you order printer cartridges?" she asks as we go down the hallway.

"They came already? That was fast. My printer at work was on its last shot of ink."

"Why didn't you ship them to your office?"

"Because Tasha is on *vacation*," I say, snarling at the word I've come to hate. "I don't know where to put them. She'll just come back and be mad that nothing is where it should be. So I'm trying very hard not to touch a damn thing while she's gone."

I'll take the printer cartridges with me and put them in the printer tomorrow. That way, I won't get in trouble from Tasha for not knowing where she keeps the office supplies or for messing with her systems. Win-win.

She flips on a light in her bedroom and opens Dad's closet.

"By the way, your new Amazon password was an easy guess," I say. "Ryderisacutie4 was one I try every time I'm guessing. Try harder."

She shakes her head. "Do you want a matte black or something with a little shine?"

"Are you going to follow this up with a Sparkle joke?"

She laughs. "No, but dammit. I should've."

"Matte back. I don't want to sparkle too much and take the attention away from Sara."

Mom comes out of the closet with a tie over her arm and a smile on her face. "You're such a sweetie."

"I know." I kiss her cheek. "Thanks for this."

"Do you have a jacket? Shoes?"

I nod. "I have a suit. It's just that my ties are yellow, lavender, and a stripey one that I hate. None of those go with red."

"No, they don't. But this one will look great." She hands it to me. "Do you want me to come over and take pictures?"

"This is not a school dance, Mother."

"Don't you want a picture to preserve the moment? Don't you want to remember it?"

I smirk. "What you mean is that you want to remember it, because I promise you that this evening will be permanently etched in my mind."

We start to go back to the kitchen when something outside the window catches my attention. I walk over to the glass and burst out laughing.

"What?" Mom asks.

Jess is attaching some kind of mesh around wooden posts that form what I think is the chicken run. He has a pencil over his ear and a measuring tape on his hip. He pauses and bends down, helping one of the baby chicks get out of a bowl. He's smiling, his lips moving like he's talking to a baby. *Is he cooing to a chicken? This is gold.*

"Look at Chicken Daddy out there." I lift the window open. "Jess, *you are the chicken father!*"

He flies me the middle finger.

I shut the window and meet Mom in the kitchen.

"So no to pictures?" Mom asks.

"Big no."

"What time are you leaving?"

"I'm not telling you. You'll come over and try to take pictures."

She laughs, pinching my cheek with the dimple. "You are so handsome, Banks."

"Thanks, Mama. You're very pretty too."

She smacks my shoulder. "Have fun tonight. Enjoy it with your lady."

"I will." I reach for the tie and she places it in my hand. "Thanks for your help with the tie and the dress."

"You should pay me back with a picture."

"I'm not that thankful," I say with a wink.

"Brat."

I head for the door. "Five thirty. You get five minutes' worth of pictures."

"I knew you'd cave."

"Don't push your luck."

She laughs. "Love you, kiddo."

"Love you, Mom."

The door slams shut behind me.

# CHAPTER 21

## *Sara*

BETSY'S ENGINE ROARS BEFORE THE CAR STOPS UNDER THE CANOPY. MEN IN suits open our doors and welcome us to the gala.

"Thank you," I say, taking the gloved hand extended to me and stepping onto the pavement.

Banks comes around the front of the Corvette with a massive smile on his face. The three women standing at the door stop their conversation to watch him. He commands their attention by just walking, and the best part—he doesn't even realize it.

I'm not sure he even cares.

I glance down at the gorgeous, fake engagement ring that Banks gave me before we left his house.

*"Where did you get this?"* I ask, laughing.

*He slips it on my finger. "From Pippa. We have to return it after the gala. I won't let any schmuck think you weren't getting an engagement ring. Wasn't happening."*

The thought makes me smile.

"Hey," I say softly, trying to quell the blip of excitement in my stomach.

He takes my hand and laces his fingers through mine. *That helps.*

"We're not too late," he says, glancing at his watch. "Just twenty-five minutes or so."

I laugh. "I couldn't say no to your mom's little impromptu photo shoot."

He groans. "I told her this wasn't prom. The woman won't take no for an answer."

"So that's where you get it."

"Maybe." He presses a sweet kiss on my cheek. "Have I told you how beautiful you are tonight? Drop-dead gorgeous, Sara."

I blush. "You have, but you're more than welcome to keep telling me."

He laughs, offering me his elbow. "Are you ready to go inside?"

I slip my arm through his and let him lead me to the door, pretending not to see the trio of cougars waiting to pounce. We climb a small set of marble steps to a landing. On the far wall is a massive set of heavy double doors with two large men standing beside them.

"Have I told you how hot you are tonight?" I ask as we walk down the hall toward the banquet room.

"I don't think so."

I nudge him, laughing. "I've told you a hundred times."

"So tell me again. I like it."

"You, Mr. Carmichael, are looking handsome and dapper in your modern classic slim-cut suit." I lean toward him and whisper. "And all I can think of is unzipping your pants, pulling your cock out, and sitting on it."

He groans, making me giggle.

"Good evening," I say to the bearish gentleman holding a tablet. "I'm Sara Willis, a guest of Mr. Petterson's."

He taps around on the screen and then looks up. "Very well. Enjoy your evening."

"Thank you," Banks says, ushering me into the dramatically decorated ballroom.

"Oh, *wow*," I whisper, taking a moment to breathe in the beauty surrounding us.

The room is long and wide but still feels intimate. An over-the-top fireplace anchors the space at the far end, working with the stretched ceilings and tall windows to exude grandiosity in every way. Crystal chandeliers hang from the ceiling. The light reflects off the glass and gives the space a warm, elegant ambiance. *Decadence.*

Beautiful people mill about, some gathering in small clusters with dark-colored drinks in their hands. Chatter floats around the room just above the quiet orchestra playing through speakers hidden somewhere amongst the decor. *I can see why these tickets are so coveted. This is how the other half lives.*

"Well, what do you think?" Banks asks.

"I think I feel out of place. Look at these people. Look at their jewelry and their gowns. It's surreal."

He takes my hand and turns me to face him. His eyes sparkle. "Imagine what every other woman must feel when they look at you. I'm surprised they don't just go home."

My heart melts when he gives me his shy smile.

"Sara, hello." A woman in a glorious gold dress approaches us. She's stunning with nude-colored lips and thick dark lashes. "I'm Jennifer McKay, Mr. Petterson's assistant. It's a pleasure to meet you."

"It's a pleasure to meet you as well. This is my fiancé, Banks Carmichael."

Banks stands tall. "Thank you for having us tonight, Ms. McKay."

"It's Jennifer, please," she says, smiling brightly at us both. "Mr. Petterson asked that I find you tonight and personally welcome you to the event. He's very pleased you could come."

"It was so kind of him to invite us. I'm honored, truly."

"We do apologize for the snafu in getting your invitation to you."

I grin. "Please, don't apologize. I'm sorry you had to go through so much trouble to deliver it. I probably wouldn't have."

"Well, Mr. Petterson is one of the most respectable men in this industry. He believes in acknowledging hard work and dedication. You deserved to be here, and he wouldn't let me go home until I found your personal email."

She laughs, making Banks and I laugh along with her.

She clasps her hands in front of her. "I will let him know you've arrived. Please, enjoy yourselves. There are drinks and appetizers on the right."

"Thank you, Jennifer," I say.

With a final nod, she disappears into the throng of people.

Banks squeezes my hand. "You've impressed Myles Petterson. You're obviously an amazing accounts rep, Sara."

I smile. *When was the last time someone simply praised my work ethic for what it is? For who I am?*

"Let's walk around a little bit and mingle. It'll keep you from standing here and overthinking every word of that conversation."

I laugh, letting him guide me through the room.

We acquire champagne from a friendly server named Ryan. He and Banks sparked a conversation about baseball that was both informative and entertaining. *Typical Banks—making friends wherever he goes.*

I sip my drink and watch him chatter away, easily charming a man who didn't need to be charmed. I'm not sure Banks even meant to do it. But Ryan, our new friend, was a little anxious when he handed us our champagne, and Banks said something ridiculous to put him at ease. Now Ryan has been invited to Sunday dinner at Damaris's.

*I wonder how often that happens.*

My gaze slides across the room, sweeping across architectural details that I add to my mental corkboard for future home ideas. But it all comes to a screeching halt when I land on a pair of dark eyes boring into me.

I turn casually like an annoyed, fiery pit didn't just ignite in my stomach and slip my arm through Banks's again. Not satisfied with that small amount of contact, he slips his arm behind me at my waist.

"Joshua is here," I say once Ryan leaves.

He looks down at me. "I know."

"How? I thought you didn't know him."

"It's funny what you notice when you have a girl you care about."

Slowly, my lips turn toward the ceiling. My insides are obliterated. I stare at him, unsure whether he's kidding—playing the doting fiancé part—or if he's serious.

*Could he be serious?*

I hold my breath and process the possibility. *What would I feel like if he were?*

Then it hits me like one of Banks's awful jokes that has me bursting into a fit of laughter at two in the morning—it would feel a hell of a lot like this.

Adored. Protected. And so damn happy.

"When you have a girl you care about, huh?" I ask, turning in his arms so we're facing one another. My heartbeat quickens. "What's that mean?"

His grin is to die for. "It means that I care about you. A lot. And unless you're completely oblivious, you already knew that."

"Maybe I'm not oblivious," I say, straightening his tie. "But maybe I thought you were just being silly."

"Babe." He chuckles. "I'd never joke about that."

My knees weaken.

"Well, hello, Ms. Willis." A silver-haired man with a grandfatherly smile stands beside us. "I'm Myles Petterson, and it's a pleasure to finally meet you in person."

I clear my throat and take his hand, giving it a gentle shake. "It's so nice to meet you, Mr. Petterson. Thank you so much for the invitation. That was very kind of you." I turn to Banks, ignoring the sharp glare directed at me from across the room. "This is my fiancé, Banks Carmichael."

Mr. Petterson's bushy eyebrows tug together. "Banks Carmichael? You must be related to Kixx. Are you one of his sons?"

"Yes, sir."

Mr. Petterson extends a hand. "Your father and brother Moss did some work for me a while back. Their craftsmanship was superb. I really enjoyed working with them."

"I'll be sure to tell them." Banks smiles. "They take a lot of pride in their work."

"That's evident in the end product. So what do you do?"

"Cars. Classic car restoration, to be exact."

Mr. Petterson nods. "Is that so? I bought a Dodge Charger at an auction a few years ago. It's been sitting in my back bay under a cover since the day I brought it home. Needs tons of work, but I don't know where to start."

"I'd be happy to come take a look at it and give you some pointers, if you'd like."

Mr. Petterson's face lights up. "That would be wonderful."

Banks chuckles. "My head mechanic and assistant both took the week off. So if you'll give me a few weeks, that would be great."

"Bad timing?"

"No, I'm a sucker." Banks chuckles. "They both work their behinds off for me, so telling them they can't go be with their families isn't something I can do. It may be bad for business and bad for my health while they're gone, but we all survive, and they come back happy."

Mr. Petterson pats Banks on the shoulder, giving it a gentle squeeze. Then he turns to me.

"So, Sara, how are you doing? Have you found a new job?" Mr. Petterson asks.

My chest wobbles. "Not yet. I'm in the process of moving too—talk about bad timing," I say with a nervous laugh. "I'll be sending more résumés out this coming week."

"Why don't you call me?"

I flinch. "Really?"

He smiles. "You're bright. Talented. Creative."

Banks squeezes my hand, sending a current of energy through me.

"I think you might just be a good fit for us," Mr. Petterson says.

The hairs on the back of my neck stands on end, and I clench down on Banks's hand. Before I can gather my wits and figure out what my instincts are trying to tell me, I hear his voice.

"Good evening, Sara and gentlemen," Joshua says, his gaze burning a hole in my forehead.

Mr. Petterson hesitates and then takes a deep breath. "Mr. Eubanks, hello. I'm glad you could make it."

"Of course," Joshua says, his sights still on me. "I'm thrilled to be here." His attention switches to Banks. "And you are?"

"Banks Carmichael," he says, smoothly. "I'm Sara's fiancé. I'm sorry, I didn't catch your name."

I try to hide my smile.

Mr. Petterson waves a hand in the air, catching us all off guard. "I'm going to have to excuse myself. Banks, I'll have Jennifer get you my number, and we'll catch up on the first of the month. Does that sound good?"

"Excellent. I'll look forward to it."

"And Sara. Use my email," Mr. Petterson says, smiling. "Good to see you all. Enjoy the party."

We say our goodbyes, and I can't help chuckling in surprise on the inside at Mr. Petterson's snub of Joshua. *Mr. Petterson truly is a respectable man.*

As soon as he's gone, the air grows tense. Banks's arm goes around my waist again, holding me close to him.

"Sara, would you like to dance?" Banks asks, searching my eyes for a hint of how I feel.

"Yes."

"Wait." Joshua's smarmy voice taints the air. "I wanted to see how you're doing, Sara."

I turn toward Banks. "I'm great."

We take one step to leave when Joshua grabs my arm. I stop in my tracks and glare at him.

Banks whirls around and squares his shoulders to Joshua's. "I *highly* recommend that you don't touch her again," Banks says, his voice low and cold.

Joshua smiles, sloshing his whiskey around his tumbler. "What is this little ruse the two of you have going on? It's quite entertaining."

"Excuse us," I say, narrowing my eyes. I place a hand on Banks's chest, urging him to go. Instead, he stays in place, his gaze glued to Joshua's.

"You know," Joshua says, arrogance dripping from each word. "Your job opened back up. I could probably get you in for an interview."

Banks bristles but defers to me.

I'd like to rip him a new asshole in front of everyone at this party, but that's unprofessional. *And that's probably exactly what Joshua is banking on.*

"Good luck filling it," I say.

Joshua's face turns beet red. He clenches his free fist and glares at Banks. Whatever composure he's managed to maintain has been eroded by the alcohol and the loss of control of the situation.

*Like he ever had control to begin with. Asshole.*

"Did you know that I was fucking your fiancée two weeks ago? Yeah, for most of this year, she was sucking my cock while apparently leading you on. Just thought I'd share."

He smirks, thinking he got one over on Banks.

Banks's eyes flood with fire but he stays cool, pulling me closer to him.

"That was you?" He laughs and looks at me. "Babe. What were you thinking? This is the guy you were with? He isn't even your type." He winks. "Although, you did say you were pity fucking for a while now, so now *that* makes sense."

I laugh, amused at how well Banks is playing this off. Except … he's not. He wants to rip Joshua's throat out.

"Your fiancée is a little whore," Joshua spits, upping the ante to get the reaction he wants.

Banks smiles menacingly. "It will take a little more than that—a little more sophistication—to get me to react here. Don't get me wrong. I'd absolutely love the experience of sending your nose crashing into your cranium with my fist, and if you'd like to arrange that later, I'm more than willing to open my calendar. Do you need my business card?"

"*Fuck you,*" Joshua says.

The two large men from earlier arrive just before Banks cuts the distance between himself and Joshua. My heart pounds as I watch the scene develop in front of me.

I grab Banks's arm and hold tight. *What's going on?*

"We've been sent by Mr. Petterson, Mr. Eubanks," the man with the mustache says.

Joshua stands tall. "Does he want to see me? Where is he?"

"He's requested we escort you out. And we'd like to do that as quietly as possible, but it's up to you, of course," the other man says.

"What?" Joshua stammers, his eyes wide.

"This way," Mustache Man says, encouraging Joshua to head toward the exit.

"Call me," Banks says, grinning ear to ear.

I glance around the room until my gaze lands on Mr. Petterson.

He's standing by the fireplace with a group of men and subtly nods to me before returning to his conversation.

I sag in relief, leaning against Banks.

"Looks like my job here is done," Banks says. There's a levity in his voice that barely masks the hesitation.

My heart pulls. "Your work here, Mr. Carmichael, has just begun."

He looks down and grins. "Is that so?"

"Dance with me?"

His smile softens. It's the one he only uses for me. "I'd love to."

# CHAPTER 22

## *Sara*



*"LOOKS LIKE MY JOB HERE IS DONE."*

We slip through the darkness quietly. No radio. No conversation. Just Betsy's engine growling when Banks hits the gas. I rest my head on the seat, Banks's hand on my thigh, and watch the moon hang in the sky.

Banks's words from tonight echo through my mind. Although I disagreed and told him he'd just begun, the hesitation in his blue orbs remained. There was a faint edge of uncertainty through the night, through his smiles and jokes. As if he were right—his role as my fake fiancé was finished.

I cover his hand with mine, stroking his flesh with my thumb. He gives my thigh a gentle squeeze.

*"What was your plan?"*

*"To make you want to be with me."*

The thing that scares me the most is that I believe him.

And it's humiliating that I'm unsure how to handle his faith in me.

*How could he possibly want to be with me? How is he so confident in assessing my character that he knows this for certain? How can he ensure I'm emotionally capable of handling a relationship?*

Because I'm not sure. Not really.

But Banks seems to look at me, and he either doesn't see my flaws or chooses to overlook them. That makes me nervous that I'll slip up and prove him wrong.

*And I don't want to prove him wrong.*

Even though I've only spent the past week in their orbit, I want to belong there. I want … I want what Ashley has, if I'm honest. I want the Carmichaels.

*I want to be worthy of the Carmichael family.*

I want them to want to include me in Christmas pictures and be proud to introduce me to their friends. I want so badly to share their inside secrets and jokes, and be on the receiving end of their pranks. I want to fit in with their brand of family more than I want my next breath.

"Big day tomorrow," he says, his voice breaking the silence.

"Really? What's going on?"

He smirks. "My brothers and I are racing."

I pull my brows together. "Racing cars? Are you racing Betsy?"

He laughs. "No. We're racing man to man. There's a sign that measures your speed going out of town, and we're all meeting there to see who is fastest."

"And why would you do that?"

"Because Maddox and Jess had a pissing match between them." He looks at me over his shoulder. "Clearly, they're wrong."

"Oh, you think you'll win, huh?" I tease.

"It's a sure thing. The only one that might give me some kind of competition is Jess, but he's not in the shape I am anymore. His cardio is ass."

I grin. "I'll vouch for your cardio."

He chuckles, squeezing my leg again before withdrawing his hand.

"You've been wonderful tonight," I say softly. "Thank you for going with me and dealing with all of that. I was really proud to be there with you."

He sits a little taller in his seat.

"You handled Joshua perfectly. It's like you knew what he wanted and refused to give it to him."

His jaw flexes. "Trust me, I wanted to tear him apart limb by limb.

But, in the end, you would've paid for that, and I wouldn't let him use me to hurt you."

My insides pull at the pure sincerity in his voice. *What an amazing, thoughtful, intelligent man.* And … I think he wants me as his. *I hope I'm right.*

"Banks …"

"Yeah, babe?"

I take a deep, ragged breath. "You succeeded."

He looks at me with a confused look painted on his handsome face. "With what?"

"You made me want you."

A slow smile slips across his lips as his hand finds my thigh again. "Really?"

"Yes. But is it okay to admit that I'm nervous?"

"It's always okay to say how you feel. But why are you nervous?"

I sigh. "You and your family are like this perfect puzzle. Each one of you has a piece, and all your edges are crisp."

He laughs.

"Have you ever worked a puzzle? Because if you have, you know how important that is."

"I'll take your word for it."

"You should. Because crisp edges can make or break a dynamic. And I'm coming into your life with a soggy edge, a wobbly one, and a weak one." I pause. "Don't get me wrong. I'm a hell of a piece. Integral to the corner, as a matter of fact."

He laughs again, louder this time.

"But what if I don't quite snap into place?" I ask. "What if I never quite fit down into the landscape like I should, so instead of looking like a finished picture of an orchard, I'm an apple that keeps popping out of the picture."

He considers this. "Okay, two options. First, we just put some glue down, shove you in, and then set a glass on top of you so you can't pop up anymore."

"Sounds painful."

"It might be. We'd have to think about that one. But you never know. It could unlock a kink."

I giggle.

"The second option is to find a frame and put the puzzle in it. That way, if the apple starts to fall, there's something to catch it. Because that's what family does." He shrugs.

*That's what family does.* I hold my breath as he looks at me with the sweetest smile. *I don't deserve you, Sparkles.*

He turns onto Honeysuckle Lane and then into his driveway. The garage door rises, and Betsy slides into her spot. Neither of us attempts to move from our seats. We just sit, listening to the gentle tick of the cooling engine, and breathing in the scent of leather.

"I've been thinking about something," he says.

"About what?"

*Is it about the puzzle frame? Is he going to extend that and tell me he wants me to be a part of the Carmichael puzzle?*

He twists in his seat. "I want chickens."

My laughter comes out loud and hard. "You what?"

"I don't know—not many. Thirty, maybe."

"You want thirty chickens? Banks." I wipe tears from beneath my eyes. "What are you going to do with thirty chickens?"

"Save them from the butcher, obviously. That and buy them chicken swings. They make those. Did you know that? There are all kinds of chicken toys. You can get chicken strollers, too. Apparently, and I quote, they are *'perfect for cruising with the finest of chicks, literally.'* We could have the finest of chicks."

My chest shakes with amusement. "I can't with you."

"They would be Jess's chickens' cousins. We could take my flock over there to graze sometimes, and he can bring his over here."

He pulls his buzzing phone from the middle console, holding it so I can see the screen.

> Foxx: Is anyone going to Shade House tonight who could pick up a key for me?
>
> Jess: ANOTHER ONE?
>
> Moss: Are you okay, Foxx?

Paige: How many is this? Three? Four?

*<Banks silenced notifications>*

"He does that to us all the time," he says, smirking.

"What's going on with the keys?"

"I have no idea. He keeps losing them around town, I guess. It's very odd, even for Foxx."

"Should someone check on him? Make sure he's mentally fit?"

Banks ponders this. "Yes, but after the race tomorrow. I want to prove his physical *un*fitness before we have him checked out."

"But do you really think Foxx will race you and your brothers? It doesn't seem like something he'd do." I sigh. "But what do I know? I don't know him very well."

He opens his door. "You wouldn't think he'd be into it. But if you challenge Foxx's manhood in something like a race, he can't back down. He has the Oldest Child Syndrome or something—always something to prove."

The overhead light catches him just right. His jaw is angular. His eyes are the perfect shade of Caribbean blue. His tie hangs askew around his thick neck, and stubble dots his previously clean-shaven skin.

Thoughts of him taking me on the car in the shop have me aching for him. Remembering his mouth on me makes me wet. Thinking about him charming Mr. Petterson, putting Joshua in his place, and telling me I'm beautiful has my heart full.

And suddenly, there's only one thing I want to do. I need to do. *I want to show this man how much he means to me.*

"Wait here," I say, opening my door.

My legs shake as I walk around the front of his car. He watches me curiously as I approach him.

I reach for his hand, take it, and turn him in his seat so his feet are on the garage floor. My gaze burning into his, I undo his button and drag his zipper down his pants.

His eyes blaze as I gather my dress and kneel on the garage floor between his legs.

He helps me free his cock before leaning back and watching me take it in my hand. His brows are tight.

"What's the matter?" I ask, stroking his length. His skin is soft around his hard length. "You look like you're thinking about something."

He hisses as I lick a bead of pre-cum off the head.

"Just that pro-athletes don't have sex for a day or two before a game because it saps their energy and testosterone," he says.

I pull away and burst out laughing. "You mean, the woman you called stunning earlier tonight is on her knees in front of you with your cock in her hand ... about to be in her mouth ... and you're thinking about sapped energy and low testosterone?"

"I just really have to beat Jess." He growls. "No, fuck it. I mean, suck it."

*This man.* Still laughing, I lower my mouth to him again. "I could stop." I flick my tongue against the underside of his shaft. "Pick it back up tomorrow."

"Nope. I'm willing to rest on my genetic superiority and risk it."

I peer through my lashes, cupping his balls with my free hand. "You sure?"

"Yes," he says, sucking in a quick breath as I kiss down his length. "This is the surest I've ever been about something."

My tongue lays flat against him as it drags back to the top. I suck the tip, flicking the underside repeatedly. Up and down, side to side, and in circles, I watch his eyes hood as my tongue delivers pulses of pleasure.

"You make me feel really good," I say, licking around the head. "I want you to feel just as good."

"Clearly, you're underestimating—*fuck!*"

I wrap my hand around the base and take him as far as I can down my throat. His body tenses as I pull my lips back up.

"This is the pinnacle of my life," he says, placing his hands in my hair carefully. "If there's a highlight reel when I die, then I'm sure you kneeling in front of me with my dick in your mouth while I'm in Betsy will definitely go in it."

I laugh, the sound vibrating against him. He tugs on my hair—the sensation sharp and urgent. A pool of arousal wets my thighs.

I moan, clenching my core, pumping him as I take his long cock in and out of my mouth. My spit coats the shaft, running down the length and gathering around my hand at the base. The sounds of my effort—sucking, slurping, kissing—fill the garage and me with a need to make him come.

Banks reaches down with his free hand and cups one of my breasts, removing it from my dress. He palms it, massaging it in the same firm, needy way I'm touching his balls.

"I could get off from touching these tits," he says through clenched teeth.

His cock pops out of my mouth. He watches as I spit on it, working the liquid along his length, and grin up at him.

"You're going to come in my mouth."

His body flexes. "Are you sure you don't want to let me inside you?"

*Fuck.* The thought of me on all fours, spread wide open for him as he takes me from behind again today has my clit throbbing for attention. But I hold firm. "I want to taste you. I want to know what it feels like to have you spilling down my throat."

His eyes beg for me to finish him. My body screams for relief. My vision blurs as he guides my head to his cock and over it until I almost gag.

"This is so fucking good," he moans, his balls tightening in my palm. "Keep doing that, and it won't take long."

Encouraged by his praise, I maintain the rhythm—sucking and licking until my eyes begin to water. My pussy clenches at the sounds of satisfaction he mutters and the almost pinching of my breast.

"*Sara,*" he groans as his cock swells.

His legs stiffen, and his body shakes. I force my eyes open to watch him fall apart.

*And it is well worth the effort.*

He moans my name again—the hottest thing I've ever heard—as

hot, salty come shoots in the back of my throat. He moves my head up and down, both hands on the side of my head now, and pumps his hips into my mouth.

I take it all, swallowing him until his body relaxes. He quivers as I give a final kiss to the tip of his cock and then rest back on my heels.

He watches every move.

"Even if that costs me the race, it was so worth it," he says, grinning.

"I'm glad to hear it." I laugh, using the car to help get to my feet. "You seemed to enjoy it."

He stands and tucks himself back in his pants. Then he pulls me into him and kisses the life out of me. Slow, methodical—intentional with every swipe of his tongue and press of his lips.

When he pulls back, I'm breathless.

"Let's get you inside," he says softly. "I'm going to blow your mind."

I let him take my hand, somehow already as satisfied as Banks. *Still* … "Yes, please."

He picks me up and carries me into the house.

"If I lose this race, it's because of you," he says, making me giggle.

"But it's worth it, right?"

He kisses me as he opens the door. "Abso-fucking-lutely."

# CHAPTER 23

## *Banks*

"I feel like we're pulling up at the O.K. Corral," Sara says, taking in the scene before her.

My brothers' cars and trucks all line the side of the highway. They're gathered, along with Brooke, Ashley, Pippa, and our parents, near the radar speed sign. All heads turn as we pull up in Betsy, her V-8 roaring and announcing our arrival.

"Wow, Foxx is here," Sara says, surprised.

I'm surprised too. Foxx hasn't quite been himself lately—losing his keys, stopping to say hello the other day, and showing up here. Maybe someone does need to check on him. He's being … almost nice.

"And Jess looks pissed," Sara says.

"Jess is *always* pissed."

I park the car on the shoulder of the road behind Moss's truck.

The sun hovers above the horizon, sending pops of purples and reds and yellows soaring through the sky. It's the kind of night that would be nice to grab a beer and walk over to Maddox's and shoot the shit.

I look at Sara.

*Or it would've been.* Things look a little different these days. A whole lot better.

She laughs as she undoes her seat belt. "It probably has something to do with you being fifteen minutes late."

"I'm icing them out."

"What the hell does that mean?"

"It means I'm making them wait. They're getting on *my* schedule. It asserts dominance."

She snorts, trying desperately to hold back her amusement.

"Haven't you ever watched football?" I ask, holding out a hand.

"Not on purpose."

*She has a lot to learn.*

I roll my eyes and take my phone out of the console. "Here. Make sure you video call Paige before the action starts. Her name is saved in my favorites. She wants to see me kick their asses."

"How do I know what your password is to get in?"

"It's sixty-nine, sixty-nine, sixty-nine."

"How very predictable of you," she says, taking the phone from me. "It's buzzing."

I stretch my arm overhead and then the other. I can't go meet my brothers stone cold. The calisthenics I did at home got me loose, but I need to get some heat and pliability back in my muscles before I get out of the car.

"Who is it?" I ask.

"Do you want me to look?"

I smirk. "Well, unless you have X-ray vision, I guess you're going to have to look."

She narrows her eyes. *Adorable.* "This one is from Tasha. It says, 'Hubs got called in to work so the trip is getting cut short. I'll be in tomorrow afternoon to try to get the office sorted before Monday. Please tell me nothing burned completely down while I was gone.'"

"*Yes.*" I pump my fists. "See? This is what you get. You do nice things for people and the universe rewards you."

"The next one says, 'Peacocks are one of the fastest running birds that can run at a speed of about ten miles per hour.'" Her brows pinch. "Do you think it's a coincidence that this is about running speeds and you're about to run?"

I sit back in my seat. *I don't know.*

I can't figure this text thing out. My instincts were leaning toward Foxx, but he's standing right in front of me with no phone. All of my brothers are. *So who the fuck can it be?*

*Who knows all my brothers and would go out of their way to send us random animal texts? Paige? Maybe, but it doesn't seem like something she'd do. She has her hands full with Nate and Ryder. Mom? Dad? I think about that. Dad's too busy with work and the couch debacle. Mom has enough to do besides looking up animal factoids. That's not her style, anyway.*

I look up. Jess is motioning for us to get moving.

"Is it a coincidence?" I ask, opening my door. "I don't know. Do coincidences exist?"

Sara shrugs as she meets me at the front of Betsy. Together, we walk toward the pack. *But not a Wolfpack, according to Jess.*

"For fuck's sake, Sparkles," Moss says. "We were starting to think you chickened out."

I look at Jess and smirk. "Hi, Chicken Daddy."

"Banks, fuck off."

Everyone laughs.

"Did anyone bring a medical kit?" Mom asks, looking around.

The group of us shrugs and voices our failure to think that far ahead.

"Just don't fall down or anything," Mom says. "And, for the love of God, don't break anything."

"Please," I say. "We're athletes. Did you forget who you are talking to?"

Dad snorts. "I hate to tell you all, but you haven't been athletes in ten, fifteen years."

"I take offense to that," I say.

Moss groans. "Of course, you do."

"Hey, maybe you guys aren't athletes anymore, but I could out wrestle every single one of you right now and beat you with one hand tied behind my back. So until you can unseat the champ, I'm still an athlete," I say.

"Can you guys just start?" Paige yells through the phone. "I have to get back to work, and I want to see this."

Dad steps onto the asphalt of the lightly traveled road. "I've already walked off thirty yards. Start here and go." He points at the sign. "And the big boy there will clock you without any interference. Fastest speed wins. Remember—this thing clocks traffic in miles per hour, so we're going for the fastest *speed*, not the fastest *time*."

I do a few walking lunges to warm up the hamstrings. "Why thirty yards? Is Foxx too old for fifty?"

"It is going to be an absolute pleasure beating you today, Banks." Foxx shakes his head. "I do have other things to do. Can we begin?"

"Like looking for your keys?" I ask, cackling.

Foxx puts one hand on his hip, his focus lasered on me. "You and I are going to have a discussion about that later."

"Why?"

He holds my gaze for a moment too long—long enough to cause a surge of anxiety to travel up my spine. *What does he want to talk to me about that for?*

"I brought your key back to you from the grocery," I say. "Didn't Mom give it to you?"

He slides his attention to Dad. "Let's get going."

I spin around toward Mom.

"I gave it to him," she says, shrugging.

*What the fuck?* But there's no time to contemplate it. It's go time.

The sun is still hot, soaking into my skin. Sweat dots my forehead as I pull off my shirt. I toss it to my girl, appreciating her appreciation of me.

"Like I said, you'll start here," Dad says, toeing a chalk line on the edge of the pavement. "Who goes first?"

"Oldest to youngest?" Maddox asks. "Youngest to oldest? Alphabetical?"

Mom comes forward with a hat. "I put names in here to avoid a war. Someone can draw the order." She looks around. "Pippa? You want to do the honors?"

"Sure."

"Are you betting anything on this?" Paige asks from my phone screen. "Or are we just doing this for bragging rights?"

"Ego," Dad says.

"Got it," Paige says.

I stand beside Sara as Pippa puts her hand into the hat.

"Let's go, Chicken Mama," I say, snaking my arm around Sara's waist. She lays her head on my arm.

Pippa points my way. "Don't think you're going to get me upset with that nickname. I love those little chickies."

My attention snaps to Jess. "Oh, isn't that a surprise."

Before he can reply, Pippa reads off the first name.

"Maddox," she says. "You're first."

Ashley claps, grabbing his shoulders and giving them a shake. "You can do this. Run fast!"

Maddox stands at the line. "I got this, Ash. No worries."

"I hope no one breaks a leg," Paige says, sounding a lot like our mother.

I stand in the middle of my family and look around. We might be here for a pretty ridiculous reason—*who races each other at our age? Foxx probably has brittle bones by now*—but everyone is having fun.

Especially me when I win.

I glance at Foxx. *I should have Mom make sure he's taking calcium supplements.*

"Whenever you're ready, Mad," Dad says, stepping out of his way.

Maddox squats, rolling his neck back and forth. Then he puts his toe at the line and launches at full speed. His sneakers slide across the asphalt. His arms pump at his sides.

"Go, Maddox!" Ashley cheers.

We all watch the sign as it starts to blink numbers. It ends with a flashing twenty-two.

"Not bad," I say, trading an impressed nod with Moss.

Pippa draws another name. "It's you, Chicken Daddy."

Everyone laughs, the sound filling the evening air.

Jess points at Pippa. "You'll pay for that one later."

"Can't wait," she says, winking at him.

He lines up on the mark and takes off. His face turns cherry red as he bounds down the highway.

"I can't believe we haven't seen any cars yet," Mom says.

An eighteen flashes as Jess passes the sign.

Maddox flicks his shirt. "First place, right here."

"Moss, you're next," Pippa says.

As Moss goes to the line, Jess makes his way back to the family.

"What happened?" I ask him. "Too many late nights with the chicks?"

Maddox snorts, turning his back to Jess so he doesn't see his amusement.

Pippa kisses his cheek. "You did great."

"I would've had you," Jess says, planting his hands on his knees and heaving a breath. "I got a bad start."

"That's what they all say," Maddox says.

Moss gets in position. Paige has Sara adjust the camera so she can see better. I stand behind my girl and hold her waist.

It's not lost on me that Sara has fit into our family so perfectly. When my brothers brought home Brooke and Ashley, it was the smoothest process ever. It's as if they were both supposed to be in our family the whole time. Like there were roles for both of them, and we were just waiting for them to come fill them.

Sara listens to something Brooke says and laughs.

*And it's like that with Sara too.*

My stomach tightens as I ponder what this means.

"Run, Moss," Brooke shouts as he hustles down the straightaway.

I pull my head from my thoughts and watch the sign. *Nineteen.*

His hands hit his knees, and he heaves.

"What was my time?" Jess asks, looking at Mom.

"Eighteen."

"He didn't just beat me," Jess says, mouth gaping. "I call bullshit."

Dad holds a hand in the air. "We all agreed this was unbiased. He beat you."

Jess throws his arms up and walks away from the group.

"Foxx or Banksy," Dad says, watching Pippa pull the last name from the hat.

She grins. "Let's see it, Banks."

I shouldn't be this nervous. I don't even know why I'm nervous. Probably because I talked a lot of shit and now I have to put my money where my mouth is.

*I'd like my mouth to be on Sara's pussy.*

"You can do it, Sparkles," Sara says.

I look at her and grin. She winks.

*No, no. Focus.* I look down the stretch of road and shake my arms. *That's not far. Let's show these boys how it's done.*

I press off the ground and *go.* My eyes focused ahead of me, back straight, my head neutral to my spine. My acceleration is quicker than I expected, and I hit my top speed just as the sign begins to blink. Twenty-three, twenty-four as I blow past it.

*God, I'm not in the shape I used to be in.*

I suck in air, fighting the urge to bend over.

*Take that, boys.*

My face is hot as I turn back to my family. "What was that? Did I see a two-four on there?" I heave a breath. "That's what it looked like to me."

Sara's grins ear to ear as I reach her. Her arms go over my shoulders, and she kisses my cheek.

"That's so freaking sexy," she whispers in my ear.

"Just wait until we get home."

"I can hear you!" Paige shouts. "And I can't see anything but the sky."

Sara giggles. "Sorry." She removes herself from me and points the phone toward the road.

Foxx is already lined up.

The road is slightly higher than where we're standing. That must be the reason Foxx looks so ... large. *Maybe I just never see him in basketball shorts.*

"Don't blow out a knee," I yell, more to distract him than anything. But, in typical Foxx style, he doesn't blink. He just focuses on the road ahead like I don't even exist.

*Maybe I don't exist in his world. Huh.*

He starts out with an explosion, ripping through the air like some kind of fucking athlete that he's not. Or I didn't think he was.

My heart pounds as he flies closer to the sign.

*Please be twenty-three. Please be twenty-three.*

Everyone's attention is tuned into the sign, waiting for the numbers to flash. *Twenty-four.*

My elation from moments before slips.

"No," I say, walking toward Dad. "He didn't just tie me."

Dad's amused. "Twenty-four and twenty-four are the same number. That means it's a tie."

Foxx walks our way, staring at me, looking like he just got through with a yoga workout or something. Not at all winded.

*What the fuck?*

"You just saved us from having to hear his mouth," Moss says. "Good work, Foxx."

"I want a rematch," I say.

Foxx walks by me and winks.

"What just happened here?" I ask, holding out my hands.

Without saying a word, Foxx climbs in his truck, turns it on, and blows a U-turn in the middle of the road. Then he takes off toward our houses without as much as a honk, wave, or a fuck you.

"That means he's disqualified, right?" I ask as my family heads to their cars. "I mean, he left without an official reading from Mom."

Mom laughs. "Oh, Banksy. I love you."

"I'm the victor here," I call out. It's met with a host of mumbles and muttering from my brothers.

Sara hands me my phone with a smile. "Paige said to tell you that you did good."

I frown. "Thanks." I point at the cars pulling out onto the road. "They're just leaving. They're acting like running a twenty-four at my age isn't impressive."

"Probably because Foxx did it at his age too."

I gasp.

She laughs and takes my hand. "But you know what you can do that's really impressive?"

My cock twitches. "A number of things."

She brings her lips to mine but doesn't touch them together. Her eyes twinkle. "Wanna take me home and show me some of them?"

"Absolutely."

After a quick kiss, we walk hand in hand toward Betsy.

"But I'll have you know that I could've done better," I say as we open our doors. "I could've won that if we had a round two. Foxx was winded. He was done."

Sara grins. "I'll give you two rounds tonight."

"Make it three."

"Let's go, Sparkles."

I sigh and get in the car.

You can't win them all.

*Or can you?*

# CHAPTER 24

## *Sara*

"Yes, Jennifer. That makes total sense," I say, grinning like a loon. "I'll be there on Thursday. Thank you so much."

"We'll be looking forward to it. Take care, Sara."

"Goodbye."

"Goodbye."

I end the call and jump up and down, squealing in delight.

My spirits soar. *Is it the sunshine? The orgasmic night with Banks last night? The job interview I just scheduled with Myles Petterson for a position that I have never even dreamed of?*

*The fact that everything seems to be falling into place for the first time in my life?*

I dance across the living room and start to press Banks's number. But, before I can, his truck rumbles up the driveway.

I toss my phone on the couch and dart into the early evening air.

"Come here," Banks says, spreading his arms wide open for me.

Launching myself into his chest, I look up. "Guess what?"

"Can I kiss you first?"

"No."

"Too bad."

He grins, palming the back of my head and bringing my mouth to his. I start to protest, mostly for fun, but melt as soon as our lips connect. He breaks the kiss well before I'm ready for it to end.

"Now, what's your news or whatever I'm supposed to guess?" he asks, his fingers laced together at the small of my back.

"Jennifer McKay called—Mr. Petterson's assistant. And I have a job interview there on Thursday."

Banks picks me up and swings me around.

"That's awesome," he says, setting me back on my feet. "I'm so damn proud of you."

My insides still.

"What?" he asks, curiously. "What did I say?"

"Just that you're proud of me." My cheeks flush. "I don't know why. Just … thank you."

He laughs. "For being proud of you?"

I nod.

"Silly girl. Come on. Let's go inside and celebrate."

We start across the lawn when a voice booms from down the street. "Sparkles! Sara! Check this out."

We turn to see Jess at the side of his house, sans shirt but with a large straw hat, waving us over.

"He's turning into a fucking farmer," Banks says, making me laugh. "What have I done?"

"How was work today?" I ask as we cross the street.

"Tasha's back so it's all good. Remind me to give her a fat holiday bonus at the end of the year because she does more than I even realized. Do you know that she even cleans the bathrooms in the place?"

I smile at him. "I did not, and I'm taking it you didn't either."

"No. I thought the mat company did it for some reason. But it's Tash. She also has the sign outside changed and deals with the accountant on taxes and shit. Reality check, I'm telling you."

"Maybe you need to promote her and hire someone else to sit at her desk," I suggest. "She could be your right-hand woman."

Banks smirks. "That wouldn't make you jealous?"

"She's not touching you with that hand or I'll break her fingers."

He laughs, the sound music to my ears.

"Could you two walk any slower?" Jess asks.

"Some of us actually ran the other night." Banks smacks him on the back as Jess guides us to the back of his house. "You don't know what that's like, I know, with your shitty eighteen seconds."

"Fuck off."

They exchange a grin.

"What do you want? I just got home and need to go play with my girl," Banks says, catching an elbow from me.

We enter the backyard, and I stop dead in my tracks. *Wow.*

"What the hell did you do?" Banks asks, his eyes wide. "Holy shit, Jess. Did you have to get a permit to build this thing?"

"I didn't, so let's hope not."

A chicken cottage has been constructed with white wood and gold metal roofing. A double door big enough for a person to walk through is latched closed by thick metal hinges. It even has window boxes with flowers.

The run where the chicks are racing around is screened in. Three little chicken swings hang from the ceiling. The What a Fuster Cluck sign Banks was telling me about hangs over the door.

"*Jess*," I coo, bending down in front of the screen. "They're so cute."

A pale yellow fluff ball runs toward me and peeps.

"You seriously built these things a chicken house," Banks says incredulously.

"I even wallpapered the inside." Jess beams. "It's not done. I'm going to add some motion detectors on the corners with floodlights in case anything tries to break in at night. And maybe chicken cams just so Pippa can check on them from at work."

Banks shakes his head like he's speechless.

I stand, brushing my hands off, and smile. "This is the most incredible thing I've ever seen in my life."

"Hey," Banks says, huffing.

I roll my eyes at him. "You built this thing fast."

"I build stuff all day at work, so it's not that hard for me, and I have access to lots of materials that are going to get tossed anyway. And, you know, chickens turn into an addiction. There's a whole thing called chicken math."

"Well, a good Chicken Dad would know that," Banks jokes.

"Pippa and Ashley are out buying new mulch for it now. I kinda built it a little bigger than I anticipated," Jess says, looking over our shoulders. His brows pull together. "Who is that at your house, Banks?"

We turn to see a white car pulled up to the curb near the mailbox.

"I have no idea who that is," Banks says, watching them closely.

I hold onto his arm as Jess comes up beside me. A door opens in the back and a little girl with blond hair starts to walk up the sidewalk.

*What the hell?*

"That's Bethany," I say, heading toward her immediately.

She walks up the steps and knocks on the door. The car pulls by us, turns around in front of Damaris's house, and then scoots out of the neighborhood.

*What the hell?*

"Hey," I call out. "Bethany!"

She turns on her heel and sees me, running back down the steps. My pace picks up, getting quicker the closer I get to her.

My heart pounds, and adrenaline shoots through my veins.

*Something is wrong.*

I sense Banks close behind but don't bother to check. He'll be here. *He's Banks.*

Bethany lunges toward me, burying her tearstained face in my chest. Her body heaves as she cries out, and I'm left holding her against me, wondering what the fuck is going on.

Banks jogs to us and places his hand on my back. He gives me a look, but I shrug.

"Hey," I say, brushing her hair away from her face. "Hey, Bethany, sweetheart. What's wrong?"

She lifts her head and looks up, tears still flooding her face.

My chest is so tight that I can barely breathe. "You're going to have to talk to me and tell me what's wrong. Who dropped you off here?"

"A rideshare service."

*We'll discuss that later.* "Are you okay? Did something happen to you?"

Banks places a hand on each of our shoulders and leads us to the porch. "Let's set down. Do you guys want a drink?"

We sit on the porch steps. I help Bethany remove her backpack and wave Banks off.

"I'll be inside," he says quietly. "Just shout if you need me."

I smile at him. *Thank you, Banks, for understanding what we need right now.*

"So ..." I prompt, curiosity killing me. "I need to know you're okay."

"I'm fine. Physically, anyway."

"I know all about that."

She smiles sadly.

"Does your mom know where you are?" I ask.

"No. That's the point. I didn't go to school today."

I swallow, giving myself a chance to stay calm. "Why?"

Tears flow instantly once again. "I don't even know, Sara. I don't know what happened. We got into a fight last night—a bad one—because I told her I wanted to cut my hair." Her eyes widen. "*To cut my hair.* That's it. I didn't tell her I wanted to do drugs or move to Antarctica. I just wanted to cut my hair."

I grit my teeth, trying not to let my sister see it.

"Her boyfriend ended up coming over," she says, sniffling. "I hate him. His name is Gary, and he's a hateful, vile man. And he came in and started yelling at me that I was a spoiled brat and I should be thankful for everything she does for me. That the only kids that make their mothers cry are entitled little bitches." She pauses. "He said that."

I pull her into my shoulder and give her a big hug. *I think I need it as badly as she does.*

Her words bring back memories of me being her age and her mother playing games with me. She'd tell my dad I was told to do something and didn't do it. That she thought I was sneaking out of the house—and I wasn't. *Always.* That my request to paint my bedroom black wasn't a goth stage, but a satanic ritual that should get me a ticket to therapy.

Therapy is the one nice thing she could've done for me. Of course, she didn't. *I never thought for one moment that she'd play the same games with Bethany.*

Bethany pulls away and then digs in her backpack for a tissue. *Sweet girl.*

The loneliness in her eyes is salt on a wound in my soul that has never healed. There's always something in the back of my brain, even now, that tells me to prepare for having my world thrown upside down. To be ready to have my safety net cut.

To be alone.

"I understand what you're going through," I say, plucking the hair stuck to her cheek away. "And, I'll be honest with you, I don't have a great solution."

"Can I stay here with you?"

I sigh. "I'd be fine with that, but this isn't my house, and your mom needs to know where you are."

"She'll kill me, Sara. I skipped school today. I know they robo-called her to tell her I was absent because they always do when you miss a day. But I just can't see her. She'll be madder than she was this morning, and I just needed some space." She dries her eyes, then drops her hands. "How hard is it to give someone space?"

I grin. *She's not as different from me as she might think.*

"Look, I can't say she won't be mad," I say gently. "But I know your mom loves you more than the universe. When she calms down, I'm sure you can have a rational conversation …"

A bright-blue sedan speeds up the road, coming to a stop at the end of Banks's driveway. Bethany jumps to her feet, a hand clutching my arm.

I stand too. "It's okay."

Sabrina and a man I've never seen before, *Gary, I presume*, get out of the car. He stays next to the door while Sabrina marches across the lawn.

"Where have you been, young lady?" Sabrina shouts, stopping at the base of the steps. "Answer me. Have you been here all day?"

Bethany swallows hard. "No. I was at the park. I just got here."

"I was starting to think you were dead. Your phone was off and your location tracker wasn't able to work, and I've been scared to death."

*I bet Bethany turned her phone on to find Banks's address.*

"Get in the car," Sabrina says, the words crisp enough to cut you. "Now."

"Sabrina, wait—"

"I'll get to you in a minute." Her eyes flare. "Bethany, *now.* I'm not telling you again."

Bethany picks up her backpack and gives me a long hug that only seems to piss her mother off more.

"It's going to be okay, sweetheart. I'll do what I can," I whisper.

"I love you, Sara."

Tears pool in my eyes, and I give her another squeeze. "I love you too, Bethany."

"Now, Bethany," Sabrina barks.

She pulls away from me, slings her backpack on her shoulder, and lifts her chin in defiance. *That's my girl. Don't let her break you.*

Sabrina follows her toward the car, saying something too quietly for me to pick up.

I descend the steps and step into the sun. Out of my peripheral vision, I spot Jess still standing in the spot we left him.

*Great.*

Bethany climbs in the car and slams the door. Sabrina whips around and storms back to the house with her finger pointed at my face.

My stomach tenses as I prepare for an onslaught.

*"How dare you talk to my daughter about anything!"* she says, almost spitting the words as she stops feet in front of me. Her finger shakes with anger, and her words get louder. "You don't have a clue what you're doing. Hell, Sara, you're a child of the streets."

*What?* I grin at her, trying to stay calm. Bethany doesn't need to see a screaming match between us. "And whose fault is that?"

"Certainly not mine, if that's what you're getting at." She drops her finger. "Your father had given up on you well before he met me."

"I was ten years old. So you know …"

We stand toe-to-toe, eye to eye. I want to run inside and away from this mess, but I can't back down to her. I won't. I've done it too many times.

Foxx's truck inches down the street. He rolls the window down. He doesn't have to say a word; I can read his question on his face. *Are you okay?*

A well of emotions rises in my chest as I wave at him. He gives me a nod, dragging his gaze across the front porch, and then pulls up his driveway at the end of the lane.

"You really still are the same ten-year-old little girl who I met back then," she says, narrowing her eyes. "You're twenty-five, Sara. You're living with a man who I didn't know you were even seeing until last week. You're unemployed. Your belongings are in my garage."

"I'll get them."

"Doesn't this embarrass you?" she asks, the words growing louder. "Do you have any sense of humility at all? Do these poor people understand who they're dealing with here?"

The door squeaks behind me. Banks. Tears fill my eyes, threatening to spill down my cheeks. Despite my practiced ability to hold my emotions, this time it's a struggle.

I don't want my little sister going home with this woman. I also don't want to fight with Sabrina. Worst of all, I don't want Banks witnessing this dysfunction, and Foxx and Jess watching as I bring all of this drama to their brother's doorstep. Literally.

"You are tainting my child," she sneers. "I shouldn't have let you around. I've been entirely too nice to you."

"And I've been entirely too nice to you by letting you stand out here for this long," Banks says, putting his arm around my shoulders. "You need to leave. *Now.*"

His eyes blaze with a fire I've never seen in them before. I didn't even see this the night in the bar that ended with his arrest.

My heart aches for my sister, for me, for Sabrina—and for Banks for having to deal with this.

"Oh, you have someone fighting your battles for you, huh?" Sabrina says smugly.

"Sara can take care of herself," Banks says. "I'm pretty sure you taught her the necessity for that."

"You don't know shit."

Banks grins. "I know that you aren't going to roll up to my house and disrespect her. I know you better not take that little girl home and treat her like this."

"She's my child. You stay the hell out of that conversation."

"Just some friendly advice."

Sabrina clenches her fists at her sides, and she walks backward down the sidewalk. "Your shit will be at the end of my driveway. Get it before morning or it's going in the garbage."

He pulls me close and kisses the top of my head. I wave at Bethany, hiccupping back a sob, as they speed off.

My emotions are all over the place, and I don't know where to start to pick them apart. All I know is that they're the tangled, messy web that I work really hard to avoid.

I've been sliced wide open, the ugliness inside me spilling out for everyone to see ... and every Carmichael on this street has watched my mortification. Not sure how things could get worse.

*"Doesn't this embarrass you? Do you have any sense of humility at all? Do these poor people understand who they're dealing with here?"*

"Let's go," Banks says, kissing me again.

"Where?"

"I'll put a pizza in the oven while you get a bath."

I look up at him and take him in. Handsome face. Kind eyes. Genuine empathy.

He nudges me toward the door. "It's so much easier not having to walk across the street to get a frozen pizza. Who knew?"

Even though I don't feel like smiling, I can't help it. Because it's Banks—the man who not only stood up for me but stood by me. The man who was kind to a little girl he doesn't know, and firm to a woman he'd naturally despise. And he did it all with grace and class.

*"Sara can take care of herself. I'm pretty sure you taught her the necessity for that ... I know that you aren't going to roll up to my house and disrespect her."*

The man who is fierce yet gentle, strong yet kind.

The man who I think I've fallen in love with.

# CHAPTER 25
## *Banks*

"Open up." I smirk, dangling a piece of pizza over the bathtub. "I'm not usually talking about pizza when I say that."

Sara gives me a small smile. I'll take it.

She's been quiet since the whole Sabrina bullshit went down an hour ago. I don't blame her at all. I have no idea what it would be like to have someone talk so much shit to you—intentionally tear you down and hitting you where they know your wounds lie—and then have to pick up the pieces and go on.

I'd probably knock them out. Not that it would help because, if it would, I would've grabbed the guy accompanying Sabrina and put him to sleep.

That's the thing—I don't know how to make this better. I don't know how to fix it. That makes me feel like a failure.

Sara leans up and bites the tiniest end of the pizza.

"How are you doing?" I ask her, putting the pizza back on the plate.

I stretch my legs, still clad in my dirty work jeans, and wish I was in the bath letting it soak my sore muscles. Wishing I was holding Sara. But there's a look in her eyes that tells me she doesn't need that right now and, right now, it's not about me.

*Who even am I? It's always about me.*

"I'm okay." She pokes a toe out of the bubbles. "I'm worried about Bethany, but I don't know what I can do."

*I feel ya on that.*

"Maybe Sabrina will be more calm when we get your stuff, and we can at least see Bethany," I offer.

She frowns. "I hope so."

I give her another bite. It's slightly bigger than the last.

"I just keep thinking about how miserable she is in that big house," she says. "Sabrina was a bit more controlled when I was a teenager because my dad was there. We'd fight, and she was cold, but she didn't completely lose her shit."

Her toes flick water against the tub.

"How old were you when you moved out?" I ask.

"Eighteen. Hence, my debt. I had to get out of there, and Dad figured I was an adult so I could figure it out on my own. Then he died shortly after that, and Sabrina inherited everything, so that was the bookend for me on that life."

*How does someone do that to their child? Or to anyone they profess to love? That screams neglect. And must only reinforce her thoughts of not being good enough.*

*Fuck all of them.*

My parents bought their children houses on the same street as them so we could all be close. *And they say I'm needy.* Our family is lucky we were able to afford to do that, but even if we weren't, I'm sure they would've supported us however they could—at the very least, they would've always been there for us emotionally.

My phone chirps. I pull it out.

Maddox: Good news. Sara's rental is ready. The tenant had a warrant and didn't want the court system involved. So I have the keys. Let me know if you want me to bring them home or if you want to meet me over there this evening.

*Fuck.* I glance up to see Sara studying me. *I have to tell her.*

My stomach tightens. "That was Mad. He has the keys to the apartment you were wanting to get."

Her brows shoot to the ceiling. "*Oh.*"

"You don't have to go, you know."

"Why wouldn't I go?"

My heart races, and I move the plate off my lap because I feel like I might jump to my feet.

"I don't know," I say carefully. "You just seem like you need someone to take care of you tonight."

I don't know what I said, but tears pour down her cheeks. My insides scream at me to do something to stop it—that I upset her—but for the love of all that's holy, I don't know how.

"Sara …"

She scoots up in the tub. Her breasts sit just above the bubbles, and I can't even enjoy them.

"I love that you want to take care of me, Banks. You *are* taking care of me—more than anyone in my life ever has." Streams of mascara streak her face. "But this … shit, this drama, is a part of my life. It's an unfortunately big part of who I am. I can't stop moving forward because something gets all fucked up or else I'd be sitting in your tub crying all the damn time."

Her words pierce my heart. The look on her face turns the knife and twists it, causing me to bleed all over the bathroom floor.

"Then sit there," I say, unsure of what else *to* say. "And I'll sit right here and remind you of how great things are on the other side of the bathtub."

At least she tries to smile.

I sit on my knees and face her, needing her to believe me. "You can't let what that nasty woman said get to you, babe. You are so much more than what she said."

"But what she said was true—"

"Look at you." I point at the mirror across the room. "If this is a part of your life, you're still here. You're here and strong and smart and beautiful. *So fucking beautiful.* You're funny and impressive and *so good* at giving head."

She shakes her head, her lips flirting with a grin.

"You're impressive and talented. You have an interview with Myles Petterson." I stop to let that sink in. "You did that. He saw you and what you're capable of, and he wants you on his team. Think about that. That's amazing."

She scoots around, her ass sliding against the porcelain.

My brain flies like it does when a new car comes in the shop, and I start mentally planning all the things I need to do and check and replace and repair. It's like that, only more frantic. More necessary.

More important.

"Sara, she hurt your confidence, but she didn't hurt *you*. Do you get what I'm saying?"

She nods slowly. "I hear you, and you're right about some of that. I know it. I'm not … totally pity-partying myself. I'm still grounded in reality."

"Good."

"But that reality includes a whole other side of the coin, Banks."

"Like what?"

She takes a long, deep breath. It's one of those breaths that someone takes in preparation for something—a speech, a negative review, something hurtful. *A bomb.*

A wave of emotions rise in my chest, and I try to think of what to say before she can get the next words out. But I fail.

"I am in my mid-twenties," she says.

"So am I. It's a great place to be."

"Okay, yes, you are. And you have a house, two vehicles, a business—a career. You have a family and Sunday dinners and pizza nights at Moss's house. A nest egg." Her eyes fill with pain. "I have … me."

"Sara, stop."

"My life is in boxes at a woman's house who hates me," she says, hiccupping back a sob. "I have a car that makes a whole lot of sounds when it's been running for a while, which makes me nervous. I have two friends that have their own lives to take care of, no job, and a hefty amount of debt."

I watch her wrestle with her words. I want to interrupt and argue all of those points—explain how we can fix them and express how fixable they all are, but I know we'll come back to this. We need to come back to this. This is the crux of the issue.

The same one I discovered during vibrator gate.

"What Sabrina said tonight is the same thing that Joshua said to me."

I get up, shaking my head. "I'm not listening to this."

"Why? Because the truth hurts? Because it's ugly?"

"Because I'm not going to listen to you talk about yourself like that," I say, staring down at her. "And you're not giving either one of those assholes any … relevance. Nothing that either of them said is true, Sara. It's what people who want to rip someone else down say because it's the lowest hanging fruit."

She leans away, and I realize I'm shouting. I take a deep breath and blow it out.

"Look," I say, crouching beside the tub. "Everyone has things about them that make them insecure. We all have wounds." I quickly try to come up with something to relate to her. "Okay, like sometimes Maddox will come home from work in his suit and tie, and I'll think, '*Shit. Maddox looks pretty handsome. I might not be the best-looking one in the family anymore.*'"

Sara grins.

"And if I didn't prove to myself that wasn't true, I might believe it. But instead, I go to a mirror and take a good gander and realize it's just my insecurities screwing with me. There's no competition. I am the handsomest Carmichael." I pause. "And that's what this shit is for you. It's not real."

She touches my cheek. Water drips down my face and onto my shirt.

"*But it feels real, Banks*. It hurts me. And you must be stronger than I am because I can't just look in the mirror and see this woman that I'm just not."

I sigh, wishing so much that this never happened. That smiley, happy Sara was with me at Jess's looking at the baby chickens.

"And do you know what else?" she asks.

I shake my head.

"It looks real." Her bottom lip quivers. "Foxx and Jess saw what was going on. They had to have heard Sabrina laying into me, and that's humiliating." She leans forward. "I'm so embarrassed, Banks."

"Why? Sabrina should be embarrassed—not you. You did nothing to be embarrassed about."

She lies back again, dejected. "I told you. This is my life. I'm not like your mom, or Brooke, or Ashley, or Pippa. I don't have my shit together. Hell, *I don't even have my shit*. It's at Sabrina's. Probably at the bottom of her driveway by now. Maybe nothing will be left by the time I get there."

I don't think that was supposed to be funny, but I crack a grin anyway.

"This is just a glaring reminder that I have a lot of work to do," she says, the words dropping into the water like a coin in a wishing well. "I have to figure out how to pull myself up by the bootstraps."

"I'll help."

"You can't."

"*The hell I can't*." I stand again, my thighs burning. "That's what happens in a relationship, Sara. They help one another. They're there when it's good and even more when it's bad."

She smiles sadly. "You don't want to be in a relationship with me."

I chuckle. "You're right."

Her face falls.

"*I need to be*." I sit on the edge of the tub and let her see into my eyes. "This is what I'm built for. This is what best friends do. And you're my new best friend and a hell of a lot more fun than Maddox when he held the title."

A tiny smile slips across her lips.

Anxiety fills me as the look in her eyes tells me that she's going to fight me on this. She's not going to just let me in. *She leaves. It's what she does.*

But I can't let her leave me. I need her. I need her with every breath I take and every plan I make for tomorrow. She's my one.

I've always imagined a relationship like the one my parents have— playful and loving and fiercely loyal. I can have that with Sara. *Only Sara.*

"Stay here," I say softly. "Let me love on you a little bit."

Her eyes widen.

My heart smashes against my rib cage, making it hard to hear anything other than the blood pouring through my ears. I'm already in this far. Might as well go all in.

"I love you, Sara."

Her eyes fog. Her lips swell like she's going to cry, and I don't know if that breaks my heart or makes me happy.

"I've never told another woman I wasn't related to that I love her," I say. "But I love you. Completely and absolutely. And I really, truly hope that you don't push me away."

"I love you, too," she says, the dark rivers flowing again. "But loving me isn't easy like it is loving you."

"I'll decide that."

She blows out a breath, her chest shaking. "Can we go get my things and then meet Maddox for the key?"

My jaw locks in place. "You're really going to block me out of this?"

"You can't fix everything."

"You won't even rely on me." My head starts to pound almost as much as my heart. "Do you think I'm incapable of helping you? Do you think I'm a flake? What is it?"

"I think there are some things people have to fix on their own." She smacks the water with her hand. "Besides, I can't see your brothers after today. I can't look at them. I can only imagine what they'd say— and they'll probably tell you to run, Banks. They'll probably tell you to get rid of the dramatic one, the one who hauls shitty behavior to their front lawn. You should prepare for that."

*I'm afraid I should prepare for heartbreak instead.*

I want to tell her that they wouldn't tell me that. I want to tell her that this family would eagerly envelop her, flaws and all. *Maybe even Foxx.* But I'm all out of words. I don't know the right ones to use here, and I don't think they'll make a difference anyway.

*"I think there are some things people have to fix on their own."*

A stack of towels is folded nicely in the cabinet. Sara refolded the ones that I did. There's something about that I love. I take one out and set it on the edge of the tub and then head for the door.

"Let me know when you're ready to go, and I'll follow you to Sabrina's," I say.

"Okay."

I don't look at her over my shoulder. I don't pause to give her a second to change her mind. Because if I know Sara, she's hardheaded, and her mind is made up.

Quite possibly like the happily ever after I had dreamed up in my head.

# CHAPTER 26
## *Sara*



"Come in," Gretchen shouts.

I push open the door and step inside Ashley's mother's house. The smell of the house—roast beef mixed with peach air filters in her vents—settles something in my soul. But as soon as I see Gretchen's face and the concern that sweeps across her features, I topple.

"Honey, what's wrong?" she says.

I sit on the couch next to her. I'm certain my heart is bleeding. *What else would explain a burn this intense?*

She hands me a tissue. "Start talking because I'm getting nervous over here."

"I don't know where to start."

"Pick the spot that's most comfortable and go from there."

I lie back against the cushions and close my eyes. They're swollen, I'm pretty sure.

Banks followed me to Sabrina's and loaded my things in my car. We made quick work of it. I was worried she'd come out of the house and make another scene, and I wasn't quite sure how well Banks would take a round two.

Especially since he's upset with me.

*"I've never told another woman I wasn't related to that I love her. But I*

*love you. Completely and absolutely. And I really, truly hope that you don't push me away."*

I don't know how I botched things so badly between us. I was honest. *Isn't honesty the best policy? If that's true, why does it hurt?*

This is why I don't do this shit.

"Oh, let's see," I say, sighing. "I'm going to give you the quick version to catch you up."

"Go."

"I quit my job. I lost my apartment. I got another apartment but then couldn't move in right away. I stayed with Ashley, as you've probably heard, and promptly moved across the street with Maddox's brother because, well, Ashley is in the honeymoon phase of life. Enough said."

Gretchen tries not to smile. "I'm following you. Keep going."

"Banks, Maddox's brother—whom I'm also assuming you know at this point since he's family now for you—which I just realized and that makes this a little weird but, really, Gretchen, I have nowhere else to go with this." I groan. "My life is one big convoluted mess."

"You can still talk a hundred miles a minute when you're stressed."

"Yay me."

She blows out a breath. "Ashley told me that Sabrina came by Banks's today."

My soul shrivels. Of course, Ashley knows. Of course, she told her mother. They're all probably talking about the circus my life brought to their happy little street and are breathing a sigh of relief that Banks dodged a bullet.

*"I love you, Sara."*

If I had any tears left, I'd cry.

"I had to tell my daughter this a while back," Gretchen says. "Right now, you're blaming yourself for what happened today, aren't you?"

"Well … yeah. I guess I am. I guess I feel like I infected them with my bullshit somehow—or I will infect them if I stick around." I sigh. "But it's even more than that, Gretchen. I can't help my sister. She's with that godforsaken woman, and there's nothing I can do about it."

"Do you think she's safe?"

"Physically? Yes. Emotionally? No. Probably not. But she did manage to keep her phone and texted me a little bit ago. She said she was okay and would talk to a school counselor tomorrow."

*That's the only reason I haven't lost my mind tonight.*

Gretchen leans forward and rests a hand on my knee. "She reminds me of another little girl I used to know."

My heart aches. "I think I was stronger back then."

"It never feels like we're at our strongest in the moment we need to feel that way, does it?"

"No."

I stand, my skin too tight, and walk aimlessly around the room. None of this feels real, even though it's absolutely par for the course of my life. Just a few hours ago, I was blissfully happy. I had a new job lined up, Banks was coming home, I felt like everything was finally on one side of me.

And now ... I'm drowning. Adrift. Cast away ... although that's on me this time.

*How quickly things change.*

"So what's going on with Banks?" Gretchen asks.

I exhale harshly. My head is foggy like it's stuffed full of cotton.

"Honestly? I don't know." I shrug sadly. "He's so sweet and kind, Gretch. He wants to ..." A lump settles in my throat. "Love me, I think."

"Ah. I see."

"What does that mean?"

She scoots to the edge of her seat. "Sweetheart, I'm going to be really honest with you right now. Okay?"

I nod warily.

"Sara, you don't know how to accept love."

*What?* I face her, my brows pulled tight. "That's ridiculous."

She smiles softly. "No, it's not. That crime is on your father's soul because he should've been there for you. You should have felt loved, protected. Cherished. I did the best I could, and loved you like my own, but he should've done all of that and more."

I march across the room and gather her in my arms.

"Oh, Sara," she says, patting my back. "I love you so much, sweet girl."

I remember all the times Gretchen has hugged me like this. That she's made me dinner. Chased me down when I snuck out and hauled my ass back home. *Because she loves me.*

How many times has Becca offered to pay for dinner—because she loves me—and I haven't let her?

How often has Ashley offered to listen to my problems—because she loves me—and I've waved her off?

And Banks ... he's only been in my life a short time, but I've known about him for much longer. Already, he's "fixed" my car, walked alongside me as a fake fiancé, defended me ... twice ... tried to protect my little sister, made me his own frozen pizza—because he loves me—and I find a reason to hide.

He sees me. He tries to show me my worth. He makes me feel cherished and loved and protected—all the things a man should ... that no one has ever done before.

It's as if my heart is delivering a message to my brain.

*Maybe Gretchen's right. Maybe I don't know how to accept love.*

I pull away, watching as she wipes the moisture from beneath her eyes.

"I love you, Gretchen."

*Two I love yous in one day? What's happening here?*

"I'm going to circle back to what I was saying before. You're blaming yourself for a lot of things. It's your fault that Sabrina came to your house and acted like a fool. It's your fault that Bethany is unhappy and trapped there. It's your fault that the Carmichaels saw a nasty woman berate a lovely woman and a little girl. It's your fault that things with Banks must end."

"Your point?"

"Sara, putting all that on your shoulders isn't giving you any more power over these situations. It's eroding your mental health—maybe your physical health too. But you don't get extra control powers if you take the blame for things that aren't your fault."

"I don't want control. You're wrong."

She lifts a brow. "You do. If you control it, it can't hurt you. You can put up your defenses and walls and feel protected. But, honey, that's not how it works." She takes my hand. "The only part of this that is your fault is if you walk away from that man who I bet thinks a whole hell of a lot about you."

I swallow past a lump in my throat.

"You'll have to break these habits," she says. "You'll have to learn to trust that giving other people a little bit of responsibility, trusting them to help you heal and to love you, isn't going to hurt you. That's your natural inclination because it's how you've been taught life works. But you were taught wrong."

I hug her again.

Breathing comes a little easier, and my stomach has settled some. If nothing else, she's given me a lot to think about.

"I need to go," I say.

"Where are you off to?"

"I have a new apartment, and I haven't even seen it yet." I shrug helplessly. "I need to get my stuff out of my car and into the building while I still have energy."

"Need any help?"

I smile. "I'll be fine." *Hell, might as well make it three.* "I love you, Gretchen."

"I love you more, Sara."

The air is hot as I make my way back to my car. The wind is balmy as it licks my skin. I get in my car, shoving a box with my elbow to make room, and take off across town.

*"Sara, you don't know how to accept love."*

Banks's face pops up in my mind.

*"You won't even rely on me. Do you think I'm incapable of helping you? Do you think I'm a flake? What is it?"*

I take a deep breath and step on the gas. I'm a gas pusher, after all.

———

Banks

·  ·  ·

"Mom!" I call out, looking around the kitchen. "Mom! Where are you?"

"What do you want, Banks?" she yells from somewhere in the back of the house.

"I'm having an emergency here."

"Oh, good grief," she says before a rustle ends with a collision.

*Shit.* "Do you need help?"

She comes down the hallway from her bedroom, giving me a mom look. "I just dumped an entire box of safety pins all over the bathroom floor. Someone better be dying or something better be on fire."

"I'm dying, and my heart is on fire. Happy now?"

She's not sure whether to laugh or hug me. And if my heart wasn't actually burning up, I'd be pleased that I could confuse her this much.

"Sit down," she says, pointing at the table. "Do you need a drink?"

"No."

"Am I going to need a drink for this?"

"Sara left, and I don't know if she's coming back except that a bunch of her stuff is at my house, but we didn't part ways super great, and I think she's mad at me, and I'm really kind of mad at her too because—"

Mom holds up a hand and then grabs a bottle of whiskey. "Hold, please."

"Can you hurry up here?"

She pours herself a shot and downs it. "Whew," she says, blowing out a long, slow breath. "Okay. Continue." She waves a hand at me. "No. Start over and breathe as you talk."

"My dumbass brother Maddox got Sara an apartment."

She sits down across from me. "Yes, wasn't that the plan?"

I just look at her.

"Never mind. Go on," she says.

"Okay. So Sara's stepmom, Sabrina, came by the house today—*my house*. Her daughter, Sara's stepsister, came over because she had been in a fight with Sabrina. Sabrina went batshit. Showed her ass. And I, I'll have you know, used class and grace with her." I think that through. "Mostly."

"I'm proud."

"Thanks." I smile at her, picking up a key on the table and tapping it against the wood. "It was hard. Anyway, so Sara gets embarrassed about Sabrina's little rampage and then Maddox chooses that moment in time to say, 'Hey, the apartment is ready.' So Sara got her things from Sabrina's and then met Maddox for the key. Meanwhile, I told her I love her, and she said she loves me too, but she has to fix this herself." I suck in a breath. "*Mom.* I don't even know what that means."

Mom's smile softens. "I'm really sorry, Banks. That must've been really hard for you."

"Yes. It was. She says she's not easy to love or something. But, Mom, she's the easiest person to love. I fell in love with her without even realizing it was happening."

"Maybe she needs a little space."

"Hello? We don't do that in this family!"

She sits back and crosses her arms over herself, looking rather smug.

"What?" I deadpan.

"Nothing. I was just wondering when this day would come."

I hold out my hands. *Can we get to the important stuff here?*

"The day my baby boy started putting someone else's happiness above his own."

"Fun. Yup. I think we're there." I lean across the table. "*Help me fix this.*"

She studies me for a long time before finally standing. "Come with me. Let's take a walk."

"A walk? What's a walk going to do? I'm panicking over here, Mother."

She laughs. "Come on. A walk will help you think. Promise. But first put Foxx's key down. The boy has been losing them left and right."

I get up and follow her outside. "You better be right about this."

"Am I ever wrong, Sparkles?"

I groan as the door shuts behind us.

# CHAPTER 27

*Sara*

"It's not *bad*," I say, taking in the mint-green walls and black-trimmed living room. "Beggars can't be choosers, I guess."

My stomach growls, reminding me that I haven't eaten since a bagel at breakfast. I was planning on making Banks the pasta dish we saw on television last night. I even figured out how to substitute ground beef for chicken since Banks is still on a *save the chickens* campaign. But now that's out, and I have no food here, so I guess it'll be fast food.

Yuck.

My arms are scratched from carrying some of the boxes from my car to the little garage attached to the apartment. It barely fits my car, and my car isn't the biggest thing ever made. So with the boxes in there—because I don't want to take my things inside until I clean it, despite Maddox telling me they had it professionally detailed—my car won't fit. *Fun times.*

*Hey, at least I have a place of my own again.*

My phone buzzes on the countertop in the kitchen. I race to it, hoping it's Banks. *Please be him.*

I look at the screen and my spirits sink.

> The Businessman: Hey, I haven't been ignoring you. I got sent to New York for a business meeting and just got back to town. Wanna meet up? 😉

My stomach churns. Bile tints my mouth.

A few weeks ago, I would've hopped into my car and said, *"See ya in twenty."* But now, that just feels … wrong.

*"You don't have a clue what you're doing. Hell, Sara, you're a child of the streets. Your father had given up on you well before he met me."*

I look at his name again and feel … nothing. "It's not you I want, Brock. I'm taken."

> Me: Take care of yourself, Brock. Our situation isn't working for me anymore.

> The Businessman: No worries. Take care. Let me know if you ever need anything—sexually or otherwise.

I grin sadly. *He's probably not a bad guy.* I hit the block button.

The apartment is a living room, eat-in kitchen, one bed, and one bath. It's the size of Banks's living room and kitchen combined. Despite the cozy nature of the place, it feels cold. Vacant. Lonely.

"Hello, loneliness, my old friend," I say, humming the line like it's a song lyric. "What do I do first? Probably should finish unloading the car so I can get some food." I pause. "And an air mattress."

*Joy.*

I grab my car keys off the counter and head for the door. As soon as I twist the handle, someone knocks on the other side.

A shock of adrenaline hits me hard, and I yank the door open faster than I should. I don't know the neighbors or if the guy who just vacated this place is pissed. *Clearly, I'm irrational.*

I gasp softly as my gaze settles on Damaris Carmichael. Her face is warm, motherly, as she stands on my tiny stoop with bags in her hands.

"Damaris?" I ask, puzzled. "What are you doing here?"

"I brought you dinner. I didn't figure you had time to get something good today, so I whipped up some sub sandwiches and a salad. I hope that's okay. I'm not sure what you like and I didn't know if you'd have a way to heat things."

*Fucking tears.* They fill my eyes, and I blink as furiously as I can to get them to reabsorb wherever they came from.

"That's …" I sigh. "That's so nice of you. You didn't have to do that."

"I know."

I step to the side, and she comes inside, moving like the matriarch she is.

"Pippa also sent you some soup," she says. "Can I stick this in your fridge?"

*Lucky that was here when I got the keys.* "Uh, sure."

I stand in the doorway and watch her take over my space. *I see where Banks gets it now.* The thought makes me smile.

"This is a chilled peach soup with fresh goat cheese." She holds a little package on top of the glass container before putting them in the fridge. "Pippa says she's in a cold soup season and makes a new soup just about every day. I didn't know there were that many soups out there."

I grin.

She goes back to her bags and pulls out a small, soft-sided can cooler, two bottles of Fresca, and a sandwich, small bag of chips, and a to-go salad container.

"The drinks are cold," she says. "I forgot to bring ice, so hopefully this will be fine."

I don't know what to say other than I should say something. "This is … wonderful. Unexpected. It's more than fine."

She finishes unloading her bags and then turns to me. "I'm going to get right to the point."

*Oh shit.* I nod hesitantly.

"Banks told me what happened today," she says, eyes searching mine. "I'm sorry."

"Me too."

She sighs. "Sabrina? Is that her name?"

I nod again.

"She better have been glad I wasn't home."

*What?* A slow smile splits my cheeks.

"Come. Sit," she says, patting the counter. "You need to eat."

"Yes, ma'am." I hop on the counter as instructed, not sure where this is going. "I apologize for the spectacle today."

She unwraps the sandwich. "What are you apologizing for? You weren't the one acting like a lunatic."

My heart swells.

"When I was in high school, I played softball. Second base. Not to sound too much like my children, but I was good," she says.

I giggle.

She grins. "My grandfather used to come to my games, and every time he'd show up, there was a fifty-fifty chance he was drunk off his behind." She digs around in the bag and pulls out plastic cutlery. "He would stand behind the batter's box and just shout all kinds of madness. Not always bad things, but he'd go over the top, clapping and whistling and yelling—the whole bit. And I became known at school as the girl with the drunk grandpa."

I take the sandwich she hands me.

"It was the worst. Kids are just mean, anyway," she says, setting a drink beside me. "I was so embarrassed by him. It was awful."

I take a deep breath. Suddenly, I see right where this is headed, and I'm not sure I'm ready for it.

I watch this beautiful, successful, powerful woman work around my dumpy apartment, bringing me a sandwich she went out of her way to create just for me. If this was for Banks or Ashley, I'd understand. *But me?* I'm so confused.

*Maybe she doesn't know Banks and I are in an argument.*

I set my sandwich on the counter beside the drink. "Damaris, Banks is mad at me, I'm pretty sure."

She smiles. "Well, this isn't about Banks. This is about you."

"I don't understand."

She leans against the counter and folds her arms across her waist. "My son is worried about you. Now, I'm not coming here to play matchmaker because you're both adults and can figure that out yourselves. But you're important to him, so you're important to me. You're important to all of us, Sara."

The lump that plagued me all evening settles in my throat again. I can barely swallow over it this time. Maybe it's because I'm trying not to tear up at the same time, and I don't multitask well.

"I don't know why you are all so nice to me," I say, my voice filled with my unshed tears.

"Well, you know Banks and his predisposition not to acknowledge boundaries." She smiles. "He gets that from me."

I laugh, wiping my nose with the back of my hand.

"Can I help you with anything?" she asks. "If you ever want to talk, I'm here. I know that can be weird since I'm Banks's mom, but you have Ashley. And now Pippa and Brooke."

She's talking to me as if I'm one of them. *As if I'm a Carmichael.*

It's a magical elation and a terrible joke at the same time. The sensations push and pull me until I'm dizzy.

"What's wrong?" she asks. "Are you okay?"

I sniffle. "I just don't think I have the emotional capacity for your family."

"That's okay. Neither do I most days."

I laugh. She pats me on the knee and goes back to her bags.

"Can I be honest with you?" I ask.

"Of course. I hope you always are."

"This will probably sound ... Well, I don't know how it will sound. But the truth is, I don't necessarily know how well I'd fit in your family."

She glances over her shoulder. "Why do you say that?"

I hop off the counter. There's too much nervous energy in my body to sit still any longer.

"I've always thought I was hard to love," I say, catching a hint of a smile on her face. "But tonight, someone told me that I have a hard time accepting it. And maybe both are true. I don't know. One does not exclude the other. But you all … you have your shit together, pardon my language. You're on top of your stuff. I live *here*. I have credit card debt, not gonna lie. And, worst of all, emotions make me itchy, and you're all full of them."

She laughs freely and spins around. Her face is lit up.

I grimace. "I wasn't joking. I know that all sounds horrible, but you have to see what we're working with here."

"We all do the best we can. Each one of us starts at a different green light in life and we have to get through the course, taking as many correct turns as we can. And none of us, Sara, get every turn right. And we're not all on the same course, either."

My breathing slows. There's a softness in her voice, in her gaze, that comforts me.

"From what I understand about your life, and I may have heard wrong and if I have, I apologize in advance," she says. "But if what I've heard is true, the fact that you're standing here, in your own apartment, relatively happy—"

I laugh.

"—healthy, successful … you've made more right turns than most people have."

She walks across the kitchen and wraps her hands around my arms.

"No matter what happens between you and my son, I'm always here if you need to talk or need advice," she says. "Promise me you'll remember that."

I nod, my nose burning with unshed tears.

"Good." She pats my arms and then picks up her bags. "Do you need anything else?"

"No. I'm truly grateful for the dinner and the words of encouragement, Damaris. Thank you."

She walks to the door. "I heard you make great brownies."

I laugh. "I mean, they're all right."

"Bring us a batch on Sunday for dinner, if you can. I'd love to taste them." She stops and looks at me. "I'll see you then."

My heart flutters. "I …" I take a breath. "I'll see you, Damaris."

She winks and pulls open the door. "Oh, crap. Here. Let me help you."

*What?* "What's going on?"

"Dammit, Banks. Why didn't you get someone to help you?"

"Because everyone was too busy." His voice filters through the room, swirling around my heart. "Ouch!"

"You are going to bust your fingers. Be careful."

I stand in the kitchen, the air filling with Luna Rossa Black.

My heartbeat quickens, and my knees weaken, and I cover my mouth so I don't say something that I'll regret later.

"This is a rental," Damaris says, moving out of the way. "Try not to put holes in the wall for crying out loud."

"I'm trying, Mom. I really am."

Banks walks in the apartment carrying the headboard from the guest bed—the one I slept in the first night. He leans it against the wall and stands tall, watching me with hopeful eyes.

Damaris slips out the door, closing it gently behind her.

He's still in his work jeans from earlier but has put on a fresh shirt. A navy-blue hat sits backward on his head.

"What are you doing here?" I ask.

"Bringing you a bed. You mentioned you didn't have furniture when I fished your vibrator out of the toilet."

*He remembered that?* I take in his smile. *Of course, he did.*

I halt my expectations and quell my hope just in case I'm misreading this situation. Banks smirks as if he can read my mind.

"I grabbed the rest of your stuff from my house too," he says. "Well, not all of it. But the stuff I think you'll need tonight."

"Thanks," I say, biting my lip to distract myself from the pain in my chest. "I can come get the rest tomorrow."

"That's fine."

*Okay.* I take in a shaky breath and motion toward the bed. "You didn't have to bring that. I mean, I appreciate it, but I'll get one as soon as I get my first check from Petterson. I mean, assuming I get the job."

A slow smile splits his cheeks, sinking his dimple deep. "If you want to get a new one, that's your call. I'll take this back home. But it's staying here until then because I'm not sleeping on the floor."

*Huh?*

He saunters toward me with a sly look on his face. It's typical Banks—a mix of sexiness and adorableness that's unique to him.

"I know you need your space," he says. "I don't love it. I don't really understand it. But I know it."

"Okay."

"And I know you need to take things slow. I remember you saying that you don't like relationships because men try to tell you what to do with your time, expect you to be a certain person, and think it might end in marriage." He leans forward. "I do kinda hope this ends in marriage, but I'll keep that to myself."

I cover my mouth with my hand.

"So maybe you need your own place for a while. Maybe you need to slowly transition into living together or whatever. I want you to be you because you are the woman I love."

I drop my hand because it can't cover my ear-to-ear smile anyway.

"Mom says relationships include compromise," he says, lifting his chin. "So I'll understand that you need your own apartment if you understand that I can't sleep without you every night. But I'll stay here sometimes if you'd like."

"Banks …" I say, laughing.

"What's it matter, anyway?" He shrugs. "It's always going to be me and you. And I'll get my whole garage this way, which is great because I've already seen what my brothers' garages look like when their girls move in. There's barely any space for tools."

I can't contain myself any longer. I burst out laughing.

He picks me up, and I wrap my legs around his waist, letting him kiss me as long, as deep, and as completely as he wants. Because he's right. It is always going to be me and him. I can't see our love story end any other way.

# CHAPTER 28

## Banks



"Well, we complicated the fuck out of this," I say, chuckling.

Sara stretches her arm across my stomach, feathering her fingers against my skin. "It's your fault. I told you I don't do relationships, and you just kept working me."

I scoff. "Whatever. I'm pretty sure I told you I'd fall for you, *and* I'm absolutely certain that I thought you staying here was a terrible idea."

"I need my toothbrush, and I don't even know where it is," she says, laughing. "Is it here? In my car? In a box in my apartment?"

"We need a system for this. Either we'll have double the essentials like toothbrushes and … whatever else. We'll keep one at each house. Or we'll have to bring them back and forth."

She plants a kiss on my sternum. "One in each house. That way, we can make game-time decisions about where we want to stay."

I roll my eyes.

"I know you just rolled your eyes at me," she says, smacking me lightly on the abs.

"How do you know that? You aren't even looking at me."

She giggles. "I just know."

She rolls onto her back and then snuggles up next to me. I bring her head to my lips and kiss the side of it.

I did something I've never done before—I called in to work. Tasha found it highly entertaining that I was calling it for a personal day and accurately guessed it had something to do with Sara. *"Maybe you can take one every month. It'll do us all some good,"* Tasha said, laughing.

"I know you hate this arrangement," she says. "It's been, what, two weeks or something, and you're already over it."

"True. But whatever. I'm hoping you'll get frustrated by not having your favorite shampoo at your convenience, and the shirt you'll want is at the other house. Then you'll give in and live with me like the way things were designed."

"Designed by whom?"

"By God."

She snorts, shaking her head. "Thank you for taking things slow." She pops up on her elbow and looks at me with her sweet, sleepy morning eyes. "I just want to make sure I get this right."

I brush a strand of hair behind her ear. "We'll get it right. We'll work on it until we do."

She sits up, planting her hands on my shoulders like she's going to straddle me when my phone rings. She reaches for it.

"Let it go to voicemail," I say, cupping her ass cheeks and urging her toward me.

"Answer it. Then turn it off."

I sigh, bringing the phone to my ear. "Hello?"

"Hey, there, sexy. What's happening over there?" Gloria asks.

I yank the blankets back. Sara grabs my cock and pumps it, sucking the pre-cum off the head.

*Fuck.* "Oh, not much, Glo. What's happening over there?"

Sara giggles. She sits up, stroking me, and then squats over my shaft. I hold my breath as she presses the head against her opening and then slides her body down the length until it fills her.

*"Fuck,"* I mouth, pulling the phone away from my mouth while I hiss.

Gloria rattles on about something, and I have no idea what's going on. I'm focused on Sara's tits bouncing as she rides my dick.

*How is this my life?*

*Thank you, God.*

I hear the word auction. "Hey, Gloria, hang on. About the auction."

I palm one of Sara's breasts and feel myself grow even harder. "I need to talk to you about that."

"What about it?"

"Well, I have an idea."

"Give it to me," she says.

"Let's talk about it this week at lunch. I'm a little preoccupied right now."

Sara's head falls back, her chin pointed at the ceiling. *She's so fucking gorgeous.*

"Pick me up tomorrow at eleven thirty?" she asks.

"Yup. I'll be there."

"Okay. I'll bring a mockup of the posters we're putting up with your pictures on them." She cackles. "They're so good. The ladies are going to lose their dentures over this."

I cringe. "That's ... great."

She laughs. "Okay, well, go enjoy your day. I'll see your handsome face tomorrow."

"See you tomorrow. Bye, Gloria."

"Goodbye."

I end the call and drop the phone on the bed.

"Quick question," I say, rolling her nipples just the way she likes it.

"What?" She breathes in through her teeth as she takes me in and out. "This feels so good, Banks."

"You do realize you didn't put a condom on my cock before you sat on it, right?"

She slows, dropping her body until I'm fully, *deeply* seated inside her. Her hips move in slow, delicious circles as she grinds on me.

Her eyes are wide. "Yeah, well, I didn't think about that."

"You do know how babies are made, right?"

She laughs nervously. "I do."

I grip her hips, feeling her move in my palms. *This is heaven. It gets no better than this.*

"This probably isn't the place to talk about this," she says, biting her bottom lip.

"Actually, I think this is the place to talk about everything. All of our meetings now take place with you on top of me while I'm buried inside you."

She laughs.

"What's up?" I ask.

She plants her hands on my pecs and looks me in the eye. I run my hands over her smooth skin and cup her ass.

"Talk to me," I say, bending forward and sucking one of her nipples.

"I can't think when you do that," she moans.

I nip the bead and then pull away. "Fine."

"Hang with me through this."

I flex my hips, pressing my cock as deep as it'll go inside her. "I'm hanging."

"I'm on birth control. So the odds that I'll get pregnant aren't great."

"Okay."

"And we've already discussed that we're both free from diseases, right?"

"Yeah," I say, pushing in again.

She leans forward and presses a sweet kiss against my lips.

"We've been together, officially or unofficially, for a month or so," she says, a twinkle in her eye. "And I don't want to move in with you ... yet."

"Yeah, yeah, yeah. Get to the point so I can bend you over this bed."

She giggles. "I want to have a baby."

I stop moving. *What the fuck did she just say?*

I think my eyeballs nearly fall out of my head. My core temperature just increased by one hundred degrees. *Holy fucking shit.*

"*Your baby* specifically," she says. "I'm not in a hurry, obviously, because I don't even want to live here yet. But the more I'm around your family, the more I want my own family. I want to change the script and have a bunch of little Banks and Saras running around, driving your brothers nuts."

I clear my throat. "Did you just tell me you want me to knock you up?"

She nods, grinning. "Not like today. Like I said, I'm still on birth control. I want to take things easy between us and not put pressure on anything—just enjoy the process. But I do want to have a houseful of your kids and marry you and live here ... eventually."

*Now, that is heaven. Sara, me, our kids ... maybe some chickens.*

"My cock is so hard that if you move, I'll come. I swear it." I grab her hips. "Don't move or I'll come in you, Sara."

She laughs, amused by my reaction.

"This isn't funny. You don't tell a man who's obsessed with you that you want him to impregnate you. That's hot as fuck."

"So is that a yes?"

"How about this?" I start to move but feel the impending explosion and stop. "My answer to everything is yes. If you want to get married —pick a day and tell me where to be. If you want to *finally* move in— tell me when to get your shit. If you want to have a baby—climb on this dick and ride it." I smile at her. "I'm here for it all with you. On your timeline. When you're ready, I'm already there."

She presses off my chest and smiles. If love isn't what she's looking at me with, then I've never seen it before.

Slowly, she turns her hips into a circle, grinding her pussy against my cock.

"Sara ..." I groan, my jaw flexing as I try to hold it back. "I mean it."

She switches direction, moving a little faster.

"Dammit," I say, squeezing her hips so hard I expect her to yelp.

*"Come in me, Banks."*

*Done.*

She meets me push for push, flex for flex. She fucks me as I growl into the air, filling her with my come. As I swell inside her, she screams, rocking against me as she rides out her own orgasm.

I try to keep my eyes open, desperate to watch her take me like this for the first time. But the climax is too sharp, too powerful, that I squeeze my eyes shut and let the sensation take over.

She falls into a heap on my chest, sucking in ragged breaths. I wrap my arms around her and hold her on my chest.

"You are literal perfection," I say, kissing the top of her head. "I mean it."

She hugs me, her cheeks pressed against my pectoral muscle. "I love you."

She could say it a million times—a billion times a day—and I'd never get sick of hearing her saying those words.

"I love you," I say, running my fingers through her hair.

Something starts buzzing under my ass. I fish around until I pull it out.

Request from *KixxDaddy for the amount of $1000.00 for the drinks you half finished, aka wasted, throughout your life. Consider this a deal.

I laugh and then turn off my phone.

"What do you want to do today?" she asks me. "I start at Petterson tomorrow, so I want to use the day to the best of my advantage."

I shrug. "We can fuck again."

She laughs. "Besides that."

"Oh." I think about it. "We need to go to the grocery store. What do you want to do?"

"I told Bethany maybe we'd come and get her for dinner tonight."

"Sounds good."

I draw faint circles on Sara's back and think about all that's happened with the Sabrina and Bethany situation. The way Jess and Foxx talked to Sara and expressed their disdain for what happened to her. Foxx even said more than five words. It was quite a day. And somehow, shortly after that, Sabrina broke up with Gary, her asshole boyfriend, and called Sara to talk. I'm not sure what took place to cause Sabrina's change of tune, but I'm happy for Sara and Bethany.

Bethany has stayed with Sara once or twice in the past couple of weeks. We've picked her up for dinner and even attended one of Bethany's cheer routines, much to my chagrin.

"Hey, Mom has some fudge hidden in the back of her pantry," I say. "It's the good pistachio kind. Want me to go get us some?"

She laughs and sits up. "No. Why don't you just buy it yourself?"

"Because I can't just go all adult at once. Mom would miss it."

"Eh, I don't think so."

"She secretly likes it when I borrow stuff from her house. It reminds her of when we were little."

Sara's phone starts ringing from the bedside table. "Gimme."

"I turned mine off for you."

"And I'll turn mine off for you—after this call."

I express my displeasure as I hand her the device.

She presses the speakerphone button. "Hello?"

"Hi, Sara. It's Damaris. Is my son with you by any chance? I saw both of your cars home."

I shake my head.

"Yup. He's right here. He can hear you."

"Banks Owen Carmichael—why did a box full of plastic spiders just show up at my house?"

I grimace. "Why did you open that?"

"They were falling out from under the tape, and I just picked up the box and almost had a heart attack."

"It's a federal offense to open someone else's mail," I say.

"Then stop sending your shit to my house. Now come and get this box. I'm setting it on the porch. Those little things look so real."

Sara's brows pull together. I wink at her.

"I'll come. Do you have any fudge left?" I ask.

She sighs. "Bring my yellow bowl back."

"Maybe."

"Goodbye, Banks."

"Goodbye, Mama."

As promised, Sara turns her phone off and sets it next to mine. "I hope our sons aren't as rotten as you."

The thought of Sara carrying my son has me hard again. I roll her over on her back, making her squeal.

"You're going to be sorry you ever said a word about having my baby," I say, sliding back into her.

She holds my face in her hands. "I doubt it."
We lose ourselves in each other, forgetting all about the world.

# Epilogue

SARA

1 MONTH LATER ...

"Kixx, that couch is downright embarrassing," Damaris says, marching through the kitchen. "It squeaks when you stand or sit down. It has thirty years of stains. *I want a new couch.*"

"That's a slight exaggeration," Kixx says. "Think of all the memories that thing holds." He looks up at all of us at the table and winks. "SpaghettiOs. Maddox's cleat marks. Hell, Banks might've been conceived on that couch."

"That's downright disgraceful," Banks says.

The room erupts in a fit of laughter.

For as loud and boisterous as the Carmichaels are, they can keep a secret. As Kixx makes another laundry list of reasons Damaris's couch is just fine, the siblings all exchange a knowing smile.

Foxx sits down beside me, a toothpick between his lips. He shakes his head at the antics of his family, but I think he secretly enjoys it. *But, really, how could he not?*

"Did you ever get your key problem sorted?" I ask him.

He shakes his head slowly. "Nope."

I have a suspicion about what's behind the key situation, but I've not voiced it to anyone. I don't want to throw out accusations carelessly, but something doesn't quite add up.

Foxx looks at me, lifting one brow. *I think he shares my suspicions.*

"Why do I care if peacocks shed their feathers?" Banks looks up from his phone. "I am so sick of these fucking texts." He looks at Foxx. "If anyone in this room is sending them, and I find out, there's gonna be hell to pay."

Foxx takes the toothpick from between his lips, his gaze trained on Banks. "Dammit. For once, I wish it was me."

"Is it you?" Banks asks.

Foxx sighs as if he's bored with the conversation already. "Yeah, Banks. I have time to sit around and find fun animal facts to send you throughout the day." He puts the toothpick back in his mouth. "Get real."

"Is Bethany coming today?" Damaris asks. "I saw her at the gas station this week. She's such a sweetheart, Sara."

I beam. "I think she is too. But, no, she's not coming. Sabrina is taking her and a friend to a concert in Atlanta this weekend."

"Fuck Sabrina," Jess says, earning a shove from Pippa. "What? She's a …" He looks at his mother. "A very mean person." He grins.

Damaris shakes her head.

I love this family. Not only have they embraced me, but they've embraced Bethany, too. And I think she's going to be okay because of it.

*As long as she can get over her crush on Banks …*

"Gloria wanted me to ask you all to come to the charity auction next weekend," Banks says. "She gave me a poster to help tempt you to come, but Sara pinned it to the bedroom wall."

I laugh.

"In which house?" Moss asks, winking at me.

Banks pouts. "Very funny."

"It's next Saturday?" Damaris asks, rinsing a bowl. "Honey was reminding me again this morning. I don't know what she and Gloria will do when this auction is over. They're obsessed with it."

Banks smirks. "Did you see the fliers? Very obsess-able."

"I did see them," Damaris says. "The rose was a good touch."

"Who's going to get in on the action?" Banks asks.

Moss and Maddox mumble their confirmations. Jess says a solid maybe, which means he will. Foxx sits stoically with no response.

"Are you going, Foxx?" Banks asks him.

He shrugs.

"Come on, you have to come. It's going to be great," Banks says.

Foxx sighs. "Probably."

Banks's face lights up in a way that worries me. I look at Brooke, and she nods.

*"When he uses that tone, he's up to something. Probably something that will cause a lot of drama around here."*

*Shit.*

"Hey, Sara. Are you going with us to the vineyard Thursday night? There's a wine tasting and painting thing," Pippa says. "Brooke and I are going."

"Is Ashley?" I ask.

"No. She's helping Honey with the event." Pippa laughs. "That thing is taking over everyone's life."

"You know, this is the first Sunday dinner in a long time that Jess and Banks haven't wanted to throttle each other over a prank," Maddox says.

"Yeah, that's true." Moss nods approvingly. "What gives?"

Banks stares at Jess. "Two things. One, he loves the chickens."

"I do. I do," Jess says, shrugging.

"And two ..." Banks smirks. "I won the race, and Jess can't hack it."

Jess shoots to his feet, hands on the table, lobbying for a second race. The two of them go back and forth while the rest of us watch, amused.

"Damaris, do you need any help?" I ask.

"Do you want to stir the tea? We're about ready to eat."

I smile. "Sure."

Every time the family is all together, I'm taken back to the day

Banks came to my house to save my rental deposit. I was convinced I was out of good luck and my life was on a downward spiral.

And maybe it was.

But when the universe is ready to show you the path you should be on, it doesn't care if you're spiraling or soaring—and that's what I failed to understand. I always counted myself out because I wasn't stable. I held myself back because I thought that if I deserved things, they wouldn't be so hard to attain.

But that's not true.

If I've learned anything, it's that you have to be willing to receive the blessings coming your way. You have to be willing to receive love, be open to goodness, be willing to take a chance on something, *or someone*, that seems all wrong.

*Take a corner that ends up being the right one after all.*

I look up and catch Banks's eye. He gives me the shy smile that's just for me.

I took a chance and got a whole wild, amazing, loving family. And soon Banks and I will start our own little branch.

As if he knows what I'm thinking, Banks's eyes blaze.

I don't have all the answers to my problems or the solutions to the things that still plague me sometimes. I don't know when I'll move in with Banks, when we'll get married, or when we'll have our first baby.

But I know enough to trust in the process.

How could I not?

It led me here.

Banks winks at me.

*To him.*

And, in many ways, to me too.

I'm learning. Some days, I must remind myself that it's okay to accept love and feel worthy of it. To watch for the moments that others show me, in their own ways, that I'm important to them.

Sometimes, it's easy to fall back into old habits, and I start building walls, telling jokes—deflecting.

On those days, Damaris is here to remind me.

And *every day*, with every kiss, every hug, every affirming word—

every suggestion that we buy chickens until we have babies, Banks helps me love myself a little more too. I love him so damn much.

*We're going to soar.*

**Don't miss Foxx's book, FLAME. Chapter One is next. Keep reading…**

Chapter One

Foxx

"Are you having fun?" Banks slides next to me, a glass of lemonade in his hand. "That apple pie Honey made was the best pie I've ever had. Did you try it?"

I cock my head to the side and stare at him.

"Want me to get you a piece?" Banks asks, a wide smile plastered across his face.

I shift my weight from one foot to the other.

The air is filled with spices from the chili cook-off that took place an hour ago to benefit the local school's arts program. Conversations flow into a giant stream of noise as people catch up, recounting old high school sports games and current gossip.

*So much wasted energy.*

And in the midst of it all, my youngest brother is up to something. This isn't a revelation, nor is it a surprise. He's *always* up to something.

In the past few weeks, I've picked Banks up from jail in the middle of the night. I watched him walk across the street covered in glitter— retribution for attaching stickers of his face to every surface of our brother Jess's house. One morning, I looked out the window to witness a giant metal rooster staring at me from across the road, thanks to Banks's handiwork and toddler-esque humor.

The guy is a menace but a predictable one. His tells are as clear as day, and right now, they're *screaming*.

"I've socialized enough," I say. "I'm heading home."

"*Already*? You just got here."

"I said I'd support the cause. I didn't say I'd stay all afternoon."

"But there's still so much to do. Did you even see my calendar? And I—"

"Why do you care what I do?" I cross my arms over my chest. I'm curious despite curiosity being against my better judgment. "I showed up. Yes, I saw your ridiculous calendar. I bought a pie. What more do you want from me?"

He points at me. "Can I have that pie, by the way? You snagged the last coconut cream."

"*No.*"

He holds up his hands. "Easy, tiger. I was kidding." He grimaces. "*Kind of.* Anyway, about you leaving …"

I look at the ceiling and sigh.

This is precisely why I avoid human interaction as much as possible. I always walk away worse for the wear. I'm pushed too far or needled too much. Things are expected of me. My time and energy become commandeered, and I'm not into that sort of behavior.

It's not that I don't understand the concept behind group activities —I do. I took enough psychology classes to wrap my brain around it. People need to share their experiences and feel seen. The potential for success rises when people work together. Groups allow for high-level problem-solving and cooperation.

But me? I'd rather not be seen. I don't want to share my experiences. And I can damn well solve my own problems without someone like *Banks* weighing in.

"Are you listening to me?" Banks asks.

"No."

We turn our attention to the makeshift platform beside us. Gloria, an older woman Banks befriended in one of his silly schemes, taps a microphone. She beams from center stage.

"Ladies and gentlemen, please take your seats," she says, the microphone entirely too close to her teeth. She smiles at *me*. "It's time for the final event—the one you've all been waiting for. The bachelor auction is about to begin!"

My stomach knots at the look she's firing my way. *What's that all about? Does she think I'm Banks?*

He waves at her from beside me. She looks at him, then back at me, before returning her gaze to my brother.

*Yeah, Gloria. It's this goofy-ass guy you're after. Not me.*

Chatter breaks out through the room, and women scramble to find seats. Banks and I are nearly trampled as a group of ladies makes a beeline for the front row.

"Let's … uh, move over here," Banks says, grabbing my elbow.

I flex my arm, and he promptly drops his hand, looking at me warily.

"Sorry," he says.

"Good life choice," I say.

"About that …"

Banks sidesteps Marla, a silver-haired woman pushing her walker across the floor. Tennis balls cover the feet like drag slicks. Head down and shoulders back, she leans into the turn around the corner of the stage before nearly knocking over a small child to take the center seat.

"Have fun getting auctioned off," I say, turning to leave. "Looks like a good time."

"Foxx, *wait*."

The way he says my name, coupled with how he takes a half step back, has my instincts rippling with anticipation. *Something bad is about to happen.*

I square my shoulders with his. "What?"

He winces.

"I would like to welcome our four eligible bachelors on stage," Gloria says. "First, we have Shawn Daze, the surf instructor we all know and love. Welcome, Shawn!"

Cheers ring out from around the room as the first contestant takes his spot next to Gloria.

"Next, we have Chef Miguel Cotto, the reason we all go to La Pachanga," she says. "Welcome, Miguel!"

The applause grows louder.

Banks rocks back on his heels. "I need to tell you something."

"Colin Hensley, the firefighter that dreams are made of, is our third bachelor," Gloria says. "Say hello to our local hero!"

"Better hurry," I say. "You're next."

"About that ..."

"And, last, our final contestant. I don't know how we got this lucky, ladies," Gloria says. "Please welcome the one and only Foxx Carmichael!"

*What?*

Cheers fill the air. Everyone in the room fixes their gaze on me. Gloria watches me expectantly.

*Oh, hell no.*

Banks grimaces, moving even farther away from my right hand.

Everything inside me stills. My jaw flexes, and my teeth grind so hard they hurt.

"Tell me she got us mixed up," I say, balling my hands at my sides.

"Look, I can't be in the auction anymore. Sara will kill me. She's dangerous when she's mad."

"And I'm not?"

"Good point." His eyes dart around the room. "Listen, Foxx, I didn't think about it until we arrived. I can't let my girl Gloria down, and none of our brothers can fill in. Maddox has Ashley, Moss has Brooke. Pippa would murder Jess if I volunteered him."

"Foxx? Can you join us on stage, please?" Gloria asks, the microphone squealing in her hand. She taps on it, making it even worse. "Can someone show me how to adjust this thing?"

The entire town stares holes in my back, waiting for me to take the trail of humiliation and occupy the spot by Colin. Hushed conversations whisper through the room. I'm sure jokes are being made over coffee and coffee cake.

"*Please do this for me,*" Banks says, holding his hands before him. "I panicked, Foxx. I didn't know what to do. You are the only one of us who's single, and I ... *I panicked, Foxx.*"

"You're repeating yourself."

"It's for a good cause, and it's not like you have a bursting social calendar."

"Foxx?" Gloria asks again.

Banks grins. "You're drawing more attention to yourself by not going up there, you know."

I take a step toward him. "Sleep with one eye open, you little fucker."

Instead of looking worried, he manages to look relieved.

I don't really have a choice because, for once in his damn life, Banks is right. I'm only creating a bigger problem by resisting. The chatter among the gossips will only worsen if I duck out the back door and leave them hanging.

*Banks, you're living on borrowed time, kid.*

I straighten my shirt, stand tall, and take a long, deep breath. *Focus on revenge. It will be so, so sweet.*

I step purposely onto the stage, carefully avoiding eye contact with the audience. My heart races as I stand next to the firefighter. He gives me a slight nod, a gesture of pity, really, before turning his attention back to the women clutching paddles with numbers written in black magic marker.

Gloria drones on and on, thanking everyone who had the tiniest hand in putting the event together. Then she gives a quick rendition of the rules. While she reads the bullet points off a sheet of paper, I exhale and finally face the crowd.

The women in my family sit at a round table near the bathroom. My mother is more entertained than she should be. Dad stands next to Jess, the only brother I really like most days, and lifts a plastic cup my way. My failure to acknowledge him results in a chuckle that he's lucky I can't hear. Banks stands next to Jess and gives me a thumbs-up. I level my gaze with his, unblinking.

His smile slowly fades, and his thumb falls from the air like a deflated balloon. I enjoy a smidgen of satisfaction from that.

"Let's start the bidding on Shawn at two hundred dollars," Gloria says. "Do I have any takers?"

Paddles are thrust into the air. It's one of the most embarrassing things I've ever witnessed.

*Could I just donate a large sum of money and spare us all the trouble?*

Sweat dots the nape of my neck as the bids for Shawn increase.

"One thousand dollars for Shawn! Going once, going twice—a date with Shawn is sold to Mrs. Ferguson," Gloria says, pointing at a petite older lady with a purse embroidered with cats. "Congratulations!"

*Fuck my life.*

*And fuck Banks's life since we're at it.*

I turn to Gloria, lips parted to announce my benevolent donation, but the wind is knocked out of me.

*What is she doing here?*

Bianca Brewer stands in the entryway, chatting with a woman holding a long roll of raffle tickets like they're long-lost friends. Except they're not. Bianca has never been to Kismet Beach before.

"On to Miguel," Gloria says. "Since the last bachelor raised so much money, let's start a bit higher this time. Do I have five hundred?"

My body catches fire as Bianca moves across the room.

Landry Security assigned me to her security detail three years ago. Despite having a binder of information before meeting her, nothing could have prepared me for the powerhouse of Bianca Elaine Brewer.

She's five foot five with shoulder-length auburn hair. Her eyes are pieces of jade that can see right through you. She has high cheekbones, deep curves, and a cute button nose.

*She fascinates me.*

The woman is wildly intelligent. Watching her bring a boardroom of men to their knees is one of the hottest things I've ever seen. She's curious and confident yet humble and kind. And she doesn't give a damn about what she should and shouldn't do. She does what she wants.

Unfortunately, that can't be me.

Bianca looks up. Her green eyes shine when they connect with mine.

*Shit.*

"*Hey,*" she says, mouthing the word from across the room.

I struggle to remain unaffected, but the corners of my lips lift. She notices. She always finds the chink in my armor. A smile creeps over her pink pout, hitting me directly in the cock.

*Get yourself together, Carmichael.*

"Going once, going twice—a date with Miguel is sold to Mrs. Daniels for twelve hundred dollars!" Gloria announces.

My brows pull together as Jason, Bianca's brother and my best friend—my only friend—enters the building. His solemn expression is replaced with amusement as he realizes what he's about to witness.

I flash him a pointed look to watch himself. It only makes him laugh.

*Maybe I don't like him either.*

"Next up is Colin," Gloria says. "Let's start the bidding at five hundred. Do I see six?"

Jason and Bianca take a seat in the back row. He folds his hands on his lap like he's settling in for a show. She takes a bid paddle from the raffle ticket lady.

This is the nail in Banksy's coffin.

"I have six," Gloria says. "Do I see seven?"

Bianca's eyes find mine again.

"There's seven. Do I have eight?" Gloria asks.

Bianca lifts a brow, pressing her lips together.

*What does that mean? Do you want a date with Colin?*

As if she reads my mind, she raises her paddle.

I raise a brow back.

"There's eight. Do I have nine?" Gloria asks the room.

Bianca shrugs innocently, daring me to react. But I don't. And I won't.

She might get under my skin like no one I've met before, but I refuse to cross that line.

I was the lead on her security detail for two and a half years, and for two and a half years the woman whittled away at my restraint. It's impossible to resist her. Her little smile and the way her nose wrinkles when she's being cheeky. Her penchant for burgers and vanilla shakes. Her perfume and her ability to wear a T-shirt and cocktail dress with the same understated elegance.

*The way she says my name.*

Our relationship shifted over time. It began strictly professionally before transitioning to more of a friendship. And then, during the past six months, we were toeing a line that shouldn't be crossed.

Conversations weren't strictly business. Smiles were exchanged when no one was looking. Our touches lingered long after contact should've been broken.

I wasn't thinking of her as my boss. I was thinking about her bent over her desk. I was imagining her in my bed wearing my T-shirt. I had visions of her in my truck, her hand in mine, doing mundane tasks like running errands.

But it was harmless. It was simply a war inside me that I was winning.

And then one night changed everything. That's the night six months ago that I asked for an immediate transfer … and I haven't seen her privately since.

"Sold! A date with Colin to Mrs. Breckenridge for one thousand one hundred dollars." Gloria peeks around the others and smiles at me. "I'm starting the bid on our final bachelor with a bid of my own at five hundred dollars. Do I have six hundred for Foxx?"

All eyes land on me. I'm not sure where to look. I don't want to see my family laughing; I want to like them tomorrow. I can't look at Banks because I'll be tempted to leap off the stage and beat his ass right here. I don't want to look at anyone bidding, lest they think I want them to spend their hard-earned dollars on a date with me. And I sure as hell don't want to make eye contact with Bianca.

"Six hundred from Marla in the front," Gloria says. "Do I have seven?"

Various paddles shoot to the ceiling. *And they stay there.*

Gloria laughs. "I see. Let's go to eight hundred?" The paddles remain in the air. "Nine? One thousand? One thousand one hundred?"

*What the hell is happening?*

"Fifteen hundred!" Marla grabs her walker to brace herself. "I bid fifteen hundred."

"Okay. Sixteen hundred, anyone?" Gloria asks. "Yes! I have sixteen hundred from the lady in the back."

Heads turn to the back of the room. Bianca sits tall in her seat, proudly waving her paddle.

I look at Jason in surprise. He shrugs as if there's nothing he can do. I send him a silent message to stop her. But instead of intervening like I've seen him do countless times in both private and combat situations, he defers.

He's helpless and at the mercy of his baby sister.

"Seventeen hundred!" Marla shouts, her voice wavering from the force of her words.

"Eighteen hundred," Bianca fires back.

"Two thousand," Marla says, her hands shaking. She narrows her eyes at Bianca.

Out of my periphery, I notice Banks snickering.

"Two thousand, two hundred." Bianca's voice is edgier than before as she stares Marla down. "I bid two thousand, two hundred dollars."

Jason gets up and stands behind her, holding his forehead.

"Two thousand, three hundred," Marla says.

"Twenty-five hundred."

Heads swing from one side of the room to the other as bids volley back and forth.

Marla scoots her walker around so she's face-to-face with Bianca. "Twenty-seven hundred."

"Twenty-eight," Bianca says easily.

Marla's finger shakes as she points at her adversary. "Respect your elders, missy!" Her gaze whips to Gloria. *"Three thousand."*

"Someone stop this," I mumble.

Bianca stands, holding her paddle in the air, and levels her gaze at Marla. "Ten thousand dollars."

*What did she just say?*

Gasps echo through the room.

"I'm sorry, hon," Gloria says, the microphone squealing. "Did you just bid *ten thousand dollars*?"

Bianca smiles sheepishly. "It's for charity, right?"

Marla flops in her chair, defeated.

Applause breaks out as Gloria struggles through her shock, her gaze switching between Bianca and me. I feel like Gloria expects me to say something, but I have nothing to say other than *what the fuck just happened?*

My head spins.

I exit the stage, ignoring curious looks from the audience as everyone gets up to leave.

I came for pie.

*Pie.*

*What went so wrong?*

My feet falter, and I stop just short of where my brother and I stood only minutes ago.

*Banks.*

*Banks is what went wrong.*

I growl into the air.

*Today can't possibly get any worse.*

Flame is live now on Amazon, Audible, and free with Kindle Unlimited.

# Acknowledgments

It takes a village to raise a child. Despite Banks Carmichael being a fictional character, it took many of us to get him (and me) through this story.

Thank you to the Creator for my life, beautiful words, my wild and chaotic family, and endless inspiration.

The Carmichael family mirrors my own family in many ways. Inspiration for this series of books hasn't been hard to come by. A huge thank you to Mr. Locke and our four sons (whose names all end in a *x* or *s*) for your understanding of what it takes to write a book, your support and encouragement, and your endless laughter, stories, and hijinx. I love you all so damn much.

Peggy and Rob Williams will never understand how much their presence in my life means to me. Thank you for checking in on me, worrying about me, and loving me like your child. I am incredibly blessed.

A big thank you to Kari March for designing yet another perfect couple. You knew exactly what I was after and delivered with fireworks. Thank you so very much.

Tiffany Remy is probably breathing a sigh of relief that this book is complete. It's rough living with Banks in your head and she had to deal with that by association. I appreciate your patience while I worked through this book and all the other things that you took off my plate.

Michele Ficht came through for me yet again. I'm so grateful that you went on this journey with me. Thank you for your kindness, professionalism, and friendship.

Thank you to Anjelica Grace for working me and this story into her days. You're always so kind, willing to bounce ideas and calm me back over the ledge.

Without Marion Archer (Marion Making Manuscripts) and Jenny Sims (Editing 4 Indies), this story would've been a disaster. Ladies, your attention to detail and sharp eyes polished this book to perfection.

Of course, Mandi Beck was a constant source of support and cheerleading through this book. My life isn't complete without her. S.L. Scott is my go-to for brainstorming, business decisions, and encouragement. Go get 'em, tiger! Ha! I write every day with Jessica Prince. If she didn't text me every day, I probably wouldn't have found my office many of them.

I'm eternally grateful for Kaitie Reister and the sunshine she brings to my inbox and All Locked Up (Goodreads group). And without routine calls from Brittni Van (Overbooked PA Services), I wouldn't stack on track and I would certainly laugh much less! Thank you for your friendship, ladies!

Thank you to Candi Kane PR for helping spread the word about my books! My appreciation for you knows no bounds.

And, last but certainly not least, thank you for picking up this book. Thanks for taking a chance on it. I hope it put a smile on your face.

USA Today Bestselling author, Adriana Locke, writes contemporary romances about the two things she knows best—big families and small towns. Her stories are about ordinary people finding extraordinary love with the perfect combination of heart, heat, and humor.

She loves connecting with readers, fall weather, football, reading alpha heroes, everything pumpkin, and pretending to garden.

Hailing from a tiny town in the Midwest, Adriana spends her free time with her high school sweetheart (who she married over twenty years ago) and their four sons (who truly are her best work). Her kitchen may be a perpetual disaster, and if all else fails, there is always pizza.

www.adrianalocke.com